THE ACE OF LIGHTNING

D0109824

THE ACE OF LIGHTNING

STORIES

STEPHEN-PAUL MARTIN

FC2

TUSCALOOSA

FC2 is an imprint of The University of Alabama Press

Inquiries about reproducing material from this work should be addressed to
the University of Alabama Press

Book Design: Publications Unit, Department of English, Illinois State
Univeristy; Director: Steve Halle; Production Assistant: Madeline Cornwell
Cover Design: Lou Robinson
Typeface: Garamond

ISBN: 978-1-57366-058-7
E-ISBN: 978-1-57366-869-9

Library of Congress Cataloging-in-Publication Data

Names: Martin, Stephen-Paul, author.
Title: The ace of lightning : stories / Stephen-Paul Martin.
Description: Tuscaloosa : FC2, [2017]
Identifiers: LCCN 2016023958 | ISBN 9781573660587 (softcover : acid-
free paper)
Subjects: LCSH: Franz Ferdinand, Archduke of Austria,
    1863-1914--Assassination--Fiction. | World War,
    1914-1918--Causes--Fiction. | GSAFD: Alternative histories (Fiction)
Classification: LCC PS3563.A7292 A6 2016 | DDC 813/.54--dc23
LC record available at https://lccn.loc.gov/2016023958

TABLE OF CONTENTS

THE REAL ENEMY

The morning sun is forcing its way through dusty venetian blinds. He gets up and struggles to make his bed for what might be the final time. Then he sits and looks at his hands. It's like he's never seen them before. Years ago, growing up in a village too small to appear on a map, he always thought he'd be using his hands to work on the farm where his family lived, the rented scrap of land they'd struggled with for generations. But here in a borrowed room in a small house in Sarajevo, he knows his hands will soon be holding the bomb and the gun beneath his bed, concealed in a Gladstone bag, the kind that doctors use on house calls.

There's a pile of books and pamphlets beside his bed. Gavrilo Princip has read them all carefully, some of them three or four times. They've convinced him that leaders of any kind are the enemy, that all political systems are delusional, destructive. He picks up a pamphlet called *The Death of a Hero*, which makes the assassination of tyrants seem like a moral duty. He tries to read the last paragraph, words he already knows by heart, urging him to sacrifice himself to set his country free, claiming that nothing else matters. He's firmly convinced that nothing else matters. But the language feels more dangerous now that he's ready to pull the trigger.

He gets up and looks in the circular mirror beside the closet door. But instead of his face looking back from the glass, there's a camera taking his picture. He's stunned and backs away, sits on his bed and blinks and shakes his head. He moves his fingers carefully over his cheeks and mouth and forehead, as if he were pressing them back into place, keeping his face from becoming a black and white photographic image. Then he looks back toward the mirror, thinks about taking it down from the wall, examining the other side, checking the space behind it. But the shock of what's just happened keeps him from moving. He's always been afraid of mirrors and cameras. They weren't familiar parts of his life on the farm where he spent his first thirteen years, and when he first encountered them in the one-room school he attended, they seemed to have magic powers, dangerous powers, things to avoid. Now he's afraid that the damage is done, that the picture will soon be developed, circulated in books, becoming a permanent part of the future. He can already feel a million faces turning published pages, looking at his face ten years from now, a hundred years from now.

Footsteps approach in the hall outside his room. He thinks at first that it's Danilo Ilic's mother, who's been nice enough to let him to stay in her house for the past few weeks. Gavrilo stands and prepares to make light conversation. But when the door opens, Dani himself steps in, looking like he hasn't slept or shaved in several days. He starts to speak, but Gavrilo says: What time is it?

Dani pulls an old watch out of his vest pocket and says: 7:34.

They look at each other tensely. When they first became friends two years ago Dani was like an older brother, recommending anarchist writers, Kropotkin and Bakunin, guiding him to cafés where students talked about revolution. But the past few weeks have been strange. Dani's been talking like he's afraid, even though he's supposed to be guiding the process, making plans. A week ago Dani insisted that nothing would happen, that the Austrian archduke wasn't really an enemy worth killing. But Gavrilo wouldn't back down, and over the next few days he assumed control, calmly and quietly steering their conversations, leading Dani to think that there was no reason to be confused, that without any doubt it was time for decisive action. Two days ago Dani was making final arrangements, deciding where to position six assassins along the Appel Quay, the boulevard that follows the Miljacka River through the center of Sarajevo, where the archduke's motorcade will soon be approaching.

But now Dani looks uncertain again. Gavrilo assumes that he's gotten bad news from Belgrade, that now the Black Hand doesn't want an assassination, even though they provided the bombs and guns a month before. It's typical of the way the Black Hand works, with everything caught up in coded secrecy, so it's hard to know what's really going on. Gavrilo tries to look like he knows what he wants, but his face feels wrong, like it might be a slice of bread that's just about to get used in a sandwich, or might be a clock whose hands have been torn off.

He says: What time is it?

Dani pulls an old watch out of his vest pocket and says: 7:34.

Gavrilo hears the festive sounds of the city through the window, people getting ready to be excited, to greet the heir apparent with cheers and smiles and Habsburg banners. He feels contempt. He tells himself that the people don't know what they're doing, that they're in a daze that only a violent action can truly penetrate. He thinks of all the risks he took a few months ago in Belgrade, working in secret with dangerous men to get the weapons he needed, then walking for days through freezing rain, dodging police and border patrols, putting his life on the line for a chance to fire the fatal shot. He refuses to act like he's grateful for the reforms coming down from Vienna, the so-called modernization of his country over the past five years, the friendly face of the enemy, offering comfort instead of freedom. It's a transformation that's been embraced by the older generation, who somehow didn't seem disturbed by the overnight annexation, when they woke to find official signs, posted all over the city, declaring that their country would now be part of the Habsburg Empire.

He says: What time is it?

Dani pulls an old watch out of his vest pocket and says: 7:34.

A fly comes in through the window, circling above the light and shade on Gavrilo's desk. Normally he would be annoyed and try to get rid of it, but now he watches it carefully, fascinated by the way it moves, the circling shifts in speed and elevation. Soon it's making figure eights, perfectly formed infinity signs, images so exact that he starts to think it's not a fly, that it's really a small machine, a spying device sent back in time, invented at least a century in the future, a time he can now imagine all too clearly, a world where everyone will be secretly watching everyone else, and no one will have a chance to get away with anything, and no one will even know what it means to get away with something, and nothing will be worth getting away with.

He says: What time is it?

Dani pulls an old watch out of his vest pocket and says: 7:34.

There's something wrong with Dani's face. It looks like it's being held in place by strips of invisible tape, or like he's just come back from a frustrating classroom, where he had to work hard to keep from blowing up at annoying students, who thought it was terribly funny to give the wrong answers to obvious questions. Dani looks like a pencil with a worn-out eraser.

He used to be a teacher. His face still shows the imprint of his job. Gavrilo wonders if his own face shows the imprint of on-going meaningless work, all the stupid jobs he's had to take in the past few years, with no hope of finding anything better in the future.

He says: What time is it?

Dani says: I just told you—7:34.

Gavrilo says: You just told me?

Dani says: I just told you four times: 7:34, 7:34, 7:34, 7:34.

Gavrilo says: You did? Why?

Dani says: You kept asking me over and over again.

Gavrilo says: Really?

Dani says: Is something wrong?

Gavrilo figures he'd better change the subject, so he quickly mentions Nedjo Cabrinovic and Trifko Grabez, his old school friends and now partners in the assassination plot, the ones who'd smuggled the weapons across the border with him a few weeks ago. Dani says they're waiting at Vlajnic's pastry shop. Then he says that he's waiting for further instructions from Belgrade, that the Black Hand seems to have changed their plans again. Things are on hold right now.

Gavrilo gets angry and starts to speak, but he knows exactly how their discussion will go. He doesn't want to talk anymore. He wants bullets and bombs, decisive action. If they don't do it now, it might not ever get done. And he knows from what he's read that the past is full of things that never got done. He's been picturing the moment he's been waiting for, the look on the archduke's face confronting the gun one second before it gets fired—the archduke with two famous country palaces and a widely photographed mansion in Vienna, Gavrilo without a single room to call his own.

Dani looks like he's getting ready to launch an explanation. He's good with explanations, playing with language. He's written clever essays in *The Bell*, the journal he edits. He's always working hard to make striking phrases, as if it were enough to find the right words. Gavrilo is tired of skillful arguments that change nothing. He's ready to really do the things they've been talking about in the cheap cafés, long nights filled with subversive declarations, Young Bosnia preparing to shape its own future, no longer willing to live in the shadows of foreign empires.

He watches the fly darting in and out of the light and shade on his desk, in and out of the dusty blinds moving slightly in the breeze. It lands on his forehead, pausing as if to make sure that it's biting the right person. Gavrilo's right hand starts to reach up, eager to kill. But something in his left hand tells him to wait, reminding him that the fly might really be more than just an insect. When it bites, the front of his brain is filled with light, confirming what he's been feeling since he woke ten minutes ago, the sense that what they've been planning has already happened, that everything has been leading up to this moment, everything that's ever happened anywhere at any time, major events and minor events and things that no one noticed. There's no turning back at this point. His confusion is gone.

He says: It doesn't matter what the Black Hand wants.

Dani looks startled and says: It does. They're dangerous people.

Gavrilo says: Are they?

Dani says: Of course they are. You know they are. You know what they can do, the people they've killed, their power over people in the highest places. You know what they're all about. Why pretend that you don't? You took the oath.

Looking past Dani's head, Gavrilo sees a hand reaching out of the mirror, giving him the finger, or giving Dani the finger, then getting sucked back into the glass with the sound of a closing zipper. The sound makes Dani flinch but when he turns everything seems normal. The fly lands on the mirror, moving its quick front feet, watching itself with more than a thousand eyes, looking like it's just about to bite its own reflection, or like it might be annoyed by the festive sounds coming in from the street.

Gavrilo says: What oath are you talking about, Dani? That time they took me into that dark basement and made me swear to take my own life after completing my assignment? Don't make me laugh. What theatrical nonsense! I don't accept assignments. I'm not some student getting homework. It's all been my idea right from the start, right from the time Nedjo and I started talking about it, back in Belgrade. Remember? The Café Amerika? The meetings with Djuro Sarac and Handsome Cigo? It was all in that letter I wrote you, all in that secret language we'd come up with. Or did you forget how to read it? And if I took an oath, so what? What's an oath? It's just a bunch of words. I'll do what I want. I always do what I want.

Dani looks alarmed and says: You're talking like a fool, Gavro. This isn't a game. That hooded man in the basement that night—he wasn't putting on an act. He's a dangerous man. They're all dangerous men. Trust me. I've been working with them for more than a year now. I've seen some scary things.

Gavrilo laughs like someone who doesn't know what laughter sounds like, someone who only knows about laughter from books. He says: How dangerous can they be? What can they take from us that we're not already losing? The cyanide is right here in my pocket.

Dani says: But what if there are better ways to make things happen? What if the Black Hand—

Gavrilo's eyes look like they're slowly assembling what they're seeing. He says: It's too late for anything else. Nedjo and

9

Trifko and I are already there, on the Appel Quay with the other three men you've hired. The archduke's Double Phaeton is approaching. Nedjo pulls out a bomb, taps it against a lamppost, exactly the way you showed him, but he throws it too soon. The bomb lands in the archduke's car, but he's still got time to knock it out onto the street, and it explodes behind him, causing only minor injuries to people in the next car. Nedjo jumps off the bridge into the river, but it's only three inches deep, and the police have no trouble catching him. The poison he swallowed a minute ago makes him sick but doesn't kill him. I can see his face as they're leading him away. He looks like he's just told a joke that nobody laughed at.

Dani says: You sound ridiculous. Why—

Gavrilo says: Don't interrupt me, Dani. I know what I'm talking about. It's already happening. I'm not predicting anything. I'm describing it. I'm walking away from the Appel Quay. I'm hungry. There's a girl waving to me outside Schiller's Café. Her name is Tanya. I slept with her two nights ago. I couldn't bear the thought of dying a virgin.

Dani says: You slept with someone? Why, Gavro? Did you forget Young Bosnia? The code of abstinence we live by? You know that sex is out of the question. It sounds nice but it's foolish. Too often it leads to reproduction. And why would we want to reproduce? Why would we want to bring more stupid and violent beings into the world? Because the sex is fun? Because it feels better than anything else? Nonsense! The pleasure is overrated. All pleasure is overrated. It amounts to this: You gave in to a bourgeois distraction.

Gavrilo slowly nods and sits on a stool beside his desk, shakes his head fiercely several times, breaking out of his trance, then stands again and says: A bourgeois distraction? You're right.

That's exactly what it turned out to be. I felt stupid the whole time I was with her. And nothing really happened. I'm still a virgin.

Dani shakes his head: And now—

Gavrilo snaps back into his trance and says: And now I'm sitting with her in Schiller's Café, and she's buying me sandwiches. I'm so hungry. Now that things have gone wrong, now that they're taking Nedjo to jail, now that they've got a body they can torture until he gives them our names, the only thing that remains is this horrible hunger. All I want to do is eat sandwiches forever. And this girl—she's tall with curly black hair—she wants to sleep with me again. She thinks she's the sexiest girl in Sarajevo. It offends her that someone had trouble getting excited with her in bed. I want to laugh in her face. I want to tell her that food is better than sex. But then there's a noise in the street. I look outside. It's the archduke's car, stalled right outside the café. I can't believe what I'm seeing. Why is he still in Sarajevo after someone tried to kill him? I step out and fire two shots. There's screaming and shouting, people knocking me down.

Dani says: Come out of it, Gavro. What's wrong with you? You're talking like that weird woman my mother knows, the one who claims she can channel the voices of the dead. Listen to me. There's something—

Gavrilo says: I know the woman you're talking about. She's a fake. I'm nothing like her. I don't care about the dead. They don't matter anymore. The only thing I care about is the future, the one we're creating. But—

Dani says: Gavro, please! Shut up and listen. There's something you need to know—

Gavrilo says: I already know what I need to know. And all the talking in the world won't make any difference. The future has already told me everything worth listening to.

Dani says: The future? It doesn't exist yet. How can it tell you anything?

Gavrilo looks like someone looking through a shop front window, slowly making out the shapes of things in the dark of the shop, distracted by his own face looking back from the glass, by the motion of reflected shapes behind him on the street. He says: I'm a ghost in a town where no one believes in ghosts. I'm reading a book on a park bench beside a wall that's not a wall, a wall that's really a book in another dimension, a book that's really a wall in another dimension, though I know that other dimensions don't exist. I'm a stray dog haunted by moonlight in a town on the other side of the world. I'm in the yes of no and the no of yes. I'm the ace of lightning.

Dani starts to speak but Gavrilo stops him, holding up his hand. He says: I'm playing cards with a woman dressed in moonlight. She's making up the rules—

Dani raises his voice: Stop talking, Gavro! Stop that insane ranting and listen!

Gavrilo looks at Dani like he's never seen him before.

Dani says: There are better ways, Gavro, much better ways. It's not enough to kill the crown prince. The emperor, his own uncle, wants him dead anyway. So do the generals in Vienna, the ones with all the real power. Think carefully, Gavro. It's Vidovdan, St. Vitus Day, the day of our martyrs. The Austrians aren't stupid. They had to know we would take it as a serious insult when they chose June 28 for the archduke's visit. They had to know that the streets would be teeming with assassins. They must have wanted him dead. Think about it, Gavro: You'll just be doing their dirty work for them. Nothing will change. Nothing—

Gavrilo says: You're just talking. As always, you're just using words to avoid significant action. Language isn't enough anymore. It's never been enough.

He leans down and takes the gun and the bomb from the Gladstone bag. He puts them in his inner coat pocket.

Dani says: I never said that language was enough. But that doesn't make it any less important. Without it, where would we be?

Gavrilo says: Nowhere. Here. The same thing.

Dani shakes his head and looks at the floor, slowly crosses the room and looks in the mirror. There's no face looking back. The room looks empty. He says: This is crazy, Gavro. It's like we're not here anymore!

The fly stops moving its quick front feet, darts away from the mirror, circles Dani's head and then Gavrilo's head and flies out the window.

Gavrilo says: In the history books of the future, this moment won't exist. We might as well not be here, having this conversation. The books will say that I shot the archduke Ferdinand. My picture will be in some of those books, beside the archduke's picture. But the words you're wasting now to try to stop what can't be stopped, the words that might have changed the course of Western civilization, those desperate words won't ever be recorded.

Dani slowly moves his hand back and forth in front of the mirror. But the room in the glass looks empty except for the bars of light and shade on the floor, gliding as the breeze comes in through the dusty venetian blinds. He says: There's an old tradition that vampires have no reflection. But we both know that's nonsense. Vampires are just another bourgeois distraction. There's something much more disturbing taking place, something that has nothing to do with fantasies and legends. If words like these are left out of history books, why bother talking? Why are we having this conversation, when no one will ever know what we're talking about.

Gavrilo says: The books will be filled with famous names, people with too much power, people who never should have had that power in the first place. There's always someone like that, like the man I'm preparing to kill, some power-hungry fool who gets to have his picture taken, some blathering idiot people can't stop writing about. But the truth is simple: Whoever the leader is, we need to get rid of him. Whatever the leader says, he's full of shit.

Dani says: The truth is never simple, Gavro. It might seem simple in print, but that's only because so much has been left out. It's—

Gavrilo speaks with his trance voice again: I'm seeing it again. What hasn't happened yet has already happened. You and I have been arrested. They don't consider us patriots or heroes. They're calling us murderers, not martyrs. They're starving us in our cells, trying to force us to confess. The Habsburg troops are terrorizing the countryside, randomly taking Serbian peasants from their farms, accusing them of being involved in the assassination, executing them on gallows erected right outside our prison windows, where we're forced to watch innocent people being killed because of the so-called crime we committed, because we won't say what they want us to say, that the Black Hand hired us to do the Serbian government's dirty work. The Austrians want an excuse to start a war. For several decades, they've wanted to attack and destroy Serbia, make it another part of their greedy empire. Everyone knows that. But they can't get us to confess to things that aren't true, and the mass executions continue. On trial I say all sorts of things, making everything even more unclear. I lead them to think we're working for the Masons, that we're all

14

Freemasons ourselves, that we're part of a brotherhood that's been secretly shaping European history since the Middle Ages, and—

Dani says: There you go again! More of that insane ranting! If you really want the martyrdom you keep talking about, you can't have a nervous breakdown.

Gavrilo says: Europe is on the verge of a collective nervous breakdown.

Dani nods and says: I've said more or less the same thing in print many times.

Gavrilo says: It's not enough to say it in print. It's time to do what needs to be done, to sacrifice our lives for a future worth living in.

Dani says: Stop kidding yourself, Gavro. *Sacrifice our lives? A future worth living in?* You're getting carried away by the sound of your own empty rhetoric. You're not a martyr. A martyr believes in something. But you've got nothing to believe in. Yugoslavia? Is such a place even possible without years and years of violence? Is that what you're willing to die for? Is that a future worth living in? What do you—

His voice is cut off by noise coming in from the street, carnival sounds, people shouting and laughing and blowing horns.

Gavrilo says: Listen to those idiots out there, Dani! They think they're at a party, a joyous occasion, even though the guest of honor is someone who's made it clear that he thinks all Slavs are pigs. How can we just stand here talking, when all the fools in this city are eager to welcome their enemy, forgetting that it's our special day, the day our countrymen died at the Battle of Kosovo. Think of them, Dani, slaughtered by the sultan's troops on the Field of Blackbirds. What would they think if they could see us today, glad to be under the thumb of another foreign power? What—

15

Dani says: It's not the right time, Gavro. Do you really think that killing the archduke will make any serious difference? He's not the real enemy. The generals and the bureaucrats are the ones with the actual power. Can you shoot them all one by one, then shoot their replacements?

Gavro says: No more questions, Dani. It's time for answers, time to see Nedjo and Trifko. They're waiting for us, aren't they? In Vlajnic's pastry shop? Let's not be late. The future is waiting for us now, but it won't wait forever.

POSSIBLY EVERYTHING

It's been a quiet afternoon, but now I can hear alarms in the distance, and I'm thinking back to the fall of 1962, the feeling of being torn awake by sirens at three in the morning, knowing that there were Russian bombs in Cuba, terrified that there might soon be an all-out nuclear war, not knowing then what seems obvious now, that the Soviets weren't really planning an attack, that JFK was the one I should have been worried about, that his thinking was being distorted by the steroids he was taking, that he should have known better than to force a confrontation, especially since he'd just finished reading *The Guns of August*, which carefully shows how major wars can start in response to minor provocations, how the murder of the Habsburg archduke in Sarajevo never should have led to the war that failed to end all wars, how the assassination would have been quickly forgotten if the generals in Vienna hadn't wanted an excuse to wage war on Serbia, issuing an absurd ultimatum, quickly dismissing a thoughtful response, plunging into what should have remained a regional conflict, but escalated with insane speed until it consumed the whole continent, and a similar series of escalations could easily take place now, a hundred years and too many unlearned lessons later, in response to any number of regional tensions, and there's no telling how far the violence would go, how much would be destroyed, possibly everything, an anxiety I've been living with for so long that I've learned to shrug it off, not an ideal response, but maybe there's no such thing as an ideal response, no such thing as a fully rational choice of action, not when there's interference coming from every direction, so much invasive media noise, so many things I'm forced to think about, combined with personal fears and absurd obsessions, so many things I'm supposed to remember to do, things I tend to put off as long as I can, but I know I can't avoid cleaning my bedroom closet any longer, so I open it and start throwing things into a garbage bag, but I stop when I find an old painting behind an old suitcase, a pseudo-pastoral picture I found in a thrift shop years ago, a canvas that looked at first like a Dutch landscape, a dirt road curving into a forest, a barn with a broken door, cows in a pasture beside a windmill, a faded, partly cloudy sky, all the things you might expect from a seventeenth-century landscape artist, except that above the barn there's a flying saucer, rendered so precisely that it seems to be spinning, humming and throbbing, as if it were preparing to release itself from the canvas and fly out my open window, spreading terror wherever it goes, people madly running down the streets in the wake of mass destruction, scenes from the black and white flying saucer movies I used to watch back in the Cold War fifties, great cities reduced to burning ruins in a matter of minutes, heaps of broken images like in T.S. Eliot's famous poem, which in some ways was a response to the Great War Gavrilo Princip never meant to start, so now I'm picturing Princip sitting on the edge of his bed looking at his hands, three hours before firing the fateful shots, looking around the sparsely furnished room like he's never seen it before, a place where a friend's mother has been letting him stay without paying rent, and the morning light is too strong so now he's closing the venetian blinds, then looking into the circular mirror beside his closet, surprised to find his own face looking back, then even more surprised that he was expecting someone else, someone watching every move he makes, tracking him with a cutting edge device that only appears to be a mirror, something that people paid to be smart came up with in a research lab, a paranoid thought he can't quite set aside, since even if it's not true it might as well be, so he carefully pulls his face away from the glass, watching to see if another face takes the place of his reflection, half expecting to hear the other face laugh at his confusion, and he puts his face in his hands to make sure it's still in place, that it hasn't been swallowed by the mirror, then turns to look at the pile of pamphlets and books beside his bed, anarchist and Marxist works he's been reading nonstop for the past few weeks, pages that have filled him with a morbid yearning, the desire to sacrifice himself, exchange a meaningless life for a meaningful death, following through on plans he's been developing for the past three months, killing the future king of the Habsburg empire, then shooting himself in the head or swallowing poison, a grand heroic gesture light years away from what he grew up with, the rural poverty his family had been struggling with for generations, a farming life that left him sick and exhausted, avoiding the fields by day, returning secretly at night, lying on his back for hours looking at the stars, knowing that there were supposed to be stories in the sky but not knowing how to read them, never having been told exactly how the stars could be connected to form pictures, so he made up his own constellations, his own map of the infinite darkness, something he frequently redesigned and expanded, learning the pleasures of creation and revision, though he doesn't remember much of it now, since education soon caught up with him, replaced his map of the sky with the standard version, but at times he can still recall what he felt, not the shapes and stories he made but the pleasure of making them, especially if he shuts his eyes and blocks out the sounds of the outside world, something he tries to do right now, pretending that Sarajevo isn't right outside the venetian blinds, that people all over the city aren't getting excited, eager to celebrate the Austrian archduke's arrival, somehow pleased that their country has been annexed by the Habsburg empire, or maybe not really pleased but not sufficiently disturbed, not angry enough to appreciate the sacrifice he's about to make, the bullets he's about to fire, so he tries to find comfort by making mental pictures, imagining that he's on a chunk of ice in the Arctic Ocean, watching iridescent spirals and waves of color fill the sky, a place I'd like to take myself right now, though not on a chunk of ice, maybe instead on the porch of a cabin somewhere in northern Wisconsin, a distant childhood memory that might be half invented, because even though I know for sure that I saw the Northern Lights, the cabin part of it could have been in a movie, but either way the image almost gives me what I'm looking for, a brief escape from the sirens that have been sounding for maybe ten minutes now, getting on my nerves in the worst way, making the world seem even more dangerous than it really is, dangerous enough to scare the big black dog I can see from the bedroom window, running down the street in my direction, as if he thought I could save him, protect him from the disaster the sirens might be announcing, and I feel like I should run outside and take him in, since after all, I've always thought of dogs as enlightened beings, wise enough to ignore the TV shows they're forced to sit through, resting at the feet or on the laps of their so-called masters, ignoring all the animals getting used as commercial images, tuning out all the other mass produced images, pictures that most of the human world can't avoid, scripted faces and voices coming from every conceivable angle, invading public space from an ever-increasing number of glowing screens, though of course it's a mistake to put all the blame on the glowing screens, since long before there were TVs and computers, long before billions of dollars got spent each day on mass deception, people were filled with images telling them who to be and what to do, like the images of martyrdom, heroic self-sacrifice, which had such a strong effect on Gavrilo Princip when he first came to the cafés of Sarajevo and got involved with Young Bosnia, a radical youth movement whose members met in groups all over the city to talk about getting rid of oppressive leaders, firing fatal shots and then shooting themselves or drinking poison, an image that appealed to a whole generation of young people in Princip's position, trapped in an ongoing cycle of desperate poverty, sleeping on streets and eating out of trash cans, but now that the plan is in place and there's nothing to stop him from dying a hero, he wants to stop the voices in his head, to find comfort in the memory of a night sky unpopulated by stories about mythic beings, but there's no escape from the stupid excitement beginning to fill the streets, no escape from the noise that the human species can't stop making, a problem that's far more serious now than it was in Princip's time, and down the street I can hear people making hideous noise with blowing machines, pushing dead leaves off lawns and driveways, work that used to be done quietly with rakes and brooms, but apparently someone figured out that noise was more efficient, a decision that seems to have gone unquestioned, so now the leaf blowers are everywhere, such normal parts of life that almost everyone just ignores them, so it's hard to imagine a protest movement, public demonstrations resulting in federal noise regulations, and

even if I wanted to confront the problem by assassinating someone, I'm not sure where I could point the gun I don't have, since
there's no Archduke of Noise planning a public tour of the places under his influence, and even if such a person really existed,
dressed in a uniform covered with ribbons and medals, filling
public space with ghost-written sound bites, many people would
probably greet him with open arms, eager to be convinced that
noise isn't really a serious problem, even as it kills billions of
brain cells every second all over the world, even as we keep telling
ourselves how brilliant we're becoming, an absurdity I can't bring
myself to laugh at anymore, especially in moments like this, with
a loud sound being blocked out by an even louder one, but when
the blowers are finally turned off, the sirens don't sound the
same, like maybe the earlier sirens have stopped and other sirens
have been turned on, an even more disturbing noise, rapidly
shifting between a high sound and a low sound, so loud I can
barely hear the fly that's come in through the window, circling the
room, circling my head, making figure eights in the afternoon
light above my desk, a sound that by itself would be annoying,
but compared to the layers of noise I've just been assaulted by,
the buzzing of the fly almost sounds like music, part of the natu-
ral world, not another example of noise pollution, though before
too long it starts to get on my nerves, especially since there's
something weird about the infinity signs the fly keeps making,
shapes that normally wouldn't be so perfect, wouldn't seem to be
evidence of careful preparation, as if the fly had been practicing,
attending long rehearsals, reaching a point of machine-like precision, like he's not a fly but a drone of some kind, a sign that
someone somewhere decided I was worth spying on, that I had
secrets and agendas worth detecting, an assumption I suppose I
could take as a compliment if it weren't so ridiculous, though of

course there are people all over the world who don't have the luxury of laughing off such possibilities, which reminds me of a woman I was dating a few years ago, who'd spent her childhood in an Iron Curtain country where it was understood that there were microphones and cameras hidden in the walls and floors and ceilings, that even in your own home you had to talk in whispers, write messages to family members using a secret language, on slips of paper that had to be quickly burned, or communicate through subtle manual signals that got revised each day, or say things that always meant something else, so that everything was a matter of coding and decoding, a situation I was appalled by when she first told me about it, leading me to feel gratitude that she was no longer caught in such paranoid conditions, but it soon became clear that she still assumed that anything anyone said was a coded version of something else, so I had to get used to being an object of suspicion, trying to make sure that nothing I said could be taken to mean something else, a problem which got worse when I started to wonder if I ever really meant what I was saying or thinking, if it was even possible to mean what I said or thought, a condition of doubt I finally got so accustomed to that it felt normal, so I'm not surprised to find Princip wondering about a mirror, if it might be allowing people to observe him, people deeply concerned about what he's up to, or people who don't really care but are being paid to seem like they care, to file reports to be read by others who then file other reports, or maybe no one reads the reports, and they just sit in file cabinets until someone throws them away, making room for other reports that no one reads, or maybe Princip's thoughts are moving in a very different direction, and he's starting to suspect that he's trapped in one of those narratives where the main character becomes aware of himself as a verbal device, knowing that someone is writing him into existence, shaping and watching every move he makes, but starting to lose control when the character starts to figure things out, picturing the author so vividly that he can even see the shadow of a pen poised above the page, carefully making phrases, crossing other phrases out, shaping a situation that didn't exist until the language made it seem to, and maybe the character finally decides to fight back, inciting the other characters to resist the author's intentions, which would make good sense in the case of Gavrilo Princip, who had every reason to rebel against the narratives he'd been written into, a phrase that makes it sound like he was nothing more than a renegade signifier, but of course he was more than that, more than a verbal construct in a carefully designed aesthetic environment, and even if he gets re-invented whenever someone writes about him, the fact remains that he was physically there in that room, independent of anyone's imagined version of him, trying to come to terms with the magnitude of what he was planning to do, probably wondering if it was worth it, if it really made sense to kill the archduke, because it was widely understood that many powerful people in Vienna thought that the heir apparent was a pompous jerk, and probably some of them even wanted him dead, in which case Princip was playing right into their hands, doing their dirty work for them without knowing it, a possibility that he probably considered but finally dismissed, in part because he didn't want to go crazy thinking about all the things that might or might not be true, knowing that if you think too much you probably won't do anything, a possibility I'm frequently tormented by, the fear of taking decisive actions without knowing the results in advance, knowing from past experience that I'm not at my best in dangerous situations, not unless I'm driven by moral outrage, convinced that the law is protecting the wrong people, convinced that I need to put myself at risk, no matter what happens, like the time I got herded into a police van and dumped off in a huge auditorium somewhere on the outskirts of Washington, detained with hundreds of other people protesting the US invasion of Iraq, all of us thoroughly disgusted by the Bush administration's military profiteering, which was triggering violence that continues even now, twelve years later, while the people who caused the insanity live in pleasant situations, protected by their wealth, but though I felt that violent action was called for, an assassination of the top Republican leaders, I wasn't ready to pull the trigger myself, probably because I thought I had too much to lose, a mostly pleasant life with good friends and a career I believed in, so I told myself it was enough to be part of a demonstration, feeling good about singing Vietnam era protest songs with hundreds of others in that chilly auditorium, knowing that it wouldn't stop the war, that the White House and the Pentagon were in the back pockets of corporations, whose leaders thought of Iraq as a business opportunity, a place to destroy and rebuild for billions of dollars, violently self-serving designs that soon became obvious even to people who supported the war at first, and I wonder if such people feel guilty now when they see footage of journalists in Iraq getting their heads chopped off, or maybe they still find comfort in all the old Republican rhetoric, clinging to assumptions that sounded shallow and stale more than half a century ago, a thought which may have something to do with old tensions that are starting to surface in various parts of my body, odd feelings of wanting to hold on to things from my past, somehow making it hard to throw out this dusty painting I'm holding, even though it's been in my closet for years, probably because I don't like it enough to put it back up on my wall, and I'm trying to remember where it was hanging before, maybe somewhere near the front door, or in the bathroom, or in my bedroom, or in all three places at different times, or maybe it doesn't matter where it was, especially now that the sirens are getting louder, coming closer, making me wonder if something in my neighborhood is burning down, or if there's been an accident, or a serious crime of some kind, and I'm thinking about something that happened yesterday afternoon, when I went to the corner convenience store to buy popcorn, pretzels, peanuts, potato chips, anything salty and greasy and gassy, but when I tried to pay my credit card wouldn't work, and I didn't have cash and couldn't find my debit card in my wallet, so I had to look sheepish and apologize, move to the magazine alcove in the back of the store, spend fifteen minutes pushing buttons on my phone, fumbling through MasterCard's deadly automated system, repeatedly being told that my call was important and to please wait for the next available representative, and I finally pushed the right buttons, purely by chance, reaching a real person, who turned out to be just as mechanical as the system itself, forced to maintain a rigidly scripted politeness, asking for my mother's maiden name and my first pet's name and my favorite football team, and then my stupid smart phone dropped the call, so I threw the goddamn thing against the back wall of the store, watched it explode in kaleidoscopic slow motion, losing myself in the colors and shapes and sounds, all that microcircuitry falling like fireworks, and I wanted to think that other phones were exploding all over the world, billions of stupid smart phones being shattered, a worldwide rejection of the worldwide web, or whatever it's called these days, but then the store clerk cleared his throat and put a grave look on his face, as if to say that I was acting like a jerk, that my first world middle class white guy problems weren't severe enough to justify my behavior, that billions

28

of people all over the world were dealing with much more desperate situations, that in the past people would have killed to have credit cards and smart phones and all the other conveniences we take for granted today, that I should get a grip on myself and apologize, then get the fuck out and never come back, and the look on his face, the open contempt, made me want to climb onto the roof of the building, stand beside the 7/11 sign and speak through a megaphone, claiming that the idiotic delays I'd just endured were parts of an ongoing conspiracy, a vast network of carefully staged annoyances designed to induce mind-rotting levels of frustration, leading people to assume that they might feel slightly better if they bought something, anything at all, so long as it gave them a feeling of power, even if it was nothing but spending power, the freedom to get stuck with credit card debt, accompanied by a never-ending fear of not having enough, something that feels especially disturbing right now, with the sirens getting closer, apparently not announcing an attack, but coming instead from police cars, and maybe I'm the one they're coming to get, a fear that's come over me many times in my life, that I've made a terrible mistake and now there's no telling how much might be taken away from me, possibly everything, even though I did little more than destroy my communication device, but of course it was all being filmed, like almost everything else these days, so probably someone reviewing the film decided I was dangerous, and I'm reminded of the shoplifting I did back when I was a teenager, when I took model battleships and fighter planes from department stores, spent awkward hours trying to glue them together, frequently getting so frustrated that I finally tore up the instructions, something that normally might be nothing more than a mildly amusing memory, but now it's got me wondering if I could still be accused of crimes I got away with half a century ago, an absurd fear that, nonetheless, gets so strong that I can keep it in check only by telling myself how many times I've moved since then, so that anyone who still wanted to press charges would have trouble finding me, which probably isn't true, since today's hi-tech devices have made it impossible to disappear, even if you're being very careful, and I haven't even been trying to cover my tracks, so I'm not surprised when I look out my open front door and see police lights flashing, approaching from the end of the street, an explosion of color that's almost beautiful at first, briefly reminding me of a light show at an outdoor concert near Mesa Verde a few years ago, where I had a very weird sexual encounter, caught up in the strangely hypnotic music of a group called Assassination Sandwich, a name they took from an art exhibit they'd seen in a small town north of Vancouver, a series of plastic sandwiches with an assassin's face on one piece of bread and the victim's face on the other, and the woman I was trying to fuck on a blanket pitched behind towering blade-like rocks was the former mistress of the artist who made the sandwiches, a young man who'd been doing them as a joke until people told him how brilliant the idea was, which led him to start issuing manifestoes and arranging interviews in art magazines, forgetting the perversely funny feeling that initially made the project happen, and, of course, it made me laugh when she first explained it to me, but the laughter got stale when she wouldn't stop talking about the terribly brilliant man who'd once been her lover, how only a true genius could have come up with such a clever concept, and no matter how insistently I kept trying to push my tongue into her mouth, she kept pulling away and blabbing about the cheese sandwich that featured Princip and the archduke, because the story goes that Princip was eating a cheese sandwich in a café right before he pulled the trigger, talking with a woman he'd gone to bed with a few days before, supposedly the only sex he'd ever had, though I read somewhere that the sandwich story was fake, and I read somewhere else that there really wasn't any sex, that when the crucial moment came, and the woman was stretched out on Princip's borrowed bed, he got nervous, began talking too much, overcome by performance anxiety, so instead of losing his virginity a few days before he shot his way into the history books of the future, he ended up making excuses for himself, just as my own passion came to a frustrating end when I asked the artist's former mistress how much the plastic sandwiches were selling for, pointing out that Princip wouldn't have enough money to buy one of them if he were still alive today, and I remember all too clearly how she pushed me off and got up and walked away without giving an answer, right in the middle of a saxophone solo that made the stage seem like a chunk of ice floating in the Arctic Ocean, the light show filling the sky like aurora borealis, a memory that's now dissolving into the flashing lights of the squad cars blocking my driveway, so I shove the fake pastoral painting back into my closet, quietly shut and lock the front door of my house, thinking that I can pretend I'm not home, which might at least delay the moment of truth, except that they'll probably figure out that I'm here, since my car is in the driveway, and soon I hear footsteps approaching, and the problem is apparently quite serious, somehow requiring the flashing lights and the sirens and the four beefy policemen I can see as I peek through the blinds from my kitchen window, wondering what I could have done that would call for such an extreme response, telling myself that they must have come to the wrong place, that they've made a wrong turn, which brings me back to 1914 again, the fateful mistake the archduke's driver made, turning right when he should have gone straight, stalling right in front of Schiller's café, where Princip was waiting with or without a cheese sandwich, saw that the crown prince was only a few feet away and pulled out his pistol, firing the fatal shots, bullets that would have remained in his gun if the driver hadn't made the wrong turn, possibly the worst mistake ever made, though it wasn't really the driver's fault, since no one told him to keep going straight on the Appel Quay, that turning right onto a street named after the archduke's uncle, Habsburg Emperor Franz Joseph, was no longer part of the plan, so the people to blame were really the military officials traveling with the archduke, the ones who forgot to tell the driver, a mistake that might have been deliberate, part of a conspiracy, an indication that someone with power, possibly people close to the top in Vienna, wanted the crown prince dead, didn't think he was fit to rule one of the world's greatest empires, but I've never been a big fan of conspiracy theories, and even if I've been known to invent such theories on my own, I assume that they tend to be developed by people with too much time on their hands, people who need to distract themselves with sinister fantasies, even when the known facts are compelling enough and logical explanations can be provided, as in the case of the wrong turn in Sarajevo, which can easily be accounted for, since the people who should have informed the driver were probably thinking of too many things at once, struggling with the kind of mental overload that so often leads to mistakes, which might be what I'm facing right now, cops with so much on their minds that they couldn't follow GPS instructions, and now they're checking the name on the mailbox beside the front door, and I'm hoping they'll shake their heads and shrug, get back in their cars, turn off their flashing lights, drive away as if they'd never been here, but instead they're nodding in agreement, so it looks like I'm the one they're looking for, and apparently I've committed such a major crime that they needed to keep their sirens on for more than fifteen minutes, disturbing the peace from one end of town to the other, and now they're knocking loudly, insistently, making me wish I knew what the charges would be, because I need to prepare myself, think about what to say in advance, the details I might need to invent, coming up with a story so compelling that even the most hard-boiled cops would want to keep listening, letting themselves be seduced by a verbal picture, a labyrinth of words they might never emerge from.

TWILIGHT ZONE EPISODE

I wake to the sound of my front door getting pushed open. I sit up quickly, not sure what to do. I throw off my blanket and put my feet on the floor. A woman wearing a sky-blue sweatsuit stumbles into my bedroom. She's tall and covered with snow and she's holding a knife.

She smiles and says: Sorry to scare you like this. Don't worry about the knife. I just used it to pick the lock on your front door.

I manage to say: Why didn't you just knock?

She says: I was knocking for fifteen minutes, and finally it was just too cold to keep standing there waiting. My feet were freezing.

I can hear wind blowing snow into the living room from the open front door. I say: I've always been able to sleep through almost anything. But that knife is making me nervous.

She shrugs and smiles and hands me the knife. I put it on the table next to my bed. I say: Okay, now I feel a whole lot better.

She says: I hope you don't mind if I stay for a minute or two and try to warm up. It's so fucking cold outside!

I say: Yeah, sure, no problem. Let's get the front door closed.

I take my bathrobe from the hook on the closet door, put it on over my flannel pajamas, then follow her into the living room. She steps outside and shakes the snow off her curly black hair and her sweatsuit. She comes back in and locks the door behind her.

I say: I hope you don't mind if I ask you what you're doing here. And maybe you can also tell me your name.

She smiles and says: Yeah, I guess I owe you an explanation. My car broke down a few miles down the road. There doesn't seem to be any cell reception out here, so I couldn't call anyone. I waited in the car for a while, hoping another driver would stop and help me. But no one came, so I finally got out and started walking. After about an hour I saw your house. It was the first sign of human life I'd seen, aside from the telephone poles. I just had to get inside. Sorry if I scared you.

I can hear the wind banging against the windows. I say: Yeah, that was a pretty weird way to wake up. But it's no problem really, now that you've explained the situation. Can I make you a cup of coffee?

She says: That would be great!

I invite her to sit on the couch. I go to the kitchen and get the coffee started, then come back into the living room and sit on a small wooden stool.

She says: It's weird to be somewhere that doesn't have cell reception.

I say: That's one of the reasons I'm living here in the middle of nowhere. I don't like smart phones. I use a land line.

She says: I don't like smart phones either. But it's hard to get by without one these days.

I say: You have to get used to it. I've been unplugged for almost three years now. I think of this house as a media-free zone.

She looks around the room quickly and says: I can see that there's no TV here. Do you have a laptop stashed away somewhere?

I say: I'm totally unplugged. I don't even get a newspaper.

She shakes her head: You don't get news?

I say: I get to town about once every two weeks for supplies. If anything important is happening in the world, I hear about it at the general store.

She shakes her head again: You only get news twice a month?

I say: That's enough for me. I'm trying to recover from information sickness.

She says: Information sickness? I've never heard that term.

I say: It was in a book I read a long time ago, I forget the title. It was mainly about people having sex with dolphins, but the term "information sickness" kept coming up.

She says: Sex with dolphins? Sounds nice, in theory anyway. But do you really believe that information is a kind of sickness? Don't you think it's important to know what's going on in the world?

I say: The first newspaper in the United States was published not far from here, some time in the late eighteenth century. It was only four pages long, and it came out only when there was enough news to report, maybe once a month or once every two or three months.

She says: But it's not the eighteenth century. For a twenty-first century person—

I say: I know what you're going to say. You can trust that I've thought about it carefully, and I think I'm better off not polluting myself with bullshit.

She laughs: There's plenty of that, no question about it.

I ask her how she likes her coffee, go to the kitchen and pour out two cups and bring them back and set them down on the coffee table. I gesture toward the wall of floor-to-ceiling bookshelves and say: It's not that I don't like learning things. But I prefer printed pages to glowing screens.

She nods and warms her hands on the coffee cup I've given her, takes a few quick sips and says: I love this coffee!

I say: It's a local brand I discovered when I moved up here.

She says: How long ago was that?

I say: I've been here five years. I came here from New York City. A few years before I left I sold a screenplay. It was never made into a movie, but I made enough money off it to buy this place. I got it for almost nothing. I invested the rest of the money and now I can live off the monthly dividends. It's not a huge income, but I keep my expenses low.

She says: What was the screenplay about?

I say: The assassination that led to World War I.

She looks disturbed, then tries to conceal the look by nodding eagerly.

I say: Is something wrong?

She tries to smile and finally says: No, nothing's wrong. It's just that I've done some reading about Gavrilo Princip and the archduke—

I say: My screenplay wasn't really about the shooting. It was focused on a conversation that took place in Princip's room three hours before the bullets were fired. One of the other assassins tried to talk him out of killing the archduke. But Princip wouldn't listen. He was convinced that—

She says: A whole movie in just one scene? Was it like *My Dinner with André*? That's one of my favorite movies.

I say: Yeah, pretty much like that. But the dialogue was more realistic, and one of the reasons the movie never got made is that I insisted on using regular people to play the parts of Princip and Danilo Ilic, the other assassin. I didn't want professional actors. I was afraid they might do too much acting.

She says: You didn't want acting?

I say: I didn't want anything theatrical or dramatic. I wanted characters who could behave like normal people having a tense and confused conversation.

She nods: No Hollywood stuff.

I say: Right. And no soundtrack either. That's why it never got made: no theatrical dialogue and no soundtrack. And I also insisted on long segments that took place in an empty mirror, just voices talking and the characters off camera.

She says: You wouldn't compromise? Even though lots of money was at stake?

I say: I saw no reason to make a movie based on trite cinematic formulas. We've already had enough movies like that. And a Hollywood movie about an important historical event would just be another Hollywood movie.

She says: That's a pretty extreme way of seeing it. But I admire your artistic integrity—almost as much as I admire your coffee. There's nothing like a great cup of coffee on a cold morning like this one.

I nod and say: You were out there in the cold for a long time. Are you still cold? Can I give you a sweater?

She says: No need. Your house is plenty warm. From the outside it looked like a solar house.

I nod: That's one of the reasons I bought it.

She smiles: It's so warm in here I'm tempted to take off my sweatsuit. But I'm not wearing anything underneath.

I smile but I'm not sure what to say. The silence lasts a few seconds too long, so I change the subject: So why are you all the way up here in northern Maine in the dead of winter. Are you taking a ski trip?

She shakes her head and says: I tried skiing once, a few years ago, when some friends treated me to a ski lodge weekend for my

41

thirtieth birthday. My first time on the slope I sprained my ankle, and that was the end of my skiing career.

I smile: So you're up here in the frozen middle of nowhere because—

She says: Can I have more coffee, if it's not too much trouble?

I nod and go to the kitchen to pour another cup. The wind bangs against the windows, lifting the snow in the yard into wild spirals. When I go back into the living room with the coffee, she's standing by the book shelf paging through a book of surrealist paintings, turning the big pages quickly with evident pleasure.

She says: I used to do paintings like these, but when someone told me my paintings were surreal, I couldn't paint anymore. It was like suddenly I had to *try* to be surreal, though I'd never tried to be anything before.

I nod and say: The word surreal is totally overused. People use it to describe almost anything that's even slightly unusual. It kept coming up in an article I was reading a few weeks ago about recently released footage based on that wall that appeared in Central Park back in June. You've heard about that, haven't you?

She says: Yeah, a little bit. It sounds pretty weird.

I hate it when people call something weird. It's even worse than calling something surreal. But I don't want to put her on the defensive, so I nod and say: It sounds extremely weird, the way it appeared out of nowhere and no one understands what it's made of or what it's doing there. The last few times I was in town getting supplies, the wall was a major topic of conversation. But like I said, I was reading this article in a film journal, and apparently this well-known documentary filmmaker—I forget his name—was making a film about the wall, and when he tried to review and edit his footage, the wall wasn't there, and footage featuring Gavrilo Princip had somehow replaced it. The guy who wrote the article kept using the word surreal, and I got so annoyed that I couldn't keep reading, even though I know a little bit about Princip from the research I did for my screenplay.

She says: What was the name of the journal? Is it here on your bookshelf?

I say: No, I don't have a copy, and I don't remember the name. Which isn't surprising, since apparently the wall has weird effects on what you remember. Even reading about it makes you forget crucial things about what you were reading.

She smiles and says: Then I'm better off not reading about it. I forget things all the time, and I don't want to make the situation worse!

I laugh and sip my coffee. She looks around the room, then says: So you don't work or watch TV or play around on the Internet. How do you spend your time? Are you working on another screenplay?

I say: I spend most of my time reading and meditating and taking walks. I'm thinking about getting a dog.

She says: So I guess all the meditating has been helping you detox from Information Sickness, right? Are things getting better?

I say: I'm making slow but steady progress, though on some days it's hard to tell. There's still so much noise in my head. I spent more than half a century getting my mind filled up with bullshit, just like everyone else. It's not something you can recover from overnight.

She says: You're over fifty? You look younger.

I say: That's what people tell me. But I'll be sixty in August.

She says: You're aging well. And I'm not just saying that to be nice.

Again, I'm not sure what to say. It feels like she might be flirting with me, maybe because she's happy to be out of the cold, or maybe because she hasn't had sex in a while. It's been years since I've been with anyone, and sometimes on summer days in town I see women in revealing outfits and I develop fantasies about sleeping with them. When she said she wanted to take off her sweatsuit earlier, I was excited, even though it also made me feel awkward and uncertain. I've sworn off serious relationships. My long-term involvements with women have always been painful and destructive. But if the aging process is supposed to reduce your sex drive, it's not working that way for me.

I finally smile and say: It's nice of you to say that, even if you *were* just being nice.

She quickly says: I wasn't. I mean, I—

I say: But you still haven't told me why you're up here in the frozen wastes of northern Maine.

Again her smile seems forced. She puts the book of paintings back on the shelf, sits on the couch and stares at the coffee table, as if the grain of the wood might give her an answer to my question. She finally says: I was down at the university for a music festival, performances of works by Holocaust era composers silenced by the Nazis. They were playing Schoenberg's "Transfigured Night," which has always been one of my favorite pieces of music.

I nod in agreement, but I'm confused. I'm familiar with the "Thwarted Voices" festival, but I'm pretty sure it always takes place in the summer, an outdoor event. She looks like someone trying not to get caught lying, someone who knows that she's messing up details that should been carefully considered in advance. I don't want to embarrass her, so I say: I've always preferred "Transfigured Night" to Schoenberg's later work. I don't like the twelve-tone stuff.

She laughs and says: Me neither. I mean, in theory it's interesting, but it's more fun to talk about than to listen to. Still, I'm glad Schoenberg got out of Germany before the Nazis got him. Did you know that he spent the last few decades of his life in Hollywood? It's very weird to think of Schoenberg in Hollywood. It would be like putting Mickey Mouse and Donald Duck in Vienna, except that Mickey and Donald are probably already in Vienna.

I smile and say: Along with Ronald McDonald.

She laughs and gets up and goes to the bookshelf again, scanning the titles. She narrows her eyes and pulls out an old thick book I don't recognize. She dusts it off and opens it and quickly turns the pages, looking puzzled. Then she stops and looks even more puzzled. She says: What's this?

She starts to hand me the book, but drops it, losing her place. I pick it up and start turning the pages. They're all blank. I say: This is weird! I mean, I hate it when people call something weird, but this time the word makes perfect sense: all these blank pages!

She says: But they're not all blank. Keep turning the pages.

I keep turning the pages. Then I see what she's talking about. There's writing on one of the pages. It looks at first like math, calculations that might have been made in a madhouse, no numbers, just a combination of images, maybe a code of some kind, or a score for music that no one has ever played before, sequences of signs that look like crescent moons and lightbulbs, traffic signs and pitchforks, greater-than signs and less-than signs and question marks turned sideways, parentheses and ampersands, pyramids, ringed planets, donuts and feathered arrows and windshield wipers. Something about it feels dangerous, an invisible finger stabbing my brain through a gaping hole in my forehead, but the longer I look the more I start to believe that I know what I'm reading, like the signs on the page are changing me into the only person on earth who can understand them, the only person who knows how to read the kind of story they're telling.

I close the book and put it back on my shelf and say: I've never seen anything like that before. In fact, I've never seen that book before. I don't know how it got here. Maybe I got it from the thrift shop in town at some point and then put it on the shelf and forgot about it.

She laughs and says: Maybe reading that article about the wall made you forget.

I smile and say: No doubt. But those weird signs on the page had some kind of power. Just now, I was starting to think I knew how to read them, and how to pronounce them, like they might have been a kind of incantation, a way to cast magic spells, a way to use words to rearrange time and space. Not that I believe in magic spells. In fact it's embarrassing to be talking like this. But it felt like the page was laughing at me, or maybe *with* me, or maybe both. It's hard to explain.

She narrows her eyes and slowly nods, like someone trying a little too hard to seem wise, or like a detective who's just about to crack a tough case. An icy branch gets blown against the window. She turns and looks outside. For a moment she looks like she might be expecting someone, a partner in some kind of crime, or someone trying to track her down, a private eye or secret service agent.

She finally says: It's amazing how warm it is in here. I'm really tempted to take my sweatsuit off.

I want her to, but something about it still feels wrong, so I ask her if she wants more coffee.

She laughs and says: No. But I really want to take my sweatsuit off.

I say: With nothing underneath?

She puts a big smile on her face and says: Yeah. With nothing underneath!

I try to return the smile, then say: But first you have to tell me how you ended up so far north. I mean, the university is more than a hundred miles south of here and—

She shrugs and says: Why don't we just fuck? It would make things a lot easier.

I say: This is starting to feel like a *Twilight Zone* episode.

She says: Is it? Yeah, I guess it is. Or maybe not. People wouldn't say "fuck" in a *Twilight Zone* episode.

I say: But if it were a *Twilight Zone* episode, we might fuck and fall asleep in each other's arms and then you'd wake up in *your* house and I'd be coming through the door with a knife and—

She says: People wouldn't fuck in a *Twilight Zone* episode. There wouldn't be any explicit imagery. There'd be strict limits on how much skin could be shown.

I nod: Did you know that Rod Serling wanted to make the show much more politically blunt, but he was forced by the network's big shots to make his left-wing statements indirectly, by developing symbolic situations that the show's sponsors wouldn't be offended by? I never even noticed political concepts in *Twilight Zone* episodes.

She says: When censorship really works, you don't notice it.

I laugh: That's a good line. Did it just pop into your head, or is it something you read somewhere?

She looks hurt: You think I memorize lines from books, so I can say them later and sound impressive? I knew a guy who used to do that, and I always felt sorry for him.

I say: It's just that the line was so exact that it sounded rehearsed, like something you got from a book, or something you thought about for a long time, then wrote down and revised until it was perfect. But it's true: When censorship really works, you don't notice it.

I look out the window through the whirling snow toward the road, which leads through several miles of thick evergreen forest to the town where I get my supplies. I say: Do you have AAA? You can use my phone to give them a call and get your car towed to the service station in town. There's a good mechanic there—

She puts her hand on my arm and says: Do you like me?

It seems like there's only one safe way to answer, so I say: Yes.

She says: You really do?

I say: I really do. I mean, I don't really know you, but I'm having fun talking to you.

She says: So there's no need for me to leave right away, is there?

I shrug and say: No, not really. I just thought we should do something about your car and—

But she's not listening. She's looking at the broad oak floor-boards, the large oval rug. She says: I love your rug. It's perfect!

I smile and say: I found it at a garage sale and had it cleaned.

She says: It's exactly right for this room. It fits your personality.

I nod and look at the rug, which is orange with a sky blue sun in the center. The sun is smiling, but it's not a joyful smile, and its light green eyes look serious, slightly puzzled, as if they were facing something that didn't make sense.

She says: It fits your personality.

I say: Everything fits my personality.

She says: It does?

I say: Yes. I mean no, not really.

She says: Then why did you say it?

I shrug and say: I say all sorts of things I don't really mean. I get nervous when I'm talking to people, but I don't want them to notice it, so I say try to say things that sound clever and strange, to make it seem that I'm confident and relaxed. I'm the kind of guy who—

She says: I hate it when people generalize about themselves. I hate "I'm the kind of guy or girl" statements.

I can feel my annoyance building. I wasn't entirely lying when I told her I enjoyed talking to her, but she seems to like making challenging statements, and I don't like being challenged, even when I deserve it, especially when I deserve it. I tell myself to conceal my annoyance and keep the conversation going. I say: Are you trying to tell me that you don't ever think about yourself in general terms? That's hard to believe.

She says: Of course I do. And the generalizations generally turn out to be false. They're quickly invalidated by things I say and do.

I say: Right. That's how it works for me too.

I look outside. The icy trees are bending in the wind. I say: It looks really cold outside.

She says: And it's so nice and warm in here! And I think I really need to take off my sweatsuit. Are you ready?

I nod and smile and we go to my bedroom, take off our clothes and start kissing with our tongues, sliding quickly beneath my warm blanket. It's awkward at first but then things work well. We start to make all the good noises.

There's a knock at the door. It kills the moment, kills the passion. We give each other a look that says that maybe it was just the wind blowing a branch against the house, though we both know it probably wasn't.

There's another knock at the door.

I look at her carefully, searching her face for secrets she might be keeping. I'm half expecting her to vanish, for the whole day to have been a fantasy or dream, but she's there in my bed as firmly as anyone has ever been in bed with me, and I'm thinking we should just start fucking again, but I know it won't be the same. I can see it in her face and feel it in my body.

On the wall above my dresser there's a thrift shop painting, which I bought because it somehow managed to combine an old red barn, grazing cows, and a flying saucer. But now there's something wrong: There's no flying saucer. In its place, there's a cartoon sun with a big smile, looking like it's just finished gobbling up half of the human race and is thinking now about gobbling up the other half. For a second I'm sure that the change is related in some way to the weird signs in the old book. But I'm not sure what the connection means, and it's not the right time to try to figure it out. It's possible that there's no connection at all.

I tell myself that if we don't make any noise, maybe the person will think there's nobody home and go away, and then we can get things going again. But now there's more knocking, and it sounds urgent, almost menacing.

I start to get up and put on my bathrobe, thinking that I'll try to get rid of the person at the door as quickly as possible, then get back in bed. But she grabs me and forcefully pulls me back onto the sheets. When I try to get back up she slams me back down. I don't want to fight with her, but the knocking is getting louder, and I know things won't work in bed until I can get rid of our obnoxious visitor. It briefly occurs to me that the person at the door is the woman I'm in bed with, that she'll disappear in my bed right before she comes through the door in her sweatsuit with a knife, and then we'll have the same conversation we had before, talking about the wall and mass information and Gavrilo Princip, and then we'll go to bed and be interrupted again by someone knocking at the door, and she'll fade from my bed and enter the house again covered with snow in her sweatsuit with her knife, and the whole thing will start over again. Time will be stuck in a moment that can't stop repeating itself, like something from *The Twilight Zone*. I know there was an episode based on a moment repeating itself, but I can't recall it in detail, even though I used to have a DVD collection of all the *Twilight Zone* episodes, and I watched each one at least twice.

I say: Listen, you've got to let me get up and answer the door. You can hide under the covers or in the closet. I'll quickly get rid of whoever it is and then we can start fucking again.

She whispers fiercely: Keep your fucking voice down! Don't answer the door!

She grabs the knife from the table and points it at my throat and says: Do you understand?

I say: Not really. And there's really no need for that knife.

She whispers: Keep your fucking voice down!

I say: What are you so afraid of?

She says: You don't want to know.

I say: You owe me an explanation.

She says: I was planning to kill someone, okay? But a friend of mine talked me out of it.

I say: Who were you planning to kill?

She says: Never mind.

I say: No, tell me. Who? If you didn't really do it, why are you worried? Lots of people think about killing other people, but if they don't actually do it, there's no real crime, is there?

She says: My friend couldn't keep her mouth shut.

I say: She told someone?

She says: Not exactly. But her husband read one of her emails. He thought she and I were having an affair—

I say: Were you?

She says: Yeah.

The knocking keeps getting louder. I'm surprised that the person hasn't just pushed the door open. Then I remember that she locked it right after she shook the snow off her sweat suit.

I say: So you're bisexual.

She says: More or less.

I say: That must have been awkward, getting caught like that. But still, why are you afraid of someone knocking at the door?

She says: Do I have to explain it?

I say: I think it's better if you do. If I know the specifics, we can make a plan to deal with the person at the door.

She says: Okay. But don't act like I'm crazy.

I say: I lived in New York for twenty-five years. I've heard everything.

She says: I wasn't planning to kill just anyone. I was planning to kill a certain high profile Republican leader. I was planning to make sure that he didn't get a chance to run for President. I mean, I'm not a big fan of the Democratic party, but this Republican guy would be worse. He's total filth. And since I lost my nerve and didn't kill him, he's still got a chance, a really good chance. He'll probably be the Republican presidential candidate later this year. And you can't count on American voters to make intelligent decisions.

I nod and say: Scary, isn't it? I try to ignore the elections. The presidential campaigns are such disgusting spectacles, and no matter who gets elected, he'll just be another tool of the corporations that own the White House. But I'm still not sure what you're so afraid of.

She says: It turns out that my friend's husband is in the CIA. I never knew it. I always thought he was just a political science professor.

I say: So you've been marked as a dangerous person? A potential threat to our so-called national security? A terrorist?

She says: I started seeing strange people following me on the streets. It went on for several weeks. So I figured I'd get as far away from everything as possible. I was keeping in touch with my friend for a while, trying to find out who was after me and what they might do if they found me. We were texting each other. But then I read somewhere that satellite communication is a dead giveaway, making it easy for people to find you. So I—

I say: That's one of the reasons I unplugged myself. I didn't like the feeling of being watched, like I was on an electronic leash.

She says: So I stopped the online messaging, but then I started wondering about my friend. I mean, she's married to someone in the CIA, and she must have known that it wasn't safe to be texting, so maybe she was secretly working with her husband, helping them track me down. So now I'm not sure who I can trust.

I say: You're figuring that the person at the door—

She says: Who else could it be?

She's probably right. People don't normally come to my door. Mail and packages don't come here. I've got a P.O. Box in town.

She's looking at me with terror in her eyes. I don't think she's guilty of anything serious, but in the Homeland Security Era, you don't have to be guilty. You just have to seem like you might at some point be capable of doing dangerous things. The fact that she allowed herself to be talked out of killing someone should be a point in her favor. She's not like Gavrilo Princip, who refused to listen, even though his friend made good arguments, or at least they were good arguments in my screenplay. The truth is that no one really knows what they talked about. It's one of those crucial moments no history book has ever recorded.

There haven't been any knocks at the door in the past few minutes, and I want to believe that the person has gone away. But when the wind dies down slightly I hear footsteps crunching in the snow outside the bedroom window, so I know there's still danger. There's a pause. I'm assuming that he's listening, and maybe wondering if it makes sense to break through the window. I'm waiting for a knock on the glass, or possibly an explosion of glass and the grim face of a Homeland Security agent, picking himself up off the floor and pulling out a gun. But nothing happens, and soon I can hear his footsteps crunching their way toward the front of the house.

I say: So now I understand why you made that weird face when I mentioned Gavrilo Princip. But you at least came to your senses. He didn't, and look what happened.

She says: You think he was wrong? I don't. I think he had the guts to actually *do* what others were only willing to discuss. I feel bad that I couldn't do the same thing. My friend and I had big plans. We were going to form a network of assassins and keep killing off Republican presidential candidates. She had a friend with some kind of hi-tech job, and she was going to get him to help us develop an army of killer nanobots, thousands of microscopic assassins, and—

I say: Seriously?

She nods and says: Yeah, sort of. I mean, I thought we were being serious at the time. And then my friend changed her mind and then she changed mine. But even before that, I couldn't quite get myself to believe it. I kept thinking that if we really tried to put our plans into action, we'd botch everything. We'd look like total idiots.

I say: That's more or less how things happened in Sarajevo too, a series of mistakes that would have been funny if the results hadn't been so sinister. It never should have worked. But somehow it did. I've always been amazed that such a slapstick event had such gruesome consequences, changing the world forever. But you said earlier that you've done some reading about the assassination, so you already know what I'm telling you—

She says: Not really. I mean, the way you're describing it makes it sound funny, but I've always thought of Princip as a tragic figure. My roommate in college was from an old Serbian family, and for her, Gavrilo Princip was a hero. There's a bridge named after him in Sarajevo, right across the street from the place where he shot the archduke. But it sounds like in your screenplay he's a just another psycho, a delusional clown.

I say: Will the real Gavrilo Princip please stand up.

She looks puzzled, so I say: There was a fifties daytime TV show that used that phrase—will the real so-and-so please stand up. I can't remember the name of the show. But it was part of the same TV world as *The Twilight Zone*—only a lot less interesting. I used to watch it when I was sick and got to stay home from school. I think it might have been called *What's My Line*. Or no, that was something else. Maybe *To Tell the Truth*. Yeah, that sounds right.

She shrugs.

There's another knock on the front door, this one openly hostile and threatening, like we've got no right to keep someone outside, even if we're afraid of what they might do to us. I look out toward the woods behind the house. If we could just get dressed and open the window without making noise, we could climb outside and escape, use a branch to cover our tracks in the snow, take a path that follows a frozen stream through hills that shine like broken teeth to the streets of a dead subdivision, where hundreds of empty identical houses have waited for decades to be rediscovered. I found the place a few years ago, and I took some walks there. It was weird to enter houses no one had lived in, imagining all the daytime TV shows that no one had ever watched, all the diapers no one had ever changed, all the sprinkler systems that never clicked on, all the stupid marital arguments about money

55

that never happened, all the dismal vanilla sex that never took place. I wanted to like the desolate post-apocalyptic feeling, but the place always felt more haunted than a ghost town. It even might have been too weird for an episode of *The Twilight Zone*, even for a fully uncensored version, for a story that didn't rely on the usual narrative strategies, no strange and surprising reversal at the end, no fully developed characters to identify with or despise, though of course there would have been powerful setting details, so unnervingly powerful that I can't imagine going there again, even if it might help us avoid the Homeland Security people.

Instead I'm thinking now about the unexpected book on the shelf, the incomprehensible images almost concealed by all the blank pages. I remember the feeling of starting to understand what I was reading, and now as I picture the signs in my head a translation quickly begins. The strange combination of images takes the form of normal language, and I'm taking over the story they seem to be telling. It starts like this: He wakes to the sound of his front door getting pushed open. He sits up quickly, not sure what to do. He thows off his blanket and puts his feet on the floor. A woman wearing a sky-blue sweatsuit stumbles into his bedroom. She's tall and covered with snow and she's holding a knife.

All I need to do now is keep telling the story, changing parts of it here and there, making sure that at the end there's no one at the door.

THERAPY

I became a killer this morning. A dog darted out in front of my car on the freeway. I didn't even have time to take my foot off the gas, let alone hit the brakes. It was a big dog, a pit bull the size of a German shepherd. He tried to jump a split second before I slammed into him. I felt him getting crushed underneath the car. Three seconds later, I looked in the rear view mirror and saw the dog on his back, legs in the air. Then another car ran him over.

There was news on the radio, something about violence in Iraq, then an advertising jingle. I couldn't tell what they were trying to sell. My body started shaking. I pulled off the freeway, killed the engine, stared at the dashboard. I wondered why the radio was silent. Then I saw the ignition key in my hand and remembered that I'd just turned off the engine. Cars were zooming past, sunlight glaring on chrome and windows. I thought of the many beautiful hours I'd spent with dogs throughout my life. I'd always thought that having a dog was the greatest thing in the world. Now I'd killed one. I knew it was the owner's fault, not mine. He never should have let his dog run off leash near a freeway. But blaming him didn't change the fact that the dog was dead and I was the one who killed him.

I left my car and walked back on the shoulder of the freeway. By the time I got to the dog, he'd been run over many times. His skull was crushed and his body was mangled. Cars kept whizzing past, running him over again and again. It would have been dangerous to go out and try to pull his remains off the freeway. I looked around for someone who might have been the dog's owner, but there was no one else there, just speed limit signs and billboard ads for booze and cars and cell phones. I didn't know what to do, so I walked back and sat in my car, shaking and crying. I hated myself and everyone else, the whole human race with its deadly machines of pleasure and convenience. I swore that after I drove myself home I would never drive again.

Getting home took three times as long as it normally would have. I took back roads I'd never been on before. I got lost twice and had to stop and try to read the county map I keep in the glove compartment. It was difficult because my hands kept shaking. When I finally got home I called in sick at my job. Then I called my friend Gabe and told him what happened. He asked if I'd been physically hurt, if my car was damaged. He tried to get me to calm down and stop feeling bad for the dog, to see that I'd been lucky it wasn't a person I'd killed. After all, Gabe said, if I'd run over someone's child I'd be facing hysterical parents and major legal complications. He also reminded me that the dog was a giant pit bull, probably used for intimidation and fighting, a dangerous animal. But I couldn't calm down. I kept seeing the dog in front of my car. I kept feeling the moment of impact. Gabe could tell I needed help, so he said he would change his plans for the day and we set up a time to meet for lunch.

That was two hours ago. Since then, I've been trying to read, but I can't focus. My hands keep shaking. I read a page, forget what I've read, read the page again and still can't remember.

Finally, I can't sit in my chair any longer. I've got to get out and try to walk the disturbance out of my body. The late November weather is perfect, stiff wind, lots of clouds, a few patches of blue sky, about fifty degrees. I live in an old seaside town, a great place for meditative walks. But nothing is helping me now, not the cupolas and gables of the old houses in my neighborhood, not the oak trees throwing patterns of light and shade on the lawns and sidewalks, not the snow-covered mountains ten miles east of town. The image keeps coming back—the dog in front of my car, the moment of impact.

I look at my watch and see that I'm due to have lunch with Gabe in forty-five minutes. I decide to go to the restaurant and wait. They almost always have newspapers there, and maybe I can distract myself by reading about what's happening in the world. The restaurant, a converted Victorian house, is only a few blocks away. It's called The View because it looks out on the ocean. Normally such places are expensive, but the owner bought the house for almost nothing forty years ago, and since he did most of the renovations himself, he can afford to keep the prices down. A good lunch is less than five dollars, and then you can sit with coffee and a book for the afternoon, listening to the ocean.

As soon as I get there I start to feel better, especially since I know that Gabe will be here soon. But the papers are full of the usual violence, threats of nuclear war with North Korea, continued conflict in the Gaza Strip, beheadings in Iraq and drones in Afghanistan. I don't need more evidence of how mentally disturbed our species is, how large a part the United States plays in sustaining that disturbance. I focus instead on the two women at the next table. I keep the paper in front of my face, pretending to read, so they won't know that I'm tracking their conversation.

Soon it's clear that their names are Colette and Patty. I haven't looked at them carefully, since I don't want to seem intrusive. But I got the impression when I first sat down that they're in their mid thirties. Patty has a deep voice and talks quickly. Colette giggles a lot but doesn't sound stupid.

Patty says: You didn't know me back then, but I used to lie all the time. I couldn't control it. I even used to lie to my therapist. But he could tell when I was lying, or at least that's what he said. I—

Colette giggles and says: Isn't it pointless to lie in therapy? Isn't it a little like cheating in Solitaire—only worse, since you're paying for it and trying to get help?

Patty says: Sure, but like I said, I couldn't control it. My therapist said it was because I didn't think people would think I was interesting unless I pretended that strange and amazing things had happened to me.

Colette says: But you're a beautiful woman, and you know it. Guys are always dying to hear anything that comes out of your mouth. Why would you need to make things up?

Patty says: My therapist said it was because my father seduced me, then made me believe it was my fault for seducing him. This led me to believe that men only wanted me for sex, that I wasn't interesting in any other way. The trouble is, I don't remember going to bed with my father.

Colette says: That's what I don't like about therapists. They always want to make it seem like your parents did something to you.

Patty says: Right. And I'm pretty sure that this therapist I'm telling you about—he was dead ringer for JFK—wanted me to seduce him, and that's why he came up with the story about my father.

Colette giggles: I remember reading a book about JFK, how he wanted sex all the time. But I always thought JFK was ugly. I hate it when I see his face in documentaries.

There's a pause. I can hear the ice in Colette's glass. Or maybe it's Patty's glass. I think Patty's annoyed because she wanted Colette to be jealous and think how great it would be to have a therapist who looked like JFK. And maybe Colette did feel jealous but didn't want to admit it, so she said that Kennedy was ugly. I've always been good at reading between the lines, figuring out the complexities of human interaction, all the concealings and distortions. At times I think I should have become a therapist. I don't remember why I didn't major in psychology.

Patty clears her throat and says: JFK was hot. And so was this therapist. His name was John Franklin Kelly, but he went by his middle name and told me to call him Frank, since he said he wanted to be frank with me. I think that was supposed to be funny, though he said it with a straight face, the same straight face he used when he gave me his seduction theory—I mean it's straight out of Freud but Frank made it seem like he came up with it on his own, since he figured a beautiful blond like me wouldn't know the first thing about psychology. But anyway, I told him about this time I was walking home at night and I saw this glowing thing descending from the sky. It looked like a huge brain, and it landed in a field between two abandoned houses. You know the place I'm talking about, don't you? One of the houses used to be a gigantic thrift shop. They always had the most amazing stuff. It's only a few blocks from here. Anyway, there was this thing in the empty field, and when I got a closer look I thought it might be a glowing mass of jelly, about the size of a king size water bed, and—

Colette giggles: You expected JFK to believe this?

Patty says: I know it sounds weird, but I swear it really happened. And Frank wouldn't buy it. He insisted that the story was a cover up for something else, a symbolic version of—

Colette giggles: The thing about your father?

Patty says: The thing about my father. Which I'm pretty sure never happened. But Frank made a big deal about the king size water bed, since my parents had a king size water bed. At least, that's what I remember. But maybe I'm only thinking they had a water bed because Frank assumed that they must have had one and I felt bad about not going along with his interpretations. I mean, after a while I couldn't tell what really happened and what didn't. It's like I was reinventing my past in therapy. It's like—

Colette says: Back when I was fourteen and my brother Mark was eleven, he got a pet turtle and kept him in an empty aquarium he found in the garage. I remember how hard he worked to clean out the aquarium and turn it into a nice place for his turtle to live. We'd had tropical fish at one point, but they all died. I guess this was Mark's way of bringing them back to life. He'd go out every day, give the turtle food and change the water, and when he thought I wasn't around to spy on him, he'd tell the turtle all sorts of things, how he couldn't stand his life and wanted to kill himself. I told my parents about it, but when they asked Mark what was wrong, he couldn't tell the truth.

Colette pauses. Patty starts to say something, but quickly stops. The sound of conversations in the restaurant gets louder, then fades. I can hear the ice in someone's glass again.

Colette says: I think because the truth was so painful, my brother needed to tell people lies about what he was feeling, long elaborate lies he'd learned to believe, except when he was talking to his turtle. Only the turtle knew the whole truth, and when the turtle died my brother killed himself. I never got over it. If only my brother had known how to tell the truth—

Patty says: If you'd been in therapy with Frank, he would have said the turtle was a phallic symbol.

Colette says: But the turtle was real. I'm not making anything up.

Patty says: Frank would have said that you're always making things up, even when you're trying not to.

I want to put my paper down and join the conversation. I already feel like I'm part of it, and I'm thinking that Frank is probably right, maybe not about the turtle story, but certainly about Patty's story. Glowing brains don't fall out of the sky and turn into king size water beds. Or if they do, experts appear on the news with explanations, making things seem normal. But something about it makes me feel strange, like Patty's telling my own story, and I can't admit it. When she mentioned the field a few blocks away, I thought back to a night a few years ago, when a snarling dog followed me home in the dark, and I stopped in front of that field and threatened him with a stick, but he kept following at a distance, snarling and almost attacking. I wasn't sure what kind of dog he was because I never saw anything more than a shadow. But now that shadow seems unreal. Something about that memory seems false, or incomplete.

I hear something shatter on the hardwood floor. It sounds like a dropped glass of water. I lower my paper to see who made the mess, just as Gabe arrives, sits down and asks me how I'm doing. But he stops in the middle of a word and looks at Colette and smiles with bedroom eyes. Colette giggles. I finally take a good look at her, and I like what I see, kind blue eyes and brilliant long red hair. He looks at Patty with obvious pleasure, says hi and tells her his name is Gabe and shakes her hand. He's always told me that he doesn't like blonds, but Patty's long blond hair is hard not to like. It looks like she spends lots of time and money on it.

Patty tries not to smile but it's clear that she likes him. Most women do. It's not that he's handsome or well-built. He's extremely short and rarely shaves and always looks like he's hungry. But in the five years I've known him, he's always had at least one lover, and sometimes two or three at once, all crazy about him. So I'm not surprised that Patty likes him. It's just that I've never seen Gabe so bluntly flirtatious. He's always extremely polite at first, letting the women make the first move. And they always do.

For twenty seconds no one speaks. The whole restaurant goes silent, as if the sound has been turned off. It's like we're all just colored forms in a painting, and people in a museum are gathered in front of us, imagining our lives, the things we might be talking about. I know exactly what kind of people they are, how they think and what they'll probably do once they leave the museum. One of them looks familiar, and though he's not someone I've met in person, I know I've seen his picture in twentieth-century history books, chapters about the beginnings of World War I in Sarajevo, a young Serbian nationalist named Gavrilo Princip, who looks so much like Gabe that it's hard to believe they're not the same person. It occurs to me that their names are almost the same: Gabriel Prince, Gavrilo Princip.

Then I realize that I can't hear the ocean outside. I look out the window to make sure the sea is still there. The water is a chilly green, gleaming in the afternoon sun. But I can't hear the waves crashing into the cliffs, a sound that normally makes The View such a pleasant place to spend an afternoon. The owner doesn't fill the space with annoying music. He lets the sound of the sea create an atmosphere of its own.

Then I remember the shattering glass on the hardwood floor. The sound cuts back in, as if someone had flipped a switch. But something is wrong when I turn my eyes from the sea back into the room. Gabe isn't here. We're not in a museum. Colette and Patty say exactly what they said a minute ago.

Colette: But the turtle was real. I'm not making anything up.

Patty: Frank would have said that you're always making things up, even when you're trying not to.

I've got the paper in front of my face, but now it sounds like they're talking to amuse me, like they know I've been listening all along. I wonder if the whole conversation has been staged. I take a chance and lower the paper and smile in their direction, as if to acknowledge the game we've been playing. But they just keep talking as if I'm not there. Gabe walks through the front door and across the room. When he sits he briefly looks at Patty and Colette but says nothing. He shakes my hand and asks me how I'm doing, if I'm still as upset as I was on the phone.

I'm not sure what to say, so I say: Yes and no.

Gabe says: Yes and no?

I nod: Yes and no.

He says: Yes meaning what? No meaning what?

I say: Just yes and no.

Gabe laughs: Yes, meaning that you're still feeling horrible? No, meaning that you're starting to see that it doesn't really matter?

I say: Yes and no.

He laughs: That's all you can say? Yes and no?

Something perverse in me wants to keep saying it, making Gabe feel awkward. I'm mad at him for flirting with Patty and Colette instead of making me the sole focus of his attention. But now they're getting up and leaving their tip, not even looking at us. Did Gabe really flirt with them? Was he really here a minute ago, right before the sound clicked off? I start to think I've added something that didn't happen, probably because if things can be added and subtracted, maybe I can subtract what happened this morning. Maybe the dog doesn't have to be dead.

Gabe laughs: That's all you can say? Yes and no?

I know I can't say it again but I really want to. It would be so good to just stay in that phrase and go through the rest of my life saying nothing more than yes and no. It's the perfect response to so many situations. But I don't want Gabe to get mad at me. After all, he did go out of his way to spend time with me.

I say: Yes, I'm still upset. No, I don't feel quite as messed up now that we're here talking. It's great that you changed your plans to make sure I'm okay.

He says: You would have done the same for me.

In fact, I already have done the same for him several times, when women found out that he was cheating on them, started throwing things and making threats and promising never to see him again. I was always surprised that it bothered him so much when they lost control. After all, he prided himself on making sure that beneath his pleasant manners and careful displays of concern, he never cared about how they reacted to him. Being with several women at once was a way not to get too involved. We talked about it many times. He liked the feeling of safety and power it gave him. But somehow he always felt hurt when the women figured out what he was up to. His feelings made no sense to me. And now my feelings make no sense to him.

In the past, I tried to reason his pain away, hoping to get rid of it as fast as possible. It never worked, but he always said he appreciated my efforts. Now I'm in the same position he was in. I know he can't reason away my feelings, but I have to let him try

68

and act like I'm grateful. I suppose it's the thought that counts, but I feel too disturbed right now to find comfort in a cliché. So I quickly say: Let's be clear from the start. There's nothing you can say to make me feel better. Today I became an accidental killer. Yes, it was just a dog, and yes, it was the owner's fault, and yes, the dog might have been dangerous. Yes, yes, yes. But I hate the way we jump in our cars and kill and pollute and talk about how wrong it is and how something needs to be done and then we get back in our cars and do it again. I can't—

Gabe smiles: You're right. It's wrong. But if you already know we're not going to change, why get so worked up?

I say: It's *because* I know we're not going to change. That's what's getting me so worked up.

Gabe says: But you *can* change. Stop driving your car and start riding a bike. It's good exercise. Either that or admit that it doesn't really bother you enough to make a simple change.

I've got no answer. He's right. It wouldn't take much to start riding a bike. It would take me longer to get to work, but so what? The sacrifice would be minor. I haven't ridden a bike in twenty years, and I'd have to get back in shape, but it wouldn't take long. Riding the bike would get me in shape. I'm sure I can find a ten-speed bicycle on craigslist. Or maybe for something that's so important, I should forget about saving money and buy something new, something state-of-the-art. They've probably got bicycles now that pedal themselves and know where you're going.

Gabe can see that he's got me thinking. He's pleased with himself. He says: There's a cycle shop a few blocks from here. I'll show you where it is when we leave.

I nod and smile, but things aren't really better. I can still see the dog in front of my car. I can still feel the moment of impact. The waiter comes and I order coffee but nothing to eat, rare for me. I love eating in restaurants, and the food at The View is great. But my stomach is still messed up.

When the waiter goes, I notice The View's owner circulating and talking. Everyone calls him Uncle Rick, though people say it's not his real name. No one seems to know how the name came about, but it fits. He looks like an Uncle Rick. Normally I don't like talking to people who aren't close friends of mine. But Uncle Rick has a way of making small talk seem therapeutic. He's a perfect person to circulate among customers, a major reason why everyone comes to this place, which is so popular that no one in this town ever goes to Starbucks or McDonald's.

In fact, we don't have chain cafés or restaurants. To find such places, you have to drive more than an hour. We've kept the big corporations out of our town. Whenever they try to open a convenience store, fast-food place, café, clothing store, bank, or real estate office, the town holds a meeting where everyone agrees to avoid the new place, and it goes out of business in less than a year. This has happened several times since I moved here in the late nineties, and Gabe, who's lived here longer than I have, says it happened many times before that. Few things are more inspiring than seeing the golden arches torn down. People often gather to watch the demolition process.

Uncle Rick looks like a lifetime hippie. He's tall and thin with long brown hair going gray, a long brown beard, wire-rimmed glasses, and a permanent stoned smile. He's more like a mascot than an owner. It's impossible to imagine The View without him. He likes it when people order coffee and sit for an afternoon of free refills. In any other place, they'd want you to order more and leave as soon as possible, making space for other customers. But Uncle Rick wants The View filled with relaxed conversations, people taking their time and enjoying themselves. It's obviously good for business, which is ironic, since The View doesn't feel like a business. It feels like a home, better than a home, a place where you get taken care of without neurotic, demanding parents.

The central dining room still looks like the huge Victorian parlor it was when Uncle Rick bought the house. It's filled with built-in bookcases and old hardcover books, great works of fiction, philosophy, and science. Uncle Rick says that he's read them all, most of them more than once. At first, I thought he was lying, but in all the books I've paged through, reading passages here and there, the words look like they've been read and re-read many times, like they've been thought about so carefully that they mean more now than they used to.

Uncle Rick smiles when he sees us. We're regulars and he knows us by name. But his smile doesn't last. He can see that I'm upset and asks me why. When I tell him my story, he's genuinely disturbed, almost angry, and it's hard to imagine Uncle Rick being angry. He's so unsettled he has to sit down. He says: I lost my dog, Noah, the same way. It was ten years ago. I heard a car braking outside, Noah yelping loudly in pain, then the driver hitting the gas and speeding away. When I got outside, Noah was almost dead on the road. I held his head in my lap and he tried to wag his tail. Then he died. I'd had him ten years, a beautiful black lab.

He looks at me as if I killed his dog. He takes a deep breath and says: And there hasn't been a day since then that I haven't found myself missing him, wanting to tell him things, wanting to go on walks with him and visit beautiful places together.

I want Gabe to know what to say. I want Uncle Rick to go back to being smiling joking Uncle Rick. But nothing happens. We all just sit there. Uncle Rick looks fifteen years older, like he's on his death bed. He finally shakes his head, stands up, and walks across the room and up the stairs to the second floor of the house, where he lives. Everyone else in the room is looking at us, like we've done something terribly wrong.

I tell Gabe that I can't stay any longer. We get up quickly. I leave twenty dollars on the table, more than twice what our bill and tip would have come to, as if the money might make Uncle Rick feel better. We hurry across the room toward the door. People stare like we're sneaking out without paying.

Outside, Gabe shakes his head and says: That was one of the five worst moments of my life. Did you see that look on his face?

I say: I was trying not to.

He says: I've always wondered why Uncle Rick looks so happy all the time. I figured the smile had to be hiding something, a romantic tragedy in his past, like Rick in *Casablanca*. Maybe that's where he got the name Uncle Rick. But the idea that his tragedy was the loss of a dog? That's a little too much. It makes me wonder—

I say: You can't understand how losing your dog would ruin your life? It has to be a *human* loss to qualify as a tragedy?

Gabe makes a face and says: People get over the loss of a dog. It's hard sometimes, but you deal with it. It's not like losing a person who means everything to you.

I say: You're assuming that everyone's feelings work the same way. Some people can't get close to other people. It's better for them to get close to a dog or a cat or some other animal. That's what keeps getting to me about the dog I killed this morning. Sure, he looked like a monster pit bull. But what if he was a nice dog? What if he was the center of someone's life?

Gabe looks at first like he wants to laugh. He probably thinks it's absurd to use lofty terms like tragedy when you're talking about the loss of a pet. He's never had pets and doesn't know how important they can be. But he wants to be a good friend, so he puts on a serious face and says: I still think the best thing you can do at this point is to get a bike and use it whenever you can. Save your car for emergencies, or maybe for big loads of groceries. Let's go to the cycle shop and see what they've got.

I say: I just want to go home right now. You've been a great guy showing up for me today. But I think I need to be alone.

He hesitates, but he knows me well enough to know that sometimes I'm better off by myself. So he gives me a hug, something he's never done before, and tells me to call him tomorrow.

Back home, I open a history book and look up Gavrilo Princip. There's a photograph that I'm sure I've seen before, one of the assassin's mug shots, taken right after he was dragged away to prison, shouting that what he'd just done was not a crime but a noble action, that he ought to be seen as a patriotic hero, someone willing to sacrifice himself for the good of his country, a martyr in the truest sense of the word. The picture answers my question: The man I might have seen at The View two hours ago looked very much like the man who shot the archduke in Sarajevo, and almost identical to my good friend Gabriel Prince. Then I remember that when I first introduced myself to Gabe at The View, it was partly because he reminded me of someone, though at the time I didn't think of Princip, and would have had no reason to, since I had no special interest in World War I or assassinations. Am I seeing Gabriel Prince as Gavrilo Princip simply because I became a killer this morning? It makes good sense and makes no sense, like so many other things I could bring to mind. But I'm really exhausted.

I take some pills and wake up at five the next morning. The sheer white drapes beside my bed are filled with cool breeze and the distant sound of the sea, like a promise that I won't be as messed up today as I was yesterday. I'm planning to drive to work and try to set aside what's happened by doing what I get paid for, writing and designing ads and brochures for a landscaping company, people whose work I respect, since they take care of people's lawns and gardens without loud machines. Most of the people in town make use of our services, and now we're getting calls from people all over the region. Promotional writing wasn't my childhood dream. Back when I was in college, I would have thought that people who did what I do were total sell-outs. I thought all advertising was evil. I still think most of it is. But I like and respect the work I do, selling a service that doesn't make noise. It's one of the things that keeps our town so beautifully quiet. You don't hear loud machines doing yard work.

I've got a lot of work to catch up on, since I called in sick yesterday, so I leave the house early. But the doors of my car won't open, even though they're not locked. I call AAA and the guy they send tries all sorts of things but the doors won't open. He says at least five times that he's never seen anything like it before. He calls a locksmith, who fails and calls another locksmith, who fails and calls another locksmith, who fails and tells me there's no one left to call. Finally, they insist that the only thing to do is break through the windows. But the windows won't break. All of us try everything but the windows won't break. Even when one of the locksmiths calls a friend, an ex-NFL defensive tackle, who shows up with the biggest sledgehammer I've ever seen and goes berserk on the windows, he can't even make the smallest crack. Everyone is stunned, unnerved.

All the banging we've done has brought the neighbors, who want to know what's going on. When I tell them, no one knows what to say. I can see that they want to sound smart and provide explanations, but the only one who has anything to suggest is the guy next door, who works at the local university and urges me to talk to one of the science professors, an expert who can use chemicals or specialized instruments to evaluate the situation.

I nod and apologize for the disturbance and thank everyone for their time and concern. I ask the AAA guy if I should have the car towed to a service station, but he tells me not to bother, that he's the town's leading expert on fixing cars and if he can't help me no one can. I call my boss and tell him my car won't start.

I'm thinking this must be another sign that it's time to get a bike, so a few hours later I walk to the bicycle shop and look around. I'm just about to try out the fanciest model when I see someone I think I know on the other side of the shop. She's smiling at me but at first I don't know who she is. Then I remember: It's Colette, the one whose kind eyes and long red hair I liked so much.

I return her smile and say: Looking for a bike?

She giggles: My car wouldn't start this morning, and for weeks I've been promising myself I'd stop driving to work and get a bicycle—I need the exercise and besides it saves money and it's good for the planet. So this morning I decided it was time to do something about it.

I'm just about to tell her why I've decided not to drive to work anymore, but then I remember Uncle Rick's reaction to my story, and I decide it's best to just echo what she said—it saves money and it's good for the planet.

She nods and says: Are you going to the concert tonight?

When I look puzzled she says: I guess it's not really a concert. But there's going to be a benefit performance at the barn tonight. Musicians I know are playing, a group called Assassination Sandwich. It's $100 to get in, but the money goes to the Animal Liberation Front. You know about them, don't you?

I say: Are those the guys who break into labs and let monkeys out of their cages?

She says: Yeah but they're not just guys. Over half of them are women. I used to work with them. But then—

I say: Is the barn you're talking about that old place near the lighthouse? I heard they were going to renovate it and turn it into a performance space, but there were complications and it never happened. Your friends are performing there tonight? Even though it's still just a barn?

She nods: It's kind of unofficial. Only a few people know about it. But the music starts at nine. If you don't have $100 you can spare, I can help you out.

I hesitate. Why would someone who barely knows me make such an offer? It makes me wonder what's really going on. Maybe I should take it at face value. Maybe she just wants to raise money to save the planet and Assassination Sandwich is a great band and she wants people to hear them play. But if the point is to raise money and promote the band, why do only a few people know about it? Why aren't there posters all over town? It's almost as if Colette and her friends are trying to keep it a secret, and secretive people always make me nervous.

I finally say: Sure. I'll see you there. And don't worry. I'm not the richest guy in the world, but I can spare a hundred dollars if it's for a good cause.

She nods: It's for a good cause.

I say: The band has a great name: Assassination Sandwich. I was just reading about Gavrilo Princip last night.

She says: Is that the guy who shot Archduke Ferdinand? I think one of the guys in the band had a distant relative who knew him. Or knew someone who knew him.

I say: What kind of music do they play?

She giggles and puts her hand on my arm and says: It's really hard to describe. You'll just have to come and hear them.

I nod, but I'm feeling awkward, so I tell her I've got some-where to go. I'm in such a hurry that I leave without buying a bike. About half way home I remember what I was in the cycle shop to do, but I feel nervous about going back and talking to Colette again, so I tell myself I can get the bike tomorrow. I'm often afraid to try new things, even when it's clear that they'd be good for me, and I know I might be avoiding something now, using my fear of Colette as an excuse. But when I get home and try again without success to break into my car, the feeling of needing a bike returns, and I promise myself that I'll get one tomorrow morning.

At first, I'm not planning to go to the barn. No matter how good Colette's musician friends are, I probably won't like them. I've got narrow tastes in music—I listen exclusively to jazz, and only jazz from the late fifties and early sixties. But my thoughts keep drifting back to the dog I killed, preventing me from focus-ing on anything I try to do. Even doing the dishes feels over-whelming. It's clear that the only way I can stay home is by taking pills and going to sleep early, and I don't want to do that again. I don't feel like calling Gabe or another friend, but I don't want to be alone, so at half-past eight I check my wallet to make sure I've got the $100, then walk a few blocks to the seaside path that leads to the barn.

I love walks at night by the sea. Tonight it's especially beauti-ful. There's a crescent moon and a stiff wind in the trees that line the dirt path. Waves crash against rocks thirty feet below. The sound makes me want to curl up under a tree and sleep forever. I walk slowly. With every step, I care less and less about where I'm going and where I'm coming from. The crescent moon seems to move as branches bend in the wind. The whole world feels thera-peutic, and there aren't any phallic symbols. Or maybe there are, but so what? They've got nothing to do with me.

When I get to the barn I'm surprised that there's no one collecting money at the door. The large open space inside is lit by moonlight flooding in through broken windows and gaps in the ceiling. The walls are filled with the moving shadows of branches. I look for the normal performance arrangement, seats in rows and a stage, but there's nothing except a card table and three wooden chairs in a pool of moonlight. Someone steps out of a shadowy corner. I'm terrified at first, but when she sits in one of the chairs and moonlight gathers around her face, I can see it's Colette, wearing nothing.

She puts a deck of cards on the table, giggles and says: Care to join me?

I know I should excuse myself and leave, but I like the way she looks wearing nothing but moonlight, so I smile and sit at the table.

She smiles without giggling and says: Let's play strip poker.

I say: But you don't have anything on. How can you strip?

She says: It won't make any difference. I never lose.

I look at the third wooden chair and ask: Will someone be joining us?

She puts on a mysterious face and says: It's hard to say. Yes and no.

I say: Yes and no?

She says: Yes and no.

I say: Yes and no? That's it? Just yes and no.

She giggles and says: Maybe yes, maybe no.

She deals the cards. I get a good hand: three jacks. But she's got an even better hand: five aces. Not four aces and a wild card. Five aces.

She says: So take off all your clothes.

I say: You can only tell me to take off one thing at a time.

78

She says: Normally you'd be right. But look carefully at the cards.

In addition to the four normal suits—spades, hearts, diamonds, and clubs—there's a fifth suit for the fifth ace. In the moonlight it's hard to tell what it is, but it seems to be a lightning bolt. Her deck has an ace of lightning. The weather forecast mentioned a possible thunderstorm around midnight. I start to think that if I don't do what she says, I'll get hit by lightning, so I take my clothes off, though the barn is unheated.

I say: It's cold.

She says: You'll get used to it.

I say: Why are we doing this? What about Assassination Sandwich? Has the music been postponed? Or was the whole thing just a way to get me out here? I'll bet it was. But why all that nonsense about the Animal Liberation Front and the $100 admission fee? You'll only play strip poker with people who care enough about animal rights to pay $100?

She nods and giggles and says: Now that you've got all your clothes off, let's play Fish.

I remember Fish from my childhood. I used to play it all the time, with great pleasure. It's a simple game, but that's the kind of card game I enjoy. I don't want to think too much when I'm playing cards, especially in a situation like this one.

After a while it's clear that we're not playing Fish. She keeps changing the rules, and the changes make the game even more enjoyable, though before too long I don't know what I'm doing. Repeatedly I forget the new rules she's invented and make mistakes. It doesn't seem to matter. The mistakes become part of the game and the game gets better. Cards keep showing up in suits I've never seen before: the two of brains, the six of trees, the nine of stop signs, the king of teeth, and many others I can't make out in the moonlight. Each one makes me feel dizzy, as if pieces of time were being added or subtracted. I keep liking the way she looks, but the feeling is more aesthetic than erotic, and nothing sexual even starts to happen. At times I think I should try to make conversation, but she's concentrating so fiercely on the game that I keep my mouth shut. I'm expecting thunder and lightning. But there's only wind and moonlight, shadows moving on the walls. No one wins or loses. It just keeps getting later.

Then footsteps approach, the shadow of someone walking in the moonlight. I start to get up in alarm, but she tells me to relax. A man walks in and sits in the empty chair. At first I think it's Gabe. He walks and looks just like him. But then I tell myself it's Gavrilo Princip, and even though I know it has to be someone else, everything about the man is consistent with what I've learned about history's most famous teenage assassin. He's even dressed in an old black suit, which reminds me of something I read about him yesterday when I was looking for his picture. Apparently, he and his radical friends in Sarajevo used to wear black suits and black fedoras when they met in cafés, talking about the need to kill tyrannical leaders. At first I thought that they were probably trying to look like Hollywood gangsters, but then I remembered that he shot the archduke in 1914, years before there was any such thing as a Hollywood gangster. He looks at Colette and motions to the cards. She nods and deals them out, leaving me out of this hand, which is fine with me. At this point I'd rather just watch, use the time to think about what's happening.

She picks up her hand and starts doing what she was doing before, improvising rules. At first Princip seems to be having fun, getting into the free-form spirit of the game, nodding and laughing, complimenting Colette on all the smart moves she's making, as if he'd played the game many times and knew what a smart move was. But then he taps the table three times with his fist and meets her eyes, a menacing gaze, the kind you might use to put a curse on someone, or induce a trance, make your victim obey obscure commands. The look is so extreme it's almost funny. But his face in the moonlight starts to look like mask, a sinister mask without a face, a mask that can't be removed. He says nothing at first, as if to let the sound of the sea get more intense, like a film director using soundtrack music.

He finally says: The two of sandwiches eats the king of teeth!

He plucks a card out of her hand, puts it in his mouth and quickly chews it, then spits it out on the floor.

She almost starts to smile, then looks amazed, then deeply offended, mad enough to tear him into bite size pieces. But he's out the door before she has time to speak.

I'm gripping the seat of my chair, thinking it's time to make a quick exit. But she smiles and the rage in her body disappears. She picks up the cards and shuffles them, starting up the same game we were playing before, inventing the rules and getting more inventive as the game resumes, encouraged by the way I'm playfully going along with the process, though of course I'm disturbed and confused. I do my best to keep my eyes on the cards, but I can't stop myself from looking outside from time to time, waiting for someone else to show up, wondering who it was that was here before, and what he was doing. I'm not crazy enough to think it was really Princip. But I'm also pretty sure that it wasn't Gabe. After all, he acted like we'd never seen each other before. And I can't imagine him chewing up a card and spitting it out on the floor. He's too polite, especially around women. That's part of his charm, his formula for success in romantic encounters.

Finally the alarm in Colette's digital watch goes off. She smiles and says: It's midnight. Time to go.

She gathers the cards, puts them in a small wooden box, walks to the door, turns and says: Thanks for a very pleasant evening.

I say: Aren't you going to put your clothes on?

She says: I didn't bring any clothes. I never do.

I say: You *never* do? You've played cards here before without any clothes on?

She says: Many times.

I say: Let me get my clothes on and I'll walk home with you.

She says: I'm not going in your direction.

I say: How do you know what my direction is?

She says: I saw you approaching earlier.

I say: But who was that guy that was here before? He looked like—

I stop myself when the rage comes back in her face. Her body tenses up like she might get violent. It's obvious that she doesn't want to talk about what happened.

Then her smile comes back and she giggles and says: Oh, by the way, you passed the test.

I say: What test?

But she's already turned and left. I want to rush out and catch up with her, get an answer to my question, but I'm nervous about being naked. By the time I get dressed and rush outside she's gone. I walk a few minutes down the path I think she took, but there's no sign of her. There's nothing to do but go home, feel good that at least I passed the test, whatever that means.

Soon I reach the road leading back to my neighborhood. I look out over the cliffs and see The View about a hundred yards down the coast. Though it's almost one in the morning, there's a light in a second-floor window. I tell myself it's got to be Uncle Rick, still upset from the story I told him. I decide to go back and say I'm sorry for triggering painful memories. I know he doesn't expect an apology, but I also know how hard it is to lose your dog. When my golden lab got cancer and died two years ago, it took me a year to even start feeling better. I'm still not completely okay. I can't bring myself to adopt a new dog, even though the animal shelter has many dogs that need homes.

When I get to The View, I see Uncle Rick through the front door. He's in the central dining room now, reading a large battered book. From where I'm standing, it looks like it might be an ancient book of spells, the kind of thing you might consult if you wanted to bring someone back from the dead. But it's hard to think of a book like that existing in a town like this, where everyone seems too progressive to believe in ghosts and magic spells. But whatever the book might be, Uncle Rick is reading it very carefully, moving his lips to pronounce the words, though I can't hear what he's saying.

I hesitate, knowing it would be more appropriate to come back tomorrow and talk to him during business hours. But I'm disturbed by what just happened at the barn, and I want to find out if he knows Colette, or knows who the other guy might have been. I knock on the door. He jumps up and looks terrified, and I hear a dog barking, but I wave and once he figures out who I am he smiles and comes to the door. The dog, a black lab, jumps up from beside the fireplace, then sits on command as Uncle Rick opens the door.

I tell him I saw the light upstairs and felt I owed him an apology.

He says: No, no, not at all. In fact, I'm grateful. The feelings you triggered were long overdue.

He turns and gently calls the dog, Noah, who rushes across the room wagging his tail. Uncle Rick tells him to sit and Noah sits, looking up at us with eager intelligent eyes.

Uncle Rick can see from the confusion on my face that I don't understand. He says: When you told me what happened on the freeway yesterday, I realized how much I missed my dog. Not that I didn't realize it before, but I didn't fully *feel* how deep the pain went, how much I was blocking it out.

He gets the book he was reading. Up close, it looks even more like a book of spells than it did from a distance. It's large and thick and looks like it might date back to the Middle Ages. It's open to a page with an abstract design, something like a spiral of lightning bolts with a star in the center. Uncle Rick says: Back when I first opened this place, I was also a therapist. This book was my principal healing tool. The people who saw me would study the book a page at a time, meditating on designs like this one.

I say: Where did you get it?

He says: A friend gave it to me. He got it from his grandfather, who was living in Sarajevo back in 1914 when Archduke Ferdinand was assassinated.

I say: Really? I was just reading about that.

He says: Then you might know that the plan to kill the archduke came from student cafés in Belgrade and Sarajevo. Apparently, my friend's grandfather was one of those radical students. But as far as I can tell, the book was made long before that, and I have no idea where the students in Sarajevo might have gotten it.

I say: But you just said the book was a healing tool. How could it be connected to a group of assassins?

He shrugs and smiles: I really don't know. From the little I've read about the causes of World War I, the assassins weren't a gang of thugs. All we know about them comes from a few sentences in history books. Who knows who they really were, beyond those sentences? I'm sure some of them had a wide range of interests. Sarajevo had been an Islamic city for centuries. Maybe some of them were interested in Rumi and the Sufis. Or maybe The Kabbalah, or the Kama Sutra, or the Book of Changes. They were teenagers. They were reading books that filled them with revolutionary ideas. Maybe they thought they were doing something heroic. I read somewhere that Gavrilo Princip thought of himself as a martyr, someone willing to give his life to set his country free. Maybe the assassination was never meant to cause a great war, and things took off in unforeseen directions once the major European powers got involved. Maybe maybe maybe. There are so many things to consider, so many possibilities. All I know is—

I say: I'm pretty sure I saw Gavrilo Princip recently.

He looks at me strangely. I feel like a fool for having said something so absurd.

He says: Before I bought The View, I wanted to find out why the place was so cheap. Sure, it was falling apart, but why wasn't anyone trying to keep such a beautiful place together? I mean, it's got so many wonderful rooms, not to mention a fabulous view of the sea. But an uncle who was visiting from Texas looked at the place with me, and told me it was haunted. I remember laughing in his face. It was hard to believe that I had such an old-fashioned relative. It had been so long since I'd heard anyone talk like that. You know how this town is, too full of progressive intelligence for people to be superstitious. I can't imagine that anyone here believes in ghosts. But the first night I stayed here, I woke to find someone standing beside my bed. He said his name was Gavrilo Princip, and he told me to visit The Other Side. You know the place, don't you? It was run by a bunch of old hippies who took the name from a song by The Doors. It used to be in that house down the street before it closed.

I nod eagerly and say: I've never been inside. It went out of business a few years before I moved here. But my friend Gabe tells me that it used to be a fantastic thrift shop, that they were selling all sorts of great things for almost nothing. A lot of the amazing stuff he's got in his house came from there.

Uncle Rick smiles: No question about it—all sorts of great things. And when I woke up the day after my Princip experience, I went there and found what I assumed was a copy of a Dutch landscape, a scene with a dirt road, an old red barn and a pasture with a battered windmill in the background. I thought it would make a great decoration. But an art historian friend of mine told me that it looked it might be more than a copy, and it turned out that a picture I'd bought for a few dollars was really an original Dutch landscape, worth almost a million dollars at the time. I've been living off the money ever since.

I say: That's amazing! But what about Princip? Did you ever see him again?

He says: Soon after the visitation, I paid someone to come here all the way from San Diego to do an exorcism. I assumed that if the place was really haunted, I could run a better business without ghosts. Though I didn't believe in ghosts at the time, and it would have been easy to assume that what I saw was just a dream, I didn't want to take any chances, and there haven't been any Gavrilo Princip sightings since I opened the place thirty years ago. Until now.

He pauses and studies my face. I'm not sure what he wants me to say, so I nod and smile.

He says: But last night I felt haunted. Something told me to look at the book, that there were answers there for me, so I turned to this page and let the image do its work.

I say: Its work?

He slowly nods: Its work. And when I woke up this morning, Noah was right where he always was before, beside my bed, wagging his tail.

I'm about to laugh, but I know he might be serious, so I quickly say: How did that happen?

He says: I let the image do its work.

I look at him to see if he's joking. He's smiling broadly. It might be a look of good-natured mischief or a sign of simple happiness. I don't know him well enough to read his face. I'm thinking that he probably knew it was time to get a new dog, so he got a black lab from the animal shelter, but he wants me to think that magic took place and Noah came back from the dead. I want to let him know that I know he's joking, but I don't want to be too blunt because I don't want to hurt him again if he's not joking, if he's really convinced that his new dog is the one that was killed ten years ago. So I say: The image really did its work.

He slowly nods and says: The image did its work. The images always do their work—if you let them.

I find this disturbing, so I ask: Will the images do any work you want? Can you make all nuclear weapons disappear? Can you fix the hole in the ozone layer? Can you make blind people see? Can you make sure that if I ever see Princip again, he'll tell me where I can find a painting worth almost a million dollars?

He laughs: It doesn't quite work that way. You have to know how to let the image work, and learning how to let the image work is the work of a lifetime. In so many ways, I'm still just a beginner. But let's talk about it more some other time.

I scratch behind Noah's ears and tell Uncle Rick how pleased I am. Then I say I've got to go home and get some sleep. It doesn't seem like the right time to ask him if he knows Colette, and he doesn't look like he wants to talk anymore about teenage assassins. I just want to crawl into bed and forget about everything for a while.

But the night isn't over yet. As I walk down the empty street leading back to my house, I hear a dog howling—nearby or far away, it's hard to tell. It disturbs me when dogs howl, since it might mean that something bad is about to happen, something only the dog is aware of. When my first wife got killed twenty years ago in a freeway accident, my dog howled all through the morning before she went out. But tonight the howling triggers a different memory.

Two years ago, late at night on the street where I'm walking now, I heard a dog snarling in back of me, following at a distance, at times coming closer, though he never quite got close enough to be more than a menacing shadow. I reached the empty lot between the two abandoned houses, the same place Patty was talking about before. The snarling stopped, and I saw something in the sky that looked at first like a shooting star. But instead of quickly disappearing, it came closer, hovering over one of the houses, probably the house that used to be The Other Side. Soon it was barely a hundred feet away, and it looked like a huge brain, glowing and disappearing, glowing and disappearing. Then it dropped silently into the empty lot, shining on and off in the overgrown grass.

At first I was afraid to take a closer look. But I told myself it might be something important, so I cautiously crossed the lot until I was standing next to something that looked like a mass of yellow jelly, maybe ten feet across and four feet deep, glowing and pulsing, lights going off and on. I waited for something to happen, and though I worried that it might be radioactive, or poisonous in some other way, I couldn't pull myself away. I felt compelled to keep looking.

I thought of calling the police, but I hated the police, ever since I got in trouble with them in junior high school for breaking into a neighbor's house and stealing his turtles. They really weren't his turtles. He'd stolen them from me a few days before, and he wouldn't admit they were mine. But when I tried to get them back, he and his family were out of town and a neighbor who saw me break into the house called the police. Thinking back on it now, it makes me laugh. But at the time the police didn't think it was funny. I remember it was only a few days after the Kennedy assassination. The whole nation was deeply disturbed, and the cops weren't in the mood to take things lightly. They treated me like I'd killed somebody. I had to go to juvenile court and answer ridiculous questions.

So calling the police was out of the question, especially since I didn't have a cell phone. Instead I just stood there watching the thing pulse and throb, the lights going off and on. I thought I heard a voice on the road, but when I called out there was no response. I picked up a large stick from the ground and thrust it into the glowing mass. It wobbled like a water bed, but it wouldn't pop, no matter how fiercely I jabbed it with my stick. I finally gave up and went home.

When I got up the next morning and went back to see the thing in broad daylight, it wasn't there. I felt stupid. I should have knocked on someone's door, explained the situation and asked to use their phone to call the police, but because of a silly childhood hang-up, I'd failed to do something that would have established beyond all doubt that I wasn't dreaming. Instead, I had to wonder for the next few days if I was losing my mind. I'd heard stories about people seeing things in the sky and feeling so disturbed that they needed UFO group therapy sessions. I'd already had years of therapy. I didn't want more.

Then I heard on the news that whatever it was had been taken to the university for observation. The scientists there didn't know what to make of it. What was it made of? Why was it invisible half the time? Was it alive? Was it intelligent? Did it want something? Did it have something planned? The radio said that at this point they could only speculate. The next day, the same questions were asked on the news, the radio voice concluding again that the experts could only speculate. That was the last I heard of it. I searched all over the Internet and couldn't find anything else.

I would have gone to the university and talked to the scientists in person, but pressures at work began to take all my attention, and soon I forgot about what I'd seen. In fact, I forgot it so fully that when I heard Patty's story at The View yesterday, I agreed with her shrink that she had to be making it up. It's only the howling of the dog tonight that's fully brought that strange night back to me. I don't understand it any better now than I did two years ago, so I try to put it out of my mind and get some sleep. But the dog's terrible howling keeps waking me up. I start to think it's the dog I hit on the freeway, that as a punishment for killing him, I'll be haunted by his howling for the rest of my life. Or maybe it's Gavrilo Princip, having taken the form of a stray dog haunted by moonlight. I finally give up and get out of bed, reach for my bottle of pills and put it back down again, make myself a bowl of buttered popcorn, my favorite comfort food. I keep wondering about the test Colette referred to. The only thing I know about her is the story she told about her brother. Does the test have something to do with her brother's suicide?

Back when I was in therapy, I told my therapist a disturbing story from my childhood, which he interpreted as a screen memory, a false memory I'd unconsciously generated to conceal something more unpleasant. Maybe Colette's story about the death of her brother was a false memory. Maybe the truth was much worse, that she seduced him, which drove him to suicide, and now she's dealing with her guilt in a misguided way, displaying herself to men in the barn, hoping to find one who won't allow himself to be seduced. I passed the test by refusing to do anything more than play cards with her, even as she sat there fully undressed.

I'm suddenly quite proud of myself, not just because I passed the test, but also because I've figured out her behavior. I tell myself that I missed my true calling, that I should have trained to become a therapist. After all, Gabe has told me many times that a talk with me about his problems helps him more than any therapy session he's ever paid for. But once I finish my popcorn, my confidence goes away, and I know that when I wake up the next day, my interpretation of Colette's behavior will probably seem stupid. And I still won't know what to make of Princip's presence and behavior, why it made Colette so angry, why a ghost from the other side of the world would be haunting a town where no one believes in ghosts.

I sleep late the next day. It's Saturday, so I don't need to call my boss and make an excuse. Gabe wakes me up with a call at half past noon. He asks me if I'm feeling better and I want to say yes and no again, not just because that's what I'm really feeling, but also because I can tell from his voice that he's got other things he wants to talk about, and I don't want him to just rush half-heartedly past my disturbance. But I tell myself not to be difficult. He really did try to be a good friend a few days ago. Besides, he's not my therapist, and I'm not paying him $200 an hour to put my emotional needs before his. So I say that I'm feeling better.

He says: I went to The View this morning for breakfast, sort of because I wanted to see how Uncle Rick was doing. And guess what? He's got a new black lab. He told me it's just like the dog he told us about, and he's calling him Noah, the same name he gave the one he had before.

I say: It's not the same dog?

Gabe hesitates, then says: How could it be the same dog?

I say: Right. How could it be the same dog? It's just that I got the feeling he was so attached to the other dog that he couldn't bring himself to get a new one.

Gabe says: He told me that he knew it was time to get a new dog when he had such a strong reaction to your story about hitting that dog on the freeway.

I want to tell him about my conversation with Uncle Rick last night, but Gabe has no tolerance for talk of supernatural events, and I know he would wonder about my sanity if I told him I was even briefly buying Uncle Rick's talk about the ghost of Gavrilo Princip, or magical images in an ancient book. Besides, for some reason Uncle Rick didn't tell Gabe I was there the night before. He might not want people to know about his book, even though in the past he used it as a therapeutic tool.

I change the subject, asking Gabe what he's been doing the past few days. It's an indirect way of trying to bring up the barn episode, seeing if he'll admit that he was there, ignoring me and playing cards with a naked woman. I suppose I could ask him directly, but I'm afraid to make him account for such bizarre behavior, especially since I know he would be embarrassed to admit that he was with an attractive undressed woman and didn't go to bed with her. Besides, if he wasn't really there, he'll want to know why I'm asking, and then I'll have to tell him what happened, and I know he'll just laugh at me, tell me that I need psychological help.

Gabe says: That's the other thing I called about. Remember that blond sitting next to us at The View two days ago? It turns out her name is Patty, and I ran into her Thursday afternoon at the supermarket check-out line. That woman was fast. Even before we'd paid for our groceries, she'd invited herself back to my house, which of course really meant my bedroom, and right after she had what sounded like one of the greatest orgasms in the history of casual sex, we were on my water bed looking out at the moon, and she told me an absurd story. She had to be making it up, but she really knew how to make a story sound real.

I know he was probably more interested in her body than her story telling skills, but I'm eager to hear the lie she told him.

He says: She said that the whole time we were fucking, the crescent moon was reminding her of a night about two years ago when she was walking home and getting spooked by a dog howling at the moon. Then she saw something strange in the sky. She compared it to a huge human brain, glowing on and off, but then when it landed it looked more like a mass of yellow jelly, still glowing on and off. She told me she tried to get a response out of it by poking it with a stick. Apparently, she was convinced it was alive. I couldn't believe she was thinking something like this during sex! How could she have such an awesome orgasm if she was thinking about glowing brains falling out of the sky and—

I want to tell Gabe that she's telling the truth, but again, I know he's not a big fan of paranormal events. Normally, I'm not either. But I know what I saw that night, and now I know that the voice I heard on the road must have been Patty's. I'm frustrated that I can't just say what happened without getting laughed at, so I take my frustration out on Gabe by asking an embarrassing question: How do you know she didn't fake the orgasm? If she's good at making stories sound realistic, maybe's she's also good at pretending to—

He quickly says: I can tell when women are faking it, and when they're in bed with me, they usually don't have to. But I meant to ask: Did you ever get that bike?

I'm too embarrassed to tell him what happened at the cycle shop, especially since if I tell him how things went with Colette he'll probably laugh at me for not having sex with her, so I say that I've got a new bike and I've been riding it all over town. I can tell he's pleased with himself. He thinks he's solved my problem.

Right after we hang up, I walk to the cycle shop and buy the best bike in the place. Since I'm planning to ride it to work on Monday, I try out the sequence of back roads and bicycle trails I'll have to take to avoid the freeway. It takes ninety minutes, three times as long as it normally takes by car, but the scenery is beautiful, pathways through a quiet forest with frequent views of the mountains and the sea. I get to my place of work sweating heavily, but one of the bathrooms in the building has a shower, so if I bring soap, a towel, and a change of clothes, and leave an extra thirty minutes, there won't be any problem. When I get home and see my car in the driveway, I tell myself I'll never drive it again.

I renew this conviction the following day, riding my bike down back roads and trails all over the region, looking for the best way to go to work, hoping to produce a pleasant feeling of exhaustion. Back in my twenties, when I lived in New York City, I used to jog every day around the reservoir in Central Park. I thought of exhaustion as therapy. When friends asked me why I wasn't in therapy like they were, I told them I was doing Exhaustion Therapy. I hated the therapy culture that ruled the City at the time, the assumption that all intelligent people had to have therapists and talk endlessly to each other about their problems. But when the Exhaustion Therapy stopped working, I decided I had to do what my friends were doing. I spent fifteen years talking to a therapist. It helped me understand myself and feel slightly better, but I stopped when it occurred to me that I wasn't really understanding myself. I was understanding a self constructed in therapy.

Thinking back on it, I wish it hadn't taken me fifteen years and thousands of dollars to figure out what was happening. Now I'm planning a new form of Exhaustion Therapy, but by the end of the day, having cycled for miles, I don't feel better. Though it's nice to be on a bike, using my legs to propel myself, moving without that enclosed feeling I always get in a car, the feeling of having killed another creature hasn't gone away. It might take years to cycle the disturbance out of my body.

It's pouring rain when I wake at five the next morning. The wind is banging hard against my windows, and the yard is underwater, filled with branches blown down while I slept. I don't see how I can cycle to work in this weather. Even with a rain coat and the cover provided by all the big trees in the forest, I'll have to contend with the wind, which is probably strong enough to blow me off my bike. This might be fatal, since some of the roads run right alongside the cliffs above the sea. I don't want to skip another day of work. My boss is a good guy and would probably try to buy whatever excuse I gave him, but I know he depends on me and I don't want to disappoint him. So I decide that just for today I'll have to take my car, forgetting that it's out of commission.

After a quick breakfast, I open the door to my driveway and see that my car is more than just out of commission. It's filled with water and tropical fish and swaying plants. It even has a pump and filter, making a peaceful bubbling sound I can hear despite the wind and rain. The fish are a language of color and motion, glowing in the dome light of the car. But I can't really call it a car anymore. It's become an aquarium.

I sit on my covered front porch and listen to the rain. It's such a relaxing sound that soon I decide that I might as well take the risk, let the gusting wind do its best to blow me off the face of the earth. I'm normally not the kind of guy who takes risks if I can help it, though sometimes I wish I was, and thinking of Gavrilo Princip now, the risks he was willing to take when he put his fateful plan into motion—choosing the violence of self-martyrdom over a desperately marginal existence—I tell myself that a dangerous ride to work might not be such a big deal.

I go inside, pack my things, and put on a raincoat, plunging into the storm on my brand-new bike. I took a life three days ago, so now the least I can do is put my own life on the line, let fate and nature do their work. Some day I might feel good again, as long as I don't kill anything else.

EXTRAORDINARY SUBJECTIVE STATES

The rain is hard on the roof of the barn. Gavro and Trifko are laughing. They've walked all night with guns and bombs concealed beneath their jackets. They're hungry, cold and exhausted, miles from anything familiar. But now they've found an abandoned barn, a place to rest and get out of the rain, and everything is suddenly very funny. They're laughing and it feels too good to stop. The silent joke that no one told just keeps on getting better. It's surging through their bodies, speeding things up and slowing things down, blending with the sound of rain, replacing the sound of rain. It drives them to their knees and makes them pound the ground with their fists. It pulls them up and spins them through the dark until they get dizzy. They meet each other's eyes and the laughter gets harder. They look away and then look at each other again and the laughter gets harder. When they try to form words the very thought of speaking seems absurd.

At some point things begin to seem slightly dangerous. What if they're losing their minds? What if the laughter just keeps going? What if they can't stop laughing even when they're with other people again? But the questions don't quite reach the point of clear articulation. They're quickly replaced by a less disturbing assumption. Maybe it's just a massive release of tension. After all, they're planning to shoot a crown prince and then shoot themselves. Why wouldn't they feel an overload of anxiety? Why wouldn't they want to laugh their way into oblivion?

They're on their own now. The two men who helped them cross the Drina River, then guided them on muddy back roads through a night of indistinct places, suddenly left without saying goodbye several hours ago, without telling Gavro and Trifko how to get to Sarajevo. Since then they've been guessing, telling themselves that they know where they're going, though they know they might have lost their way, that they might be laughing now because they've really been walking in circles, making figure eights, infinity signs. They can't be sure, not in the middle of the night with no stars to guide them, with cold rain coming down with blinding intensity. If they hadn't found this abandoned barn, the rain might have torn them to pieces.

The laughter finally fades and Gavro leans against a rotting post, looking at his hands and rippling his fingers. Then he counts them one by one, making sure they're all present and accounted for. He takes a deep breath and says: Trifko, what the hell is going on? I've never felt so out of control in my life. You know me, Trifko. I almost never laugh.

Trifko sits with his back against a wall, slowly shaking his head. He looks in the direction of Gavro's words, as if he were slowly tracing them back to their source. He finally says: It's true. You're not a laughing kind of guy. Sometimes I can see in your face that you think something is funny, and sometimes you say funny things, but I don't think I've ever seen you laugh out loud. I remember when we first met at school and you were going from classroom to classroom, organizing that demonstration that got us all in trouble, and you kept making sick jokes with a blank face, like you might be in pain if you laughed or even smiled—

Gavro says: But now that I know what it's like to laugh my brains out, I want to do it again. I want to do it at least once a day. It's the kind of thing that everyone should do at least once a day.

Trifko says: I don't think it's the kind of thing you can *make* yourself do.

Gavro says: No, probably not. I mean, it seemed to just come out of nowhere, and then it took over. It felt dangerous, like we might have been going mad. And what if someone had heard us and found us here with these weapons? We'd have been in serious trouble. But I didn't care. All I wanted to do was keep on laughing.

Trifko nods: The laughter itself was making me laugh. Your laughter was making me laugh because my laughter was making you laugh. It just seemed to go on and on, and all I could do was wait until it was over. But I didn't want it to be over. It might be the strangest thing I've ever felt.

There's a pause defined by the sound of rain. Then Gavro takes a deep breath and says: No question about it—the strangest thing I've ever felt. And now I'm wondering if it's connected in some way to that strange device I found in the park, back in Belgrade. Did I tell you about that? That little magic box I found right after Nedjo and I had our picture taken last month, when we got the weapons from Handsome Cigo?

Trifko says: You had your picture taken right after you got the weapons? You never told me. A magic box?

Gavro says: You know I don't believe in magic. It's just a bourgeois distraction, a stage act or a bunch of parlor tricks. But something was strange about that device. The whole experience was weird.

Trifko says: What was so weird about it? Was it just that you don't like having your picture taken?

Gavro says: It went beyond that. The photographer was wearing strange clothing. He looked like he didn't know where he was or what he was doing. And then he wasn't there, like he got sucked into a crack in the afternoon light. But right before he disappeared, something fell out of his pocket.

Trifko shrugs and says: What was it?

Gavro says: I don't know. It was about the size of a deck of cards, made of some kind of shiny, smooth material. One side of it was white and had a picture of an apple. The other side was a glowing screen with colored squares arranged in rows. I fussed around with it for a while, and then the screen started changing. First, there were colorful pictures of smiling people wearing strange outfits, then other pictures of people who weren't wearing anything. Then a small keyboard with letters and numbers, like a miniature typewriter. But the weirdest thing happened when I pressed one of the colored squares and held the the device up to my ear. I heard strange voices, saying things I didn't understand. When I showed it to one of my teachers back in Belgrade, he told me they were speaking English, and he translated a few words and phrases for me, casual things like *Get back to me when you get a chance* and *What's happening tonight*, though other voices were more rehearsed and sounded like they might have been trying to sell things.

Trifko makes a puzzled face and says: Do you still have it?

Gavro shakes his head and says: After a few days it wouldn't work anymore. The screen wouldn't light up. I took it to a repair shop, and they had no idea how to fix it. They'd never seen anything like it before. Then they couldn't find it. It got lost in the shop somewhere.

The rain keeps getting harder, and now there's wind, gusting through the cracks in the old wooden walls. Gavro and Trifko are shivering. But after a brief search, they find old blankets on a rotting shelf. They smell bad, but at least they're dry, and soon the two young men are feeling warmer. They settle down into a corner, and before too long they're drifting off. Gavro speaks in a sleepy voice: I just remembered something, a voice I heard several times on the device, someone who called herself Betty saying something about her best friend Susan, flying in from San Diego. Just imagine: a best friend who can fly. I'd really like to meet this Susan person. Some day I'll have to visit San Diego.

Trifko yawns and rubs his eyes and says: Susan—nice name.

Gavro says: Does Susan have wings? Or does she have her own flying machine, one of those cigar-shaped German things I remember reading about...

Gavro can't quite keep the sentence going. He's falling asleep. The sound of the rain on the roof is deeply relaxing now that he's warm and dry. Sleep is like a painting in the dark of a closed museum, fragments of a whispered conversation: *I'm not making anything up.* And then: *You're always making things up, even when you're not trying to.* He can almost see the shapes of the people talking. He can almost hear the sound of the ocean somewhere in the distance. Then there's lightning, a brief pause and a savage thunderclap. He sits up quickly, not sure where he is. For maybe five seconds, he might be anywhere. The parts of his brain that give time and space a familiar shape aren't functioning yet, and instead of the smells of the barn and the sound of rain, he can hear quick footsteps on a sidewalk. Something tells him they might be Susan's footsteps, thousands of miles away, a century later.

She's feeling strong and excited. Five minutes ago, she made a brilliant speech, telling her very obnoxious boss that she was quitting. Now she's looking forward to collecting unemployment, doing what she loves best, historical research. Susan feels her smart phone vibrating in her pocket. Her first response is to ignore it, figuring it's probably just her boyfriend, Duke Archer, and she doesn't want to talk to him because she's planning to end the relationship, once she works up the courage to have an honest conversation. Then she remembers a call she's expecting from Betty, an old college friend, so she starts to pull out the phone to check the number. But in the chaotic motion of the lunch-hour crowd, she bumps into someone and her phone gets knocked onto the sidewalk, where a man accidentally steps on it with the sound of a snail getting squashed. He quickly apologizes, bending to gather up the shattered pieces, handing them back, offering to reimburse her. He's tall and slender, wearing a navy blue blazer and a white fedora. There's eye contact, a look of shared interest, another apology, another look of shared interest, another apology.

Susan starts to move on. He reaches into his pocket to get some cash to pay for the phone, but she stops and shakes her head and says: No, it's not necessary. I'm not hurting for money.

The man says: No?

She says: No.

He says: Isn't everyone hurting for money these days?

She says: Yeah, sure, but I just quit my job because I've got enough money saved up for now and I don't want to work in an office with a boss I can't stand.

He unfolds a wad of bills and says: I insist.

She shakes her head again, grabs his wrist and moves the money firmly back toward his pocket. When he tries to offer the money again, she tightens her grip and says: Really, no. I hate smart phones anyway.

He says: But you'll probably need a new one, won't you?

She says: I might not. Like I just said, I don't really have to start looking for jobs right away. I might even cancel my Internet when I get home.

He smiles: And go unwired? That almost sounds impossible—

She says: But it's not. I've got plenty of things I'd rather do than look for another job I don't really want.

He hesitates. Her hand is still gripping his wrist. He says: If you don't mind my asking—What kinds of things?

She says: Historical research.

He says: Historical research without the Internet?

She says: I read books. I like going to the library.

He smiles: What kind of research are you doing?

She says: I'm investigating the causes of World War I.

He says: Why World War I?

She says: It never should have happened. And if it had never happened, the world would be a totally different place today.

He says: Didn't that war start because some guy shot someone.

She says: Supposedly. But the real reason was that European military leaders were looking for an excuse to start a war.

He says: Just like today. People with guns and bombs want to use them.

She says: I'm not interested in the guns and bombs. I'm more interested in what the assassin did *before* he fired the fatal shots.

He says: What did he do?

She says: He walked all night through freezing rain with a friend, smuggling guns and bombs across a well-guarded border. Then he had a visionary experience.

He says: Is there really any such thing as a visionary experience?

She says: Yes and no. Do you have time for a cup of coffee?

He says: I know a nice place right around the corner.

Susan goes with him to the nice place right around the corner. They sit down and pick up right where they left off. She agrees that there might not be any such thing as a visionary experience, but she emphasizes that she's not using the term in a religious sense.

He says: But that's usually how it's used. Why not find a different term?

She shrugs: Like what? Mystical?

He says: Same problem: religious connotations that started going stale hundreds of years ago.

She says: The assassin we're talking about, Gavrilo Princip, used the word mystical at his trial, but he refused to explain it. I think he meant that he'd been willing to face incredible hardships and take serious risks to complete what he considered a necessary mission to free his country from foreign tyranny.

He says: Sounds more heroic than mystical.

She says: Right. But once they'd crossed the border into Bosnia, Princip and his friend, who was also part of the assassination plot, found shelter from the freezing rain in an old barn, and they collapsed into insane laughter, which Princip described as an altered state of consciousness, a release from the limits of rational perception.

He says: Princip used those words at his trial?

She says: No. But that's what he meant.

Susan pauses and looks at her new friend, making sure he's fully engaged in what she's saying. He's clearly not faking his interest. She's already had more fun talking to him than she's had in any conversation with her boyfriend, Duke, in the past year, and she likes the man's white hat, which he hasn't removed. He's the only man in the café wearing a hat. It looks like it's part of his head.

She says: As I see it, Princip's experience in the barn was more significant than the assassination, which was meaningful only because it gave the military leaders of the Austro-Hungarian empire an excuse to wage a war they'd wanted for at least two decades. But Princip's extraordinary state of mind in the barn isn't even mentioned in most history books, while the assassination has been widely described and discussed.

He says: So your interest isn't really the causes of World War I.

She says: Not really. I just said that for the sake of convenience. I didn't expect the conversation to continue.

He nods: I didn't either. But I'm glad it has.

She says: Me too.

There's a pleasantly awkward pause. Then she says: Anyway, I think at this point we need a new way of describing the past, a history of extraordinary subjective states.

He says: Didn't William James already write a book like that? I think we had to read it in a philosophy class in college, and it later came out that William James was taking nitrous oxide.

She nods: He focused on the varieties of *religious* experience. It's a good book, nitrous oxide or not, but what I want is a history of extraordinary mental states that aren't defined in religious terms and aren't the result of taking drugs.

He smiles: I'd say you've got your hands full. It sounds like a challenging subject. I'm not even sure what kind of research you'd have to do. But how did you get interested in Princip?

She says: I used to date a guy who used to date a woman who was once married to a guy who'd lived with a woman whose sister was sleeping with a guy whose houseboy was getting blow jobs from a stripper whose most regular customer was making wax replicas of sandwiches with Princip's face on one slice of bread and Archduke Franz Ferdinand's face on the other.

He laughs: Why a sandwich?

She says: There's a version of the assassination story that

has Princip in a café eating sandwiches right before shooting the archduke.

He laughs again: Really? It's like the version of the JFK assassination where Oswald is eating a leg of chicken at the book depository window right before shooting Kennedy.

She says: This is the first time I've heard about Oswald's leg of chicken. But the Princip sandwich story is historical fact for some people and an urban legend for others.

He says: What's your opinion?

She says: Of course there's no way of knowing for sure. But I like to imagine Princip in a state of disturbance deciding to get a sandwich. He's just learned that one of the other assassins has unsuccessfully thrown a bomb at the archduke's car. There's panic and commotion everywhere, and Princip isn't sure what to do next. What could be more human than to sit down with a sandwich and try to figure out the next move? When I'm confused or upset, I often get something to eat. Why would Princip be any different, especially since he must have been really hungry. He didn't have any money and often went for days without food.

He says: Some people would get a drink in a situation like that—

She says: Princip didn't drink. He was part of a network of secret societies called Young Bosnia, and they practiced abstinence. They regarded drinking as a bourgeois indulgence.

He says: I get the same feeling about the word bourgeois as I get about visionary. Both words sound dated to me and hopelessly vague, not to mention boring.

She says: Lots of words are like that.

He says: Too many. It puts limits on what you can say.

She says: Necessary limits.

He says: But getting back to the assassination sandwich—Is

it actually in a gallery somewhere? Can you buy one if you're an art collector? How much would it cost? I'm not sure I like the idea of people selling jokes about historical tragedies.

She says: As far as I know, there's a whole series of assassination sandwiches, and you can buy one for $450, which is cheap by art world standards, but it would be way beyond Princip's budget if he were alive today.

He says: He probably wouldn't have wanted one. After all, his face is on the bread.

She says: If you're hungry enough, you'll eat anything.

He smiles and tilts back in his wooden chair so far that it looks like he's about to fall over. But Susan can tell it's a move he's mastered, and she likes how relaxed he looks. She notices for the first time that everyone in the café is eating eagerly from large bowls of popcorn. She says: I've never seen a café like this, where everyone eats popcorn. Is it like this all the time, or is it a special treat for the day?

He says: It's like this all the time. This is the original popcorn café. The owner here decided that if he put free bowls of heavily buttered popcorn on every table, he could attract a large group of regulars. It worked, and the idea quickly spread. Now there are popcorn cafés all over the city. I'm surprised you haven't heard about them.

She says: Everyone here looks happy. I'm not surprised. Buttered popcorn always makes me happy.

He says: Me too. But I'm still not sure I like the Princip sandwich idea. It's too funny to be true.

She says: I think it's funny too, but not too funny. I don't see why we have to assume that history is an entirely serious process. The more I study past events, the more I see how the laws of history are obscured by the accidents of history, and it was only because Princip took the time to get a sandwich that he was in the right place at the right time, and—

He says: I like your way of putting it: The laws of history are obscured by the accidents of history. Is that something you read in a book, or did you just think of it now?

She smiles: I think it's something Trotsky said. Or it might have been Tolstoy. I get them confused. I tried to slip it into the conversation as if it came to me just as the sentence came out. I tend to do that. I want people to think I'm smarter than I really am. Normally, I wouldn't admit something like that. But I feel so relaxed with you that I don't mind being honest, which is rare, believe me. Usually people get a carefully edited version of me, with lots of awkward stuff left out.

He shrugs and says: You seem pretty smart to me, with or without the awkward stuff. It's not every day that you meet someone doing research on the history of extraordinary subjective states.

The rest of the conversation moves from history to oral sex to real estate to the job market to the likelihood of the earth getting hit by an asteroid. They get along well throughout. Even when they disagree, they do it gracefully. About thirty minutes into their conversation, she notices that something is missing: their names. Normally, in an interaction like this one, the exchange of names would have already happened. But she doesn't want to know his real name, since she's having fun assuming that his name is Chet, which for no special reason strikes her as the perfect name for men with white fedoras, and she doesn't want to be disappointed. She assumes that Chet is thinking the same way, that he's got a name he wants her to have and doesn't want to find out that her real name is something else. Soon Chet invites her back to his place, and Susan sees no reason to refuse. She's got a black belt in karate, and she's confident she can handle the situation if things get difficult.

He leads her through a series of industrial neighborhoods to a pleasant residential area filled with old but well-maintained homes. Soon they're turning down a street of brownstone row houses with small porticos. Chet's house has a living room, dining room, kitchen and bathroom on the first floor and two large bedrooms and a bathroom on the second. The furniture and rugs are comfortably old and go well together.

He makes coffee and they talk pleasantly for another two hours. He wears his white hat the whole time, and Susan wonders if he ever takes it off. But she likes the way it makes him look, so she doesn't say anything about it. He invites her to spend the night. She doesn't feel like walking home and she's not sure how she would get there, so she accepts his invitation and sleeps soundly in the guest bedroom. The next morning, still wearing his white fedora, Chet cooks a nice breakfast of eggs, bacon, toast and coffee, then says he has to go to work and invites her to stay and make herself at home. Susan spends the day reading his books and magazines, listening to his extensive collection of jazz and classical records, and taking a walk in the neighborhood, which is filled with tree-lined streets and old houses with wraparound porches. She eats his food for lunch and dinner, then goes out to the corner store to replace what she's eaten, since she doesn't want to seem like a bad guest.

When he hasn't come back by ten that night, she gets in bed and sleeps, figuring he'll be back later. But Chet's still not there when she wakes up the next morning. Susan spends another fine day with books and food and music, takes another walk through a neighborhood that's actually much larger than she thought it was, filled with fascinating old architecture and lively cafés. She stops at one of them and drinks beer and hears live music. Between sets, she talks to a group of young men and women. They're fun to be with and they clearly enjoy her company. Everyone is eating popcorn, and it's some of the best popcorn she's ever tasted. They tell her about other great cafés in the neighborhood, and how they spend most of their nights going from place to place eating popcorn.

Later, Susan goes back to Chet's house. He's still not there, so she goes to bed. When he hasn't returned the next morning, she spends her day the same way she spent the day before, then goes back to the house and sleeps and wakes the next day and he's still not there. She thinks about reporting his disappearance to the authorities, but she doesn't want them to know that she's living in a stranger's house and eating his food. She stays there for days and he doesn't come back, and finally she decides that the house is hers. She buys new clothes, finds a great library only a few blocks away, and starts her research again. She loves her new life: the neighborhood, the new friends, and all the great popcorn. And now she won't have to formally break up with Duke, since after a while he's bound to forget about her and move on to someone else. She mails a check to her landlord with a note saying that she won't need her apartment anymore, giving him permission to sell her second-hand furniture.

Over the next three months, Susan keeps meeting nice people in popcorn cafés at night. During the day she goes to the neighborhood library and continues her research on extraordinary states of mind, how they constitute an alternative history of the world, a narrative that isn't based on the cause and effect logic that drives most historical writing. She decides that extraordinary subjective states aren't ultimately what's important. She becomes more interested in the pattern they form—or don't form—over time, since she's beginning to suspect that although the amazing mental events appear to exist in relation to each other, they don't form a pattern in the conventional sense of the term. She decides that this is the real focus of her project: to question what people mean when they talk about patterns, and to speculate on what the human mind might look like if it wasn't studied in terms of pattern formation.

When Susan shares her new conceptual focus with her friends at a café, they nod eagerly, as if they all had their own research interests and knew exactly how exciting it was to have entered a new phase in a mental project like this one. But with the buttery smell of fresh popcorn that fills the café, Susan can't be sure that her friends are giving her ideas the careful attention she's hoping for, since they all might be so stoned on the scent and taste of popcorn that they'll agree with almost anything. In fact, it even occurs to her that her new ideas on pattern formation have emerged under the influence of melted butter and salt, the rich smells that popcorn makes as it pops and gets poured into large bowls and passed around the room. She knows she should be disturbed that the shape of her thinking might be influenced more by pleasure than by logical discipline, but it's hard to care when everyone in the café seems blissed out on what they're smelling and tasting. It's nice to just be there and share ideas in a happy atmosphere.

The only person who seems confused is a new member of the group, a thirty-something guy named Gabe, who moved in a few days ago from a different part of the city. He looks like he's paying attention, but Susan can tell that he's not taking anything in. She's always been attracted to difficult people, and though things have never worked out when she's drawn to someone's suffering, she knows Gabe has a story to tell, and she can't help wanting to hear it.

Before too long, they've moved to their own corner table, and Gabe says: I almost killed a guy three months ago.

113

She tries not to look shocked, and quickly asks: By accident?

He says: No. Not by accident. On purpose.

She says: On purpose? Really?

He says: Really. I wanted him dead. I had a gun barrel stuck in his mouth and I was ready to pull the trigger. If it hadn't been for a Steely Dan song on the CD player in the guy's car, he'd be dead right now and I'd be on death row.

Susan says: That's—I don't know—That's pretty scary.

Gabe nods: That's pretty scary. I mean, he had it coming to him. He'd treated me abusively, and I wanted him dead. It was—

She says: He treated you abusively? What exactly did he do?

Gabe says: He didn't like my driving. So he cut in front of me, slammed on the brakes, got out of his car and started yelling at me. So I got a gun and tracked him down and put a few bullets in his feet and made him beg for his life. It was great to see him shaking uncontrollably while I had a gun in his mouth. And then he said I could sleep with his girlfriend, but when he tried to reach her on his cell his calls kept going straight to her voicemail. By then, I wasn't planning to pull the trigger. It was enough to see him shitting bricks when the girl didn't answer the phone.

Susan says: So did you end up having a male bonding moment about Steely Dan? My ex-boyfriend was a Steely Dan freak, but I always thought they were boring, not all that different from other big-hit groups.

Gabe shakes his head and says: After we talked for a while and I didn't want to shoot him anymore, it turned out that we liked Steely Dan for different reasons, and we didn't have anything else in common. I let him go with the promise that he wouldn't press charges against me, and I also made him swear to enroll the next day in anger management classes.

Susan can barely keep herself from laughing: What about you?

Gabe says: What about me?

Susan says: He didn't make you promise to take anger management classes?

Gabe says: How could he make me promise anything? I was the one with the gun. Besides, I didn't have an anger problem until he dumped his anger on me. But then afterwards, when I thought about what a raging fuck he was, I got worried that he'd find out where I lived and get revenge. For weeks I tried to tell myself that I was just being paranoid and he'd learned his lesson and was probably still recovering from the gunshot wounds and wouldn't want to mess with someone who'd almost killed him. But then I thought I saw his car a few times passing by on my street, so I decided to move. So far I like it here. It seems friendly, though you're the first person I've had a real conversation with.

Susan hesitates, then carefully says: Have you ever almost murdered someone before?

Gabe says: Not that I know of.

She shakes her head: Not that you *know* of?

Gabe says: There's a lot I don't know about my past.

Susan says: Why?

Gabe shrugs: I wish I knew. All I can say is that the day after Steely Dan saved me from killing someone, chunks of my past began disappearing, and at this point, it's like my early twenties never happened. There's just this big gap. And no one has been able to tell me why.

Susan almost laughs: I'm trying to imagine what it would feel like to suddenly realize that a big chunk of time was gone from my memory.

Gabe shakes his head: Like I said, it didn't happen all at once. I mean, I started having trouble remembering parts of things right away. There were gaps in things I know I used to remember fully, and the gaps kept getting bigger, and there was nothing I could do to stop them.

She says: Did you tell anyone? Did you talk to doctors?

Gabe says: Yeah, but they didn't know what to say. They asked me about stress, eating habits, sleep deprivation, stuff like that. Then I went to a hypnotist, and after a few sessions a memory surfaced that didn't seem like anything I might have done, though when it started coming back to me in the guy's office, it had the feeling memories have when they suddenly come back. Do you know what I'm talking about?

Susan hesitates, then says: I *think* so. I mean, I've had memories resurface after years of not even knowing they were gone, and in each case there was the same feeling of something familiar suddenly falling into place. Is that what you mean?

Gabe says: Yeah, except that in this case, once the feeling established itself, I was left with something I didn't understand. It felt at first like it should have been familiar, but then it clearly wasn't.

Susan says: It felt wrong? Out of place? Like something that definitely happened, but not to you?

Gabe shrugs: It's hard to talk about.

He tries to change the subject several times over the next two hours, but she keeps bringing him back to the missing years and the hypnotist's office, and soon he's telling her about the restored memories, which made it seem that at some point in his early twenties he was living in an abandoned brick school building on a rocky peninsula north of Vancouver, where the classrooms were still set up as if lessons were being taught, even though the place was filled with dust and cobwebs and it was clear that no one had been there for years. In one of the classrooms, there was extensive writing on the blackboard, teaching him a number of things he never knew before about snapping turtles. A few days later, the lesson had been replaced by information about shirts. Soon after that, he got a brief history of refrigeration techniques. Then there were three straight days on the pre-Columbian occupation of the Western hemisphere. He figured someone else had to be living there, sneaking into the classroom to erase the lessons and write new ones, but he never saw anyone else in the school or near it. Soon the situation was getting on his nerves, and he stayed away from the classrooms.

Susan struggles not to laugh, but she finally has to ask: So I guess you believe in ghosts.

Gabe shakes his head: I don't.

She says: Then who was doing the writing?

Gabe shakes his head again: No one. I mean, I stayed in that classroom one night waiting for someone to show up and erase the board and start writing. But I couldn't stay awake, and when I woke up there was a new lesson on the board.

She says: You didn't try staying there again, forcing yourself to stay awake and see what would happen?

Gabe says: No. Like I said, the situation started feeling way too creepy. I couldn't get myself to spend another night in that classroom.

Susan slowly shakes her head: Why would someone keep writing things on a blackboard in an abandoned school? And why those subjects?

Gabe shrugs: Your guess is as good as mine. But after a while it got to be too much, and I started staying on the school's outdoor patios, wrapping myself in blankets I found in a storage room in the basement. Each afternoon the wind from the sea would get stronger and stronger, but the blankets kept me warm. On clear nights the stars were brighter than I'd ever seen them before, and I stayed outside watching them until I fell asleep. The wind kept getting harder and colder, but the blankets kept me warm.

Gabe looks around the café, which is almost empty at this point, but still maintains the delicious smell of buttered popcorn. He looks at the high ceiling and watches the big fans turning slowly.

Susan says: Then what happened?

Gabe says: That was it. The memory didn't seem connected to anything else. I mean, it led to other memories without seeming directly related to them. Like you were saying earlier about pattern formation in history—

Susan says: What were the other memories?

Gabe says: They weren't as complete as the first one. I remembered working in a hardware store in Omaha, Nebraska. I remembered editing an anarchist journal in Detroit. In another memory, I was breeding Saint Bernards, in Scotland I think. And then I was working as a studio musician, a keyboard player based in L.A. See what I mean? It was like I was remembering things that a bunch of other people did. They didn't seem to add up to one person's life, or at least not *my* life. I mean, I don't play any keyboard instruments, I don't know anything about hardware, and I'm not even sure what an anarchist is.

Susan says: What about Saint Bernards?

Gabe says: They're really cool dogs. My older brother had three Saint Bernards, and I always loved hanging out with them when I visited. But I can't imagine breeding them. They need too much attention.

Susan says: And you've never been to Scotland?

Gabe says: Not that I know of.

She says: What do you really do?

He says: I've been a driving teacher for the past ten years. But once all the weird memories came up, it was hard to remember what my real job was. I had to make up a reason to call my boss at the driving school and talk to him for a while, just to confirm that, in fact, I'm a driving teacher.

Susan doesn't want to sound like she's conducting an interview, but she knows that if they stay there in the café eating popcorn, she'll want to keep asking questions. She decides that a change of setting might help, so she invites him back to the house. She feels weird about asking such a strange guy back to a place that isn't even hers, but there's something baffled about Gabe that feels more endearing than menacing, and besides, it's been almost four months since she had any sex, and she's always liked going to bed with baffled men.

It's a cold night, and they walk as quickly as they can, even though it would be more enjoyable to walk slowly and admire all the beautiful houses and trees in the neighborhood. When they reach the street of porticoed brownstones, Gabe stops and stares and says: I've seen this street before. It was in that school I was telling you about before, a picture in one of the classrooms. Either that, or I'm having a very intense déjà vu.

Susan says: Now that you mention it, I had the same feeling the first time I came here. I couldn't say exactly where I'd seen it before, but I knew the street looked familiar. I felt as if I'd always known I would come here.

Gabe says: Really?

Susan nods: I dismissed the feeling because it seemed silly at the time, but now that you're having the same experience, it doesn't feel so silly.

Gabe says: Maybe this is one of those extraordinary subjective states you were talking about earlier.

She nods and takes his hand and leads him down the street to Chet's brownstone. As she opens the front door Gabe admires the portico and says: I've always wanted a house with one of these. But this is the only time I've ever seen one, except in pictures.

Soon they're in the kitchen making popcorn. Then they move to the living room, and right before Susan can start asking questions again, Gabe looks at a framed old picture above the fireplace and says: Who's that?

It's a picture of a smiling man with messed up hair and a beard. In the background there's a red barn and a silo, a crescent moon above distant snow-covered mountains. She doesn't know who he is, but she's concerned that if she admits this, he'll wonder why she's put the picture in such a prominent place, or why she's got the picture at all. She might end up admitting that she's living in someone else's house, that she doesn't know who he was or where he went, and this might spoil her chances for having sex with Gabe later. She considers telling him that it's just a picture she found in a thrift shop, but then he'll probably raise a question she's had many times when she sees portrait paintings in thrift shops: Who would buy a picture of someone they don't know and hang it in their living room, or anywhere else in their house for that matter? Of course, art collectors and museums pay huge sums of money for portraits of people they don't know if the painting was done by a famous artist. But the painting Gabe is asking about isn't in that category.

He's looking at her strangely, puzzled that she's not answering a simple question. He says: Is something wrong?

She laughs and says: Sorry! It's just that the picture brings back sad memories. That's Uncle Rick. He's dead now, but he was one of my favorite people in the world. He used to own this amazing seaside café called The View, and my family always went there for special occasions. I didn't know him at the time that painting was done. In fact, it's not even a good picture of him. But it still brings back sweet memories.

Gabe nods and takes her hand. She tries to look like she's having sweet memories. There's a long silence. Gabe finally says: Can we make more popcorn?

She sees that the bowl is empty, so she goes to the kitchen and makes another batch in the microwave. He comes up behind her and puts his arms around her waist, moving his hands down toward her crotch. Then the microwave buzzer goes off and he jumps back, as if startled, and says: What was that?

She laughs: Relax! It was just the microwave buzzer telling us that the popcorn's done.

She's wondering if he always has such extreme reactions to simple domestic sounds, but then she decides that he probably gets disturbed by all intrusive technological noises, since they remind him of the sound his gun would have made if Steely Dan hadn't saved the day.

He smiles as she pours the popcorn into the bowl. He says: I love the sound popcorn makes when it's getting poured into a bowl! Let's put lots of butter and salt on it. Then you can tell me more about your uncle.

She's annoyed that now she'll have to keep inventing details, but she's afraid it might seem strange if she doesn't provide at least one fake memory. The problem is that she never had any uncles, so she can't just take a real memory and plug it into the context she's invented. She doesn't want another weird pause, so she puts a distant look in her eyes and says: My Uncle Vaso was an amazing guy. He grew up in Bosnia and he was in Sarajevo when Archduke Franz Ferdinand got shot. In fact, he was part of the assassination plot. He'd been involved in an underground youth movement, and he was a regular in cafés where students drank coffee all night and talked about revolution, and one night he met this guy who recruited him to put a bullet in the archduke's head, but then—

Gabe looks puzzled: I thought you said his name was Uncle Rick.

She quickly says: We always called him Uncle Rick, but his real name was Vaso. I think he changed his name to Rick—Rick Barnes—because he didn't want to be associated with his past.

Gabe says: Barnes? That was his new last name? Maybe that's why there's a barn in the picture!

Susan nods and says: Yeah, I never thought of that. But sure, why not? Anyway, he didn't want to be connected with his past and—

Gabe nods: I can see why. Most people don't want to be known as foreign assassins, especially if they've moved to America from a place that was communist at some point. I mean, was Uncle Rick—or Uncle Vaso—did he come to the States after doing time for his part in the assassination? Was he running away from a communist dictatorship? Did he get to the States back in the fifties, when people were getting accused of being communist spies?

She's annoyed that she has to answer a new set of questions, making a partly imagined person seem to be someone she really knew. It's not just a matter of being consistent, not getting caught in another lie. It's also a matter of shaping an impression, something that's not only realistic but also compelling, worth listening to, with certain things being highlighted and other things getting downplayed or left out altogether, then locating that impression in a detailed historical context. She thinks of saying that the laws of history are obscured by the accidents of history, but she's worried that Gabe might sense that she's trying to impress him with a clever line, even if he's never read Trotsky or Tolstoy.

She says: Uncle Vaso got lucky. He was only seventeen in 1914, so even though he did some jail time, he didn't get lynched like some of the others, since according to Bosnian law people under twenty didn't get the death penalty. I mean, he didn't really do anything. He just stood there with a gun in his pocket and then didn't have the nerve to shoot when the archduke drove by. But he still would have been strung up if he was a few years older. Several other guys got put to death just because they helped Gavrilo Princip smuggle weapons across the border. One of them didn't even know that Princip had weapons. And this other guy, Danilo Ilic, tried to talk Princip into calling off the assassination, but he still got lynched because he was over twenty, and Princip just did jail time because he was only nineteen, even though he was the one who pulled the trigger. I mean—

Gabe says: But when did Uncle Vaso come to the States? Was he fleeing communism?

She says: I'm not sure. I know that once he got out of prison he got involved in politics, and he wrote a famous essay advocating ethnic cleansing in Yugoslavia. But I think that might have been before Yugoslavia became communist. And I don't know exactly when he came to the States. I just know he had this great café—

Gabe says: Is the bedroom upstairs?

He's got his hand on her leg and it's getting her excited, so she laughs and says: Yeah, both bedrooms are upstairs. I was going to say that you could stay in the guest bedroom—

He laughs: There's no fucking way I'm staying in the guest bedroom!

She smiles: Just kidding!

Soon they're in bed and finding that they like the same kinds of pleasure. They've got a bowl of popcorn on the nightstand, so they can celebrate when they finish. The only thing that's not quite right is that Susan thinks Gabe would look better in bed with a white fedora, and she decides that she'll get him one if they keep seeing each other and fucking. They're moving toward a shared climax when someone starts pounding on the door downstairs. She wants to ignore it and keep the passion going, but Gabe is too startled to continue, especially since the knocking keeps getting louder.

He says: Who the fuck is that?

She says: I have no idea.

He looks at his watch and says: It's almost three in the morning. Were you expecting someone?

She says: It's probably just some idiot who's too drunk to know that he's banging on the wrong door.

He says: You're sure it's not a husband or boyfriend you managed not to tell me about earlier?

Gabe looks annoyed, like he's pretty sure that his suspicion is correct, and a skeptical look remains on his face even when she insists that she's not married or involved with someone else. The knocking keeps getting louder. Finally she says: Okay, I can see you don't believe me. Let's get dressed and answer the door, so you can see that it's not some husband or boyfriend.

Gabe says: I really don't want to get out of bed. I might lose my erection, and sometimes when I lose it I can't get it back. Why don't you just open the window and lean outside and see who it is? Or just lean outside and tell them to get the fuck out of here.

Susan says: It's so cold outside I don't want to open the window. Besides, if they're knocking at the door, they're beneath the portico, and I won't be able to see them. And I don't want to yell out the window at three in the morning. It might antagonize the neighbors. Let's just keep having fun here in bed and ignore the knocking and hope that whoever it is will just go away.

But the knocking keeps getting louder and louder, and Gabe keeps looking at Susan skeptically, so she finally says: I guess I'll have to go down and see who it is. You can stay here and play with yourself until I get back.

She puts on a robe and goes downstairs and opens the door fiercely, like she's angry at being jerked awake in the middle of the night. She expects her visitor to be at least mildly apologetic, but he looks at her like a general doing an inspection. He moves what looks like a sky blue ping pong ball in front of Susan's face, taps the device with his finger, making it flash. Susan feels like she's had her picture taken. Then he pops the ball into his mouth and calmly swallows it. He's wearing a skin-tight uniform she doesn't recognize, bright orange from top to bottom with a smiling sky blue sun in the center of his chest. The sun's light green eyes look alive, as if they were reading her face with fierce precision. Framed by the portico, the cold night looks like the background of a painting, briefly creating the feeling that the man is nothing but a colored form created by an artist. For a second, Susan wants to reach out and touch him, just to confirm that he's more than a flat painted shape, but the stern look on the man's face gives her the feeling that he'd be offended if she made even the slightest move in his direction.

He finally says: I have an important message for you.

He hands her a sealed orange envelope, blank except for the same sky blue sun in the center, the same precise green eyes.

She says: Is the message really meant for me? Does it matter that I don't officially live here?

He says: Of course it matters! What are you doing here?

She hesitates, not sure if it's wise to tell the truth, but something about the blue sun's probing green eyes makes her feel that she better just blurt things out, so she says: I met the guy who lives here when we collided on the street. We had a good conversation, I liked the white hat he was wearing, so I came back here with him, and when he left I stayed because it's a great place to live.

He says: Then give me the envelope. If you're not the person the message was intended for, it would be dangerous for you to read it.

She says: What's dangerous about it?

He says: The envelope has no inside. It's just an exterior.

She says: So if I opened it—

He says: If you opened it, there wouldn't be anything there. The inside of the envelope doesn't exist.

She says: So? I've seen empty envelopes before and—

He says: You don't understand. The envelope isn't empty. It has no inside. Your eyes aren't equipped to handle a situation like that.

She says: And?

He says: You'd shut down completely. You wouldn't die, but when you began functioning again you'd be someone else entirely. You'd have to get used to being someone you wouldn't know and might not even like. I don't recommend it.

She doesn't know whether to believe him. She tries to read his face, but quickly gives up, knowing it's the kind of face she won't remember later. She thinks about Gabe in the room upstairs, imagines him jerking off or eating popcorn. She thinks about Chet and his white fedora. Both faces disappear when she tries to form clear mental pictures.

She says: What would happen if Chet—I mean, what would happen if the guy who really lives here opened it?

He says: Since he was the one the envelope was intended for, he'd be fine with it. In fact, he would gain from it.

She says: What would he gain?

He says: It's hard to know for sure. He might not ever get a cold again. This house might start to clean itself. He'd never need brooms or mops or vacuum cleaners ever again. Or—

The man's voice cuts out. His mouth remains open.

Susan says: Or?

The man's mouth closes. He says: I can't waste any more time answering questions.

The night air framed by the portico has solidified into a dark wall of translucent plastic. Thousands of small fish seem to be swimming behind it. She doesn't want to return the envelope now that he's made it sound so mysterious, but he snatches it out of her hand before she can stop him. He stands there for a moment, looking at her like she's a page of prose that needs revision, with certain details deleted and others given more emphasis. She wants to ask him to explain the look he's giving her, and also the uniform he's wearing, which seems to indicate that he represents an organization of some kind. The smiling sun on his chest is watching her closely, as if it were about to speak, deliver a verdict. But the man turns and leaves without further comment. The doors of night open slightly, and he slips through the crack just before they click shut. There's something final about the sound. It's clear that she won't be able to open the doors and find out where he's gone.

There's nothing to do but go back upstairs and hope she and Gabe can get things going again. She's gotten so cold from standing in the open doorway that she can't wait to get back under the blankets and snuggle up with Gabe's warm body. She climbs the stairs, enters the room, starts to say something sexy, but she stops when she sees that Gabe is asleep. He's snoring with his hand in his crotch, a half-eaten bowl of popcorn on the floor beside the bed. She starts to reach down to shake him awake, but then hesitates, knowing he'll want to know who was at the door and what he wanted, and he probably won't believe her if she simply tells him what happened. The truth won't work, and for once in her life she doesn't feel like making things up.

She tries to remember exactly what happened—the man's commanding attention, the sky blue ping-pong device, the blue sun's fiercely intelligent eyes, the dangerous orange envelope, the sound of the closing door of night. But the more she tries to form a firm mental picture, the more the details blur and fade and change. She tells herself that the mind is its own place, and can make a heaven of hell and a hell of heaven. She likes the way the line sounds and imagines saying it to her new friends at a popcorn café, except that someone might know that it's not an original thought, that it's something she read in a book, and besides, she doesn't believe in heaven and hell, not even as states of mind.

She watches Gabe sleeping on the bed, snoring as if he might never wake up, as if the whole world were asleep and had no reason to wake up any time soon. It makes her want to laugh as hard as she can, like Gavrilo Princip finally finding shelter after a night of rain. She's always liked it when people laugh a long time, how after a while they're not sure what they're laughing at, going beyond the social construction of rational perception, or whatever it was that her version of Princip must have meant to say at his trial. But she knows that even laughter won't change what should have been obvious right from the start, that some things aren't just states of mind. Some things really happen.

BECAUSE OF THE WALL

Jack woke up and made coffee, then tried to go online. He needed information for his project, a documentary film about the wall in Central Park. But when he clicked on his browser the screen went white and started growling. A hairy hand came up from the bottom of the screen and gave him the finger, then vanished into his normal desktop image, the Dutch landscape painting with cows and a barn and a windmill. He tried to go online five times and exactly the same thing happened.

He thought at first that he must have had a virus in his computer, but soon he learned that the problem was larger than that. When he grabbed his landline phone and made some service calls, he couldn't even reach an automated answering system. There would be two rings, a click, then someone clearing her throat. He didn't have a TV so he turned on the radio. He carefully moved the dial from station to station but got only static.

The day looked sunny and hot from his living room window. He hated muggy weather and wanted to stay in his air-conditioned apartment. But he needed information for his film, so he got dressed and walked five blocks to the Astor Place newsstand. They didn't have the morning paper. He asked if they had yesterday's paper, the day before yesterday's paper, or papers from other cities. But the guys who worked there smiled and shrugged and pointed to their shelves, empty except for a few old magazines and a pile of tabloids. Jack walked five blocks to another newsstand and the same thing happened. He walked to five more newsstands and the same thing happened. He didn't like reading the papers, but he knew that every day new theories appeared about the wall, ideas that might have a strong effect on how he was making his film.

He was just about to give up and go home when he found himself face to face with Ron and Peter, old friends he hadn't seen in years. They quickly said the things people say when they haven't kept in touch. He always found meetings like this awkward, but this one was more than awkward because Peter shouldn't have been there. He died of AIDS in 1994, twenty years ago. Making sure to smile the whole time, Jack looked him up and down carefully, trying to make sure it was really Peter and not someone else who strongly resembled him.

But it was definitely Peter, having aged of course, but in all other ways identical to the person Jack remembered, tall and thin with blue eyes, a long fat nose, big ears and short brown hair. He chopped the air with his hands as he talked, like someone guiding a plane onto an aircraft carrier, and he spoke so precisely it almost seemed that he'd memorized everything in advance. His shirt was buttoned all the way up, even though it was a hot summer day. The terrible irony was impossible to miss: Peter had always been buttoned up but couldn't remain zipped up, especially not in Central Park after dark. Jack looked at Ron to confirm that it couldn't be Peter, that they both knew he was dead. But Ron acted like nothing strange was happening.

Ron had been Peter's lover for seventeen years. For the two final years, Ron did everything possible to keep Peter alive. He was desperate to make Peter believe that he wasn't going to die, though Peter himself wasn't fooled for a second, and frequently told Ron that it was better to face the truth. Ron didn't want to face the truth and almost lost his mind when Peter died. Jack worried that Ron might kill himself, so he tried to stay in close touch for the next few months. But things weren't the same for Ron without Peter in the world. Before too long he began to prefer his own company, and no doubt Peter's imagined company, to anyone else's. He stopped returning Jack's calls.

Now they were standing in front of Jack looking delighted that they'd run into him. The conversation was just as fluid as it always was in the past. They talked about the wall, its unexplained sudden appearance in Central Park five months ago, and also about President Obama, how surprising it was that one of America's teeming population of racist monsters hadn't murdered him yet, how disappointing his foreign policy had been, keeping the wars in Iraq and Afghanistan going, continuing the Republican violence, costing the country almost half a billion dollars a day.

Jack told them about his problems with the media. Peter said that when he'd tried to go online, the computer screen had been filled with footage of someone's mouth slowly opening and closing. Ron said that all the TV channels were stuck on a single image, a sky-blue smiling cartoon sun on a bright orange background. The radio was all static except for a station with news from the previous month.

Jack looked at the people rushing by on the street. They all seemed even more dazed and disturbed than usual. He wanted to find out if they were having media problems too, but Ron looked at his watch and said they were late for a meeting with their lawyer. Jack paid special attention to his parting handshake with Peter. The skin and bones in Peter's palm and fingers felt solid, not ghostly. Jack had never been the hugging type, but he thought that the full body contact of a parting embrace would help him further confirm Peter's physical existence. He was just about to spread his arms and move closer when they backed away and excused themselves, urging Jack to keep in touch, quickly moving down the street. He followed them with his eyes, expecting Peter to suddenly vanish, return to the land of the dead. But they just kept walking and talking, stopping briefly to point at something in a shopfront window, then turning onto St. Mark's Place two blocks away.

Jack was afraid that he looked like he'd just seen a ghost, but when he checked his reflection in the window of a small café, his hair wasn't standing on end. He looked like he normally looked—curly, short, blond hair with a long thin face, tall and lanky and slightly bent over, as if he'd spent his life playing up-right bass in a jazz band. He turned and looked at the sidewalk, half expecting to see Peter's footprints pressed in dry cement. Had it all been in his head? He knew it hadn't been. Clearly, Peter was physically real, and talking with him felt exactly like it did in the past, when Peter worked as a screen writer for a well-known film director. That was how they'd gotten to know each other. Jack worked on the set design team for the same director, a pub-licity hound whose professional name was George Washington.

When Peter died, George Washington lost his best writer, and his films got steadily worse and more successful. Jack started making more money. But the richer Washington got the more obnoxious he became, so Jack found work with a better direc-tor, someone whose need for power and control wasn't quite so extreme. Thinking of movies reminded Jack that he needed a pa-per, the latest information for his film, which was currently called "Up Against A Wall: What It Means When We Don't Know What

To Say But We Know That We Have To Say Something," an aggressively cumbersome title he was planning to make even longer. He told himself that the wall deserved at least another fifteen words. Or maybe no words at all. So many things about it were uncertain: Who built it? How was it built? Why was it in Central Park? Why hadn't anyone seen it under construction? Questions like these had dominated the airwaves for the past few months, and many theories had been proposed. But beyond what anyone said, the wall didn't seem to serve any purpose. It was standing in the Great Lawn section of the park, not keeping anyone out or in, made of an indestructible material no one had ever seen before, not even the smartest people in the world.

In fact, the smartest people in the world had been invited by the US government to visit the wall and say intelligent things about it. Their visit was front-page news in every paper in the nation. But soon they agreed that they didn't know what to say. No matter what they tried, they couldn't even begin an investigation without changing the wall in subtle or obvious ways, producing alterations in color, size, and texture, though nothing seemed to alter the fact that the wall was immovable. A demolition team had tried to take it down with a bulldozer, then dynamite, then a wrecking ball, without success. A distinguished physicist, after a thorough but confused examination, concluded that the wall would even survive thermonuclear explosions, though for obvious reasons it was impossible to put this claim to the test.

It was hard to test any claim about the wall, but after several weeks of observation, the experts felt they could safely say that the wall was almost always between two and four feet thick, between a hundred and two hundred feet in length, between ten and twenty feet in height. It had first appeared on June 28, 2014, between three and four in the morning. No one had seen it pop into existence, a silly phrase which even the experts couldn't improve on, since there was no evidence that construction of any kind had taken place. Had there really been a *pop*—a rather loud *pop*—when the wall took its place in the world? Jack wanted to think so, and he wanted to think that someone in the park in the dark had heard the sound and wondered what it was. But the people who first discovered the wall heard nothing. They simply bumped into the wall at four in the morning, swearing when questioned later that it hadn't been there an hour before, when they passed through the same section of the Great Lawn, near Turtle Pond and Belvedere Castle.

A day later, City Hall officials declared that the wall had not been erected by the city, and that there was no record of any construction company having a permit to build a wall in Central Park. Most New Yorkers then assumed that the wall was a hoax of some kind. But all talk of pranks and schemes disappeared once it became clear that the wall was made of a substance even the world's foremost authorities couldn't identify. This led inevitably to claims that the wall must have come from another planet. Some scientists even speculated that the wall wasn't really a wall at all, but an alien spacecraft, or perhaps an alien life form. But if the wall had really come down from the sky, it had appeared above a place where many people would have seen it, even at four in the morning, and no one on the night of June 28 had reported anything unusual.

Initially, Jack thought that the situation was absurd, straight out of the tabloids. He told himself he had better things to think about. But in fact he didn't have better things to think about. He was tired of designing sets, tired of working on other people's movies. But he didn't know what else to do with himself, until he read in *The Village Voice* that his ex-boss, George Washington, had been deeply confused the first time he saw the wall, and had gotten even more confused each time he went back, finally becoming so disturbed that he planned to make a film in which the wall was destroyed by God as an act of vengeance. Jack was highly amused. He'd always seen George Washington as a control freak, someone who never failed to make sure he got exactly what he wanted, even if others had to pay the price. It was good to see him so disturbed and confused. Jack's feelings about the wall began to change. He wanted to see it.

He was afraid there might be crowds, so he went to see the wall on a Wednesday morning, when he figured people would either be sleeping or going to work. He was right. He was there by himself, except for two policemen sitting on a bench, looking bored and useless. He'd heard that the Great Lawn had been roped off at first, then fenced off, but the ropes and fences kept disappearing, as if the wall didn't want to be set apart from the rest of the world. Finally City Hall gave up. The only remaining precaution was a handwritten cardboard sign, warning people to approach at their own risk.

At first he thought the wall was made of white brick. Then he decided it wasn't brick but plaster, then more like some kind of plastic, or maybe unbreakable glass, or maybe its substance was changing just as its color seemed to be changing, white becoming sky blue shading into an aqua green, then slate green darkening into royal blue becoming black, paling into gray and white and silver-blue and turquoise, all the changes taking place in a second. For a minute the wall was translucent, nearly transparent, and he thought he might be looking at a huge aquarium, filled with swaying plants and the darting and gliding of tropical fish. Soon he found himself touching it without planning to. Its surface almost seemed to be breathing, moist and smooth like a dolphin's back, yet it also felt harder than stone or steel. He was so amazed that he couldn't get himself to escape the summer heat and take the air-conditioned subway home. Instead, he walked more than eighty blocks downtown to his East Third Street apartment, sweating and squinting his way through the loud mid-morning sunlight, talking himself into making a documentary, even though he'd never done one before.

He started making phone calls later that day, and over the next few weeks he got lots of interview footage. But getting pictures of the wall itself was a problem. He soon found out that everyone who tried to film or photograph the wall got the same result: no images of the wall, only shots of themselves with their cameras focused on the wall, apparently taken from the wall's point of view, as if the wall were a camera. When the same thing happened to Jack, he tried to be clever. Using skills he'd developed in art school years before, he made a photo realist painting of the wall and shot the painting. The result was footage of Jack at an easel painting, apparently shot from behind the painting, showing only Jack's face and moving arm and the back of his canvas. He was stunned at first, but soon he was laughing at the situation, planning to make it a major part of his project, the thing that made his film unlike any other. After all, how many documentaries offered no images of their subject?

From that point on, Jack focused mainly on reactions to the wall. There was no shortage of people in New York with ideas about it, well-known experts of various kinds and people with no official expertise, all eager to explain themselves on camera when Jack got in touch with them. Jack also planned to include his own theories in the film, and now that mass information seemed to be dead, now that he'd just seen someone who should have been dead, he was tempted to think that the wall's appearance in Central Park had something to do with the media's disappearance and Peter's reappearance. Though he knew that the three things might be unrelated, he wanted to see connections. Before he ran into Peter and Ron he'd been ready to rush back to his air-conditioned apartment. But now he had to keep looking. He had to find out if the news was really dead. He needed news about the death of news.

The day was getting hotter and hotter, but he kept working his way downtown, rushing from newsstand to newsstand. The lack of information was getting on his nerves. It was getting on everyone's nerves. The Manhattan streets were even crazier than usual, as people tried in vain to cope with the absence of a media system they had come to depend on. Some were howling at the sun. Some were butting heads and laughing. Some were on their hands and knees, drooling on the sidewalk. Some were driving cars or busses or trucks into brick walls, fire hydrants, dumpsters, and telephone poles. Some were sitting in a daze getting bitten by mosquitoes. Some were biting their fingers off one by one. Jack told himself to keep going, despite the insanity. Then he heard a loud noise in the sky and saw an airplane near a cluster of downtown buildings.

The plane was so low it made him think of 9/11, and he braced himself for another disaster. But the plane veered sharply to avoid the soon-to-be-opened One World Trade Center, slanting down in Jack's direction, getting smaller as it approached, finally becoming the size of a hot dog, bouncing harmlessly off Jack's forehead, crashing onto the sidewalk. Doors opened in the small fuselage. Little people ran out screaming in all directions. The plane burst into flames, burning rapidly, leaving nothing on the pavement but a flattened cigar. Jack picked it up and tried to examine it. But it smelled like charred human flesh, so he tossed it into a garbage can, then rushed into a bathroom in an office building lobby and washed his hands. It took lots of soap to clean off the horrible smell.

Clearly, things weren't safe, so he rushed back to his apartment. He felt glad that he had four walls to protect him. He shuddered when he thought about life without walls, the continuous exposure that people who couldn't afford walls had to live with. Back in the late sixties, he and his hippie friends talked eagerly about breaking down walls between people. Now he felt grateful that he had enough money to pay for a living space firmly separated from the rest of the world.

His need for insulation had grown more extreme as he got older. He'd thought many times of getting rid of his phone because it allowed people to penetrate his walled off space with their voices, simply by pressing buttons. It wasn't enough that he could refuse to answer. The mere thought that the phone might ring had made him nervous, reminding him that people might try to impose themselves on him whenever they wanted to, for reasons he couldn't control. He kept his landline phone unplugged until he wanted to use it. He couldn't understand how people could tolerate cell phones, eagerly turning themselves into moving targets.

But now his phone started ringing, even though it wasn't plugged in. He was so confused that he answered, the first time he'd taken a call in more than a year.

The voice on the other end said: Hi Jack. It's Barbara.

Jack hesitated, then said: Oh hi, how's it going?

She said: Not so well. Do you have a few minutes to talk?

Jack said: Sure.

He didn't know who Barbara was, but she had a lovely voice,

so he figured that if she needed help, he would do what he could.

She said: I just ran into someone who died a few years ago. We had a long conversation in City Hall Park. I thought at first I was losing my mind. But she was really there, my college roommate Amy Van Buren. I don't think you ever met her. We were close in college, but over the years we fell out of touch. Then I got a call a few years ago from a mutual friend who said that Amy had died in a plane crash. I went to her funeral and there were intense testimonials and everyone was upset. She was only thirty-five, too young to die. But then, about thirty minutes ago, I was walking in City Hall Park and there she was, looking just like I remembered her, except a bit older, and we talked about all the stuff we used to do in college. It turns out that she's living in Southern California now, in a small town in the Mojave Desert, and she's involved with an eco-terrorist group and has a great boyfriend. I kept thinking I was imagining the whole thing. But this guy rushing past us frantically pushing buttons on his phone bumped into her, and the physical contact made a definite sound, a firm thump, so I knew I wasn't seeing a ghost. We hugged when she had to go and hugging her felt just like it used to feel, so—

Jack said: The same thing happened to me about an hour ago.

She said: Really?

Jack said: Really. I ran into an old friend who died of AIDS sixteen years ago. I know he was physically real. We didn't hug, but we shook hands and his ex-lover was there acting like nothing was wrong.

She said: I wonder if the same thing is happening all over the city. Maybe it has something to do with that creepy wall people keep talking about.

Jack said: Yeah maybe.

She said: Maybe the wall that used to separate the living from the dead was moved to Central Park, so now there's no separation between life and death, and dead people can freely circulate among the living.

Jack said: I was thinking along those lines myself. But who moved the wall? And why? Why would someone let dead people back into the world? We've already got a serious overpopulation problem.

She said: I don't know. I don't have that part figured out yet. But my friend Susan in San Diego called me a few days ago and said that she'd run into a guy named Gavrilo Princip. Does that name ring a bell?

Jack said: Gavrilo Princip? The guy who shot the archduke in Sarajevo?

She said: Yeah. And, at first, Susan just thought it was a weird coincidence, a guy with the same name as a famous assassin. But they were sitting in a café talking, and when the guy pulled out a gun, stepped outside and started shooting, she started to think it might have been the real Gavrilo Princip, somehow come to life again. And now I'm starting to think that it might be because of the wall. I'm not sure why—

Jack said: Wait a minute. Let's go back a few sentences. This contemporary version of Princip stepped outside of a café and started shooting? Who was the target? A contemporary version of the archduke?

She said: I'm not sure. Susan didn't say.

Jack said: Think about it: If Princip were alive today, who would he shoot? There aren't any archdukes anymore. If he really wanted to perform a meaningful assassination, he'd have to destroy our mass communication system. He'd have to be the ultimate cyber criminal.

She said: Whenever people use words like cyber, my brain shuts off.

Jack said: I know what you mean. But think about it: If Princip is somehow back in circulation, he might be the one responsible for all the media breakdowns.

She said: And it's all because of the wall, since the wall gave him a doorway into the present? It sounds like this awesome sci-fi movie I saw recently, I think it was by George Washington, and there was this guy who—

Jack wasn't listening. He always tried to block out any mention of George Washington, and the talk of Gavrilo Princip was triggering a memory, a weird story about an early attempt to make a film about the wall. A guy who'd won awards for his documentaries in the past, focusing on things like Abu Ghraib and the Vietnam War, had quickly tried to collect footage and testimonials about the wall, but found that his film was corrupted when he tried to do preliminary editing. It went beyond the usual confusion people experienced when they tried to capture the wall with cameras. In place of what he thought he'd filmed, he found an extended substitution, a short film about a meeting beside the wall with Gavrilo Princip. At first he'd been confused and frustrated. But then he saw the substitution as an opportunity, and he'd explained the meeting with Princip in detail to someone from a high profile film magazine, a conversation that was soon published as feature article and triggered controversy, though most people forgot about it within a few weeks.

The substitute footage began with a guy named Bill McKinley in a small Manhattan apartment reading, hearing footsteps in the corridor, someone sliding an envelope under his door, a cryptic invitation: *Meet me at the wall at midnight*, signed by Gavrilo Princip. Bill McKinley called an ex-girlfriend and told her about it. She told him not to go, reminding him that Central Park was dangerous after dark, and besides, the note had to be a joke of some kind, since there was no way a dead person could have written and delivered it.

But Bill had been a history major in college, had written his senior thesis on the Princip assassination, and was too curious to play it safe. When he got there he saw someone sitting beside the wall on a park bench. He was dressed in a dark suit with a dark tie and a dark fedora, precisely the way Gavrilo Princip appeared in a picture Bill had seen on the Internet several times while doing his thesis research, the assassin seated on a park bench in Belgrade with two of his fellow conspirators.

Princip motioned for Bill to sit down beside him. Bill could barely control his shock. Now that he was close enough to reach out and touch him, he had no doubt that the person was Gavrilo Princip, not a mental projection, not someone dressed up to impersonate him.

There was silence at first. Then Bill asked the obvious question: Are you Gavrilo Princip?

The man said: Yeah.

Bill said: Haven't you been dead for almost a hundred years?

The man said: Yeah.

Bill said: So what are you doing here?

Princip said: I have permission.

Bill said: Permission? Someone can give you permission not to be dead?

Princip said: Yeah, sort of. Not *someone* really. That's a misleading way of putting it. But yeah, you can get permission.

Bill said: Did you come here through the wall?

Princip said: Not *through* it. Again, that's a misleading way of putting it. But yeah, the wall was part of it.

Bill said: So why are you here?

Princip said: To finish what I started before, to get the job done right.

Bill said: What job? The assassination? You succeeded, didn't you?

Princip said: Not really. Things went all wrong after I killed the archduke.

Bill nodded: Sure, I can see that. But you can't really change things now, can you? What's done is done.

Princip shrugged: Things can always be changed—maybe not the past, but there's no question that what we make of the past can have a profound effect on the future.

Bill said: Okay, so how do I fit in? Why did you contact me and not someone else? I'm just a normal guy. My powers are limited.

Princip said: I'm just a normal guy too. But look what happened—

At this point, the film apparently stopped. A large part of the article that appeared in the film magazine was focused on the famous director's speculations about whether the sudden ending was intentional, or whether a final segment of the footage had been lost. Jack remembered being frustrated, wishing that the footage had been made public, so he could have reached his own conclusions. But the director had insisted on keeping it for himself, claiming that he was planning to use it in another film he was making, which had yet to be released.

The memory was becoming so vivid in Jack's mind that he'd almost forgotten that he was on the phone with someone named Barbara. He didn't want her to know that he'd been tuning her out, so he quickly said: I'm making a film about the wall. Maybe we can get together some time in the next few days and I can film you explaining your theory, once you've got it all figured out.

She said: You make movies? I thought you were just a set designer.

Jack said: I've always made short films that I don't show anyone else. But with this new film, I'm planning to talk to people I know about having it shown next year at the New York Film Festival.

Barbara said: I've never been in a movie before. I've never even taken acting classes. You think I'm right for the part?

Jack said: I'm making a documentary. There's no acting involved.

She said: So all I would have to do is talk on film about my theory?

Jack said: Right. Would that be okay?

She said: Oh yeah, sure. And maybe after we're done filming we could have sex or something.

Jack said: No problem. Call me back when you've got things totally figured out, okay?

She said: Okay Jack. Thanks for talking to me. I feel much better now, like I'm not going crazy.

Jack said: You're not going crazy. Let's talk again soon, okay?

Jack hadn't had sex in a long time. Though he didn't know if he and Barbara would have the right sexual chemistry, he was so horny that he figured it wouldn't matter. Things looked promising. After all, Barbara's voice was so beautiful it could make his phone ring even when it wasn't plugged in.

The prospect of filming Barbara for his documentary made Jack want to review the footage he already had and do some preliminary editing. He opened his laptop and started watching, taking careful notes, making outlines and diagrams. His editing software was working well, even though the Internet was still gone. He knew he needed to keep gathering information, so he worried about the absence of all the websites focused on the wall, but for now he had compelling footage to work with. He'd filmed several interviews with famous scientists sounding brilliant as they talked about how baffled they were. They knew exactly how to use elaborate phrases to make their confusion sound impressive. Jack was pleased with how intellectual his film would sound when he finally put it together. He hated himself when he tried to sound smart, especially when he failed, but he knew that brainy talk by people with credentials would make his film sound more authentic.

He was even more pleased with the many nonprofessional theories he'd collected. He was planning to claim in his film that because the experts were thoroughly confused, their opinions were no more important than anyone else's. Jack hoped that at some point in the near or distant future, when the mysteries about the wall had been reduced to answers, a nonprofessional theory would be the one that solved the problem.

There were many strong candidates. A cabbie from Staten Island argued that the wall was really a door that would open if the proper words were spoken, and he'd worked up hundreds of incantations and tried them out on the wall, so far without success, but he felt he was getting closer. An aging high school gym teacher from Sheepshead Bay claimed that the wall had slipped through a crack from another dimension, that it was here by mistake, just like Stonehenge and the Sphinx and the huge stone heads on Easter Island. A guy who ran a bowling alley in Queens compared the wall to the Vietnam War Memorial in Washington, arguing that the wall had been issued by the universe as a moral complaint, that once the wars in Iraq and Afghanistan were finally over, all the names of the people killed in those wars—and not just the names of all the dead Americans—would suddenly appear on the wall, along with names of the people whose lives had been ruined, accompanied by an ironic statement of thanks to Presidents Bush and Obama for the roles they played in orchestrating the violence. An ex-dancer who ran an Internet school for the occult sciences calmly explained that the wall was a magic object, that the world had lost so much magic over the years that the wall had appeared to balance things out, that people should start meditating on the Great Lawn to restore their magic powers. An unemployed train conductor was convinced that the wall was a book that contained all other books—even those books that hadn't been written yet—but to read this vast collection of texts people wouldn't turn pages, but instead would slowly project their thinking into the depth of the wall, which was really a densely packed collection of transparent pages, each page a thousand times thinner than a piece of toilet paper, filled with symbols made of other symbols, asking of readers nothing less than the willingness to learn a whole new signifying system, reading each symbol hundreds of ways.

The thought of learning to read all over again made Jack so nervous that he started shivering. He turned off his air conditioner and opened his windows. He wanted to hear Barbara's voice again but he didn't have her number. He didn't like feeling so horny, so in need of another person, but he didn't want to masturbate because it might make him lose his concentration, so he transformed his anxiety into aesthetic energy and stayed up most of the night working on his film, falling asleep right before the sun came up, right in the middle of thoughts about Gavrilo Princip, about footage that might never be made available, and might not even exist, for all Jack knew.

He woke at noon sweating heavily with his head on his laptop and his pillows on the floor. He tried to get online, but a hairy hand appeared on his growling screen and gave him the finger. He made a number of service calls but again got someone clearing her throat. Then he failed to find the radio station Ron mentioned the day before. He finally decided to go back out and try to find a *New York Times*. At the newsstand on Astor Place, the two guys who worked there looked at him like he was crazy. The same thing happened at the next three places he tried. None of them had papers. They acted as if the very notion of selling news was absurd. Jack finally got mad. He asked them what a newsstand was if there wasn't any news to sell. They smiled as if they'd heard the question a hundred times before.

Jack decided to go home and get his camera. He wanted to film the newsstand people claiming that news was a thing of the past. His theory about the wall and the death of news was looking strong, though he didn't know why it was only now, five months after its initial appearance, that the wall was infecting the instruments of mass communication. Had the wall made a conscious decision to start breaking down the mass media? Did it make sense to think of the wall as a being that made decisions? Or was its mere presence in the world having a slow but gathering influence on the way things happened, finally reaching a point where it began to shut down or distort mass information? Was Gavrilo Princip somehow behind the whole thing, finishing a job he'd started a hundred years before? Jack knew these questions would have to be raised in his film. A voice-over segment rapidly began planning itself in his head. Then he saw Ron at a bus stop.

Ron smiled: We're not in touch for years, then we run into each other two days in a row!

Jack said: I read somewhere that when things don't happen for a while, it's unlikely that they'll happen again. But once

149

something happens, it's likely to happen again and again, simply because it's happened.

Ron said: So we'll probably keep running into each other for a while?

Jack said: I guess so, if what they say is true, whoever *they* are.

Jack had always thought Ron looked like Abraham Lincoln, and had even asked Ron at one point why he'd never starred in an Abraham Lincoln movie. But Ron had changed. He didn't look like Honest Abe any longer. He'd shaved off his beard, put on weight and become a dead ringer for Millard Fillmore. Or maybe Jack only made this connection because the former site of the Fillmore East was a few blocks away, and Jack remembered a great Pink Floyd concert there forty years ago. Or maybe Pink Floyd had never played at the Fillmore, and he was only thinking of Pink Floyd because one of their greatest albums was called *The Wall.* He wondered if this album had started selling heavily again, now that everyone was thinking about the wall in Central Park.

Ron said: Peter told me this morning that the new George Washington film he's been working on isn't working out.

Jack had to know the truth. He gently placed his hands on Ron's shoulders and said: Ron, let's get serious. Hasn't Peter been dead for twenty years? I mean, didn't he die of AIDS after two horrible years? Weren't you taking care of him the whole time? Weren't you in the hospital when he died?

Ron smiled and said: If Peter's dead, who's the guy in bed with me every night?

Ron paused and the smile disappeared. He looked angry. Then he said: Anyway, Peter's thinking of dropping the film altogether, even though he's not finished with the screenplay and he might have to deal with a law suit. But when he mentioned it on the phone last night, George Washington quickly offered more money.

Jack dropped his hands and looked at his feet. He told himself he should probably make Ron confront the truth, but he had to admit it was really Peter he'd talked to the day before, and he had to admit that he didn't know what the facts were anymore, so he took up Ron's train of thought and said: Ever since George Washington sold out, he's been convinced that money is the answer to everything. He thinks he sees his own face on every dollar bill he makes.

Ron said: The film he's making now is sure to gross more than half a billion. It's about the Central Park wall getting hit by lightning, a sign from God that the wall is an abomination, like the Tower of Babel.

Jack nodded: I heard about it a few months ago, typical Washington bullshit. But what's the problem?

Ron said: Whenever Washington's set design team tries to build the wall, it caves in before they can finish. So they tried to shoot the whole thing on a smaller scale, with a miniature replica. It looked like it was working. The five by ten inch wall held together. They did the fake lightning, and the wall blew up. But when they looked at the footage, there was no wall getting hit by lightning. Instead they had a shot of a plane flying past the new tower, the One World Trade Center building, shrinking down to the size of a hot dog, crashing into someone's head. They tried it three more times and the same thing happened.

Jack looked at Ron like one of them must have been crazy. Ron looked back like both of them must have been crazy.

Jack said: So Peter's finally admitting to himself that working with George Washington is a huge waste of time?

Ron said: He's known it all along, and he was skeptical about this new film from the start. He's always hated doomsday special effects movies. But he had what I thought was a brilliant idea, and Washington turned it down.

Jack said: Sounds like George Washington. He turns down everyone's ideas, then he comes up with the same ideas a few months later and thinks they're brilliant. But what was Peter's idea?

Ron laughed: Peter thought that if they filmed a miniature plane crashing into a guy's head, they'd get the shot of the lightning bolt striking the wall.

Jack shook his head: Why wouldn't Washington at least give it a try? Nothing else was working, and besides—

Ron's bus pulled up, so he and Jack shook hands and Ron was gone. Had the sky been filled with storm clouds, Jack was sure that lightning would have darted from the sky and blown up the bus. Fortunately, there wasn't a cloud in the sky.

Jack remembered that he'd been planning to get his camera, so he went back home. But when he made the rounds of the newsstands again, they were all closed. At first he was disappointed. Then it occurred to him that footage of closed newsstands might be quite useful at some point, so he shot each of the places he'd visited that morning, planning in his head a voice-over narrative about the wall and the death of news. Was the wall a symbol for the need to shelter the human race from the domination of mass information? What was it about information that had become so deadly that an indestructible wall was needed to block it out?

Jack wanted clever things to say in response to this question. But when he got home, sat in his favorite easy chair and tried to write down a few pithy remarks, he felt like his efforts were functioning as a wall. He was trying too hard to sound profound.

He'd always tried too hard to sound profound, and over the past few months he'd been hating himself when he caught himself doing it. He admired people who felt no pressure to perform and didn't go out of their way to sound intelligent. A number of the nonprofessional people he'd interviewed were like that. His favorite was a nursing student he'd filmed in her rent-controlled room in Washington Heights. He'd watched her speaking on film the night before. Now he wanted to watch her again. He opened his laptop, typed a few commands, and her narrow, pock-marked face appeared on the screen, staring at the floor, speaking so softly that Jack had to turn up the volume. She said: The wall exists for the sole purpose of giving the human race a chance to watch itself scrambling to figure things out, when in fact there's no need to figure out anything about the wall. It's there in Central Park for good, and it doesn't make any difference.

He was shocked by the final sentence, so he looked at the segment again: *It's there in Central Park for good, and it doesn't make any difference.* He knew she hadn't used these words when he filmed her statement, and he knew these words weren't on the footage he'd looked at the night before. Had the mere mention of the wall made the footage unstable? Had all his other material been corrupted? Would a Princip segment suddenly appear in place of something else he'd filmed? The thought of reviewing his footage made him tense. What if all the statements he'd collected now had the same ending, with people saying that the wall didn't make any difference? Of course he could simply cut it, but what if it kept coming back? It would make him look ridiculous, and besides, it wasn't true. The wall had made a huge difference. His life had changed—the world had changed—in major ways. And before too long, because of the wall, he would probably get laid.

THE ROYAL SCAM

It begins with seven grim young men walking in slow motion toward the camera, ominous hard rock guitar music churning in the background. A snarling voice-over declares, "This is the Black Hand Gang. Gavrilo Princip is their leader, a trained assassin." The actor playing Princip is frowning fiercely, a face that could win against death in a staring contest. The camera shifts to another scowling member of the gang, and the growling voice returns: "Nedjo Cabrinovic is a suicide bomber." The guitar keeps getting louder, driven by furious drums and crashing cymbals.

Jeff is quickly annoyed by the theatrical presentation. He's ready to shut off his DVD player and do something else, even though he's been looking forward to seeing this documentary for several weeks, ever since he re-read *All Quiet on the Western Front*, which led him to further reading about the causes of World War I. He first encountered the book in high school, when a history teacher made him read it as a punishment for misbehaving in class. Back then he hated reading, but the book made a strong impression on him, leaving him with an ongoing sense of horror about the so-called Great War, all the slaughter and destruction, resolved in such misguided ways that an even greater war broke out only twenty years later. But he still didn't understand what made it all happen, even after examining the standard explanations. So he thought it might help to watch a BBC documentary on the assassination of Archduke Ferdinand, which is always cited as the event that triggered the First World War.

The film has gotten rave reviews. But Jeff has done enough reading to know that crucial distortions have already been presented, just in the first ninety seconds. There was no organized gang for Gavrilo Princip to lead. The Black Hand, a secret Serbian terrorist organization, was only indirectly involved in the assassination, and at the last minute may have tried to prevent it. Princip was not a trained assassin. He was a high school student with nothing more than a few informal lessons in shooting a gun. His close friend, Nedjo Cabrinovic, didn't think of himself as a suicide bomber. He'd probably never even heard the term, which wasn't in common use at the time. Before he got involved in the assassination plot, he'd never touched or even seen a bomb. His inexperience became obvious when he tried to kill the archduke. He threw his bomb so awkwardly that he missed his target at point blank range. The bomb went off in back of the heir apparent's open car, leaving him uninjured. Cabrinovic was no more of a trained assassin than Princip was. Yet the urgent narrating voice wants a menacing feeling, the tension and suspense of a prime-time cop show. Jeff has already seen enough to decide that what he's watching is not a documentary but a schlockumentary, a reduction of history to kitsch entertainment.

He ejects the DVD and thinks about throwing it out the window. He's always wanted to throw something out a window in disgust. He thinks it would make him look forceful, like someone willing to take a decisive action, someone ruled by passion and conviction. But he lives on the tenth floor, on a busy street in Brooklyn Heights, and he worries that the disk might land on someone's head, so he does the civilized thing and carefully puts it back in its case. Then he finishes off the bowl of buttered popcorn in his lap and goes to the kitchen to make more. He loves the sound of popcorn popping, and he listens to it with mouth-watering anticipation, gazing out the window at the nearly completed One World Trade Center, shining in the late morning light across the river. He tries not to imagine hi-jacked planes attacking it, but he knows that all over the world there have to be angry people who see the new building as an obvious target, a resurrected symbol of US global domination. He was on the Brooklyn Bridge on 9/11 when the towers collapsed. He remembers the terrible panic and confusion, the feeling that nothing would ever be safe again. Tall buildings partially block his view of the new tower, and he remembers a realtor telling him that to get a full view he'd have to pay twice as much. But even if money weren't an issue, he'd want the obstructions. He doesn't want a clear view if 9/11 happens again.

He wolfs down the new batch of popcorn, licks his greasy fingers one by one, then goes back to his bedroom and sits at his computer. But he doesn't want to think about the deadlines he ought to be meeting. His job has always been a source of confusion. Though he hates the way mass advertising has turned the world into a battlefield of images, he's done promotional work for more than thirty years, and he's good at what he does. Over the past ten years he's developed his own business. He can do almost all of his work from his own apartment, and he makes a decent living. Yet he spends lots of time feeling guilty, trying to convince himself that the online publicity campaigns he directs aren't really hard-core parts of the capitalist process. After all, he specializes in promoting activist groups concerned with animal rights and the environment. With clients he respects he keeps his fees as low as he can. Over the past few years he's been in demand, and he's got projects that he should be completing over the next few days. But the BBC schlockumentary has put him in a bad mood, so he calls his girlfriend, Betty, and arranges to visit her.

They've been sleeping with each other for the past six months, and they're still at the stage in their relationship Jeff likes best. They're not hating each other yet. Betty is twenty years younger than Jeff, so he tries to be realistic about their so-called future, knowing that she's attractive enough to be with almost any man she wants. Even though she sometimes complains that she's "past her prime" and "not what she used to be," she takes good care of herself, dresses well, and knows how to project a sense of physical confidence, something Jeff has never learned to do.

When Jeff arrives, Betty's playing with her computer. He's not surprised, since Betty directs one of Apple's tech support teams and knows things about computers that very few people know. Right now she's making a picture of a Steely Dan album take different shapes: a triangle, an octagon, a circle, two overlapping circles, a circle within a circle. Then she makes it three-dimensional. The illusion of depth looks like it's become real depth.

He says: Is that *The Royal Scam* on your computer? It's always been my favorite Steely Dan album. But it looks like it's become a physical space, like I could walk right into it and live there, if I were small enough.

She smiles and takes his hand and says: You can, and size won't be an issue. Just sit down and try it. I was in there a few minutes ago.

She seats him in what looks like a brand-new computer chair. He gives her a hesitant look, but she returns it with a "trust me" smile and he decides to do what she wants.

He says: Is this like a virtual reality set-up?

She says: Beyond that. You'll see.

She types a complicated sequence of commands and the screen turns bright orange. A pulsing dot in the center quickly grows to become a sky blue sun, smiling with sharp teeth. The chair feels alive, like it's giving him a subtle massage. He can see a small version of himself, sitting in the chair, gazing back at him from the dark depth of the sun's opening mouth. There's a soft pop and the smell of something burning, a brief blurring of his vision, and then he's in the world of the Steely Dan album cover, where the tops of skyscrapers have become the snarling heads of various beasts, menacing a homeless man sleeping on a park bench. The street feels firm beneath Jeff's feet, and he can move and breathe normally. He walks for maybe ten minutes, down at least ten streets, but no matter how many corners he turns he always ends up facing the same park bench where the home-less man is sleeping. He can't avoid the sharp smell of the man's battered shoes and torn gray coat. What's happening is not a mental fantasy. Jeff is physically there. The tops of the buildings are snarling loudly. Huge fangs flash in three-dimensional sun-light. Snapping jaws are frothing. Bestial heads twist and dart and weave and dart again, cutting the air into bite size pieces. In the sky above their heads Jeff sees a phrase, *The Royal Scam*, floating as if a plane wrote it there as an advertising gimmick. The words remind him that he's in a Steely Dan album cover, and then he's moving backwards through an orange transparent membrane. He's back in Betty's computer chair. The massage is over.

She takes his hand and says: So, how was it?

For a few seconds, Jeff isn't sure where he is or who she is. He wants to say *cool* or *wow*, but he's always thought such words were idiotic, even when they're used by intelligent people. He finally says: I'm not sure what to say. The more I walked around, the more the space seemed real. I could move straight ahead, side to side or backwards. I could hear my shoes on the pavement. I could see my reflection in the shopfronts. There was air I could breathe and the sun felt warm on my skin. There were shadows and breezes. There were dead leaves getting blown down the streets. There were shouts and honking horns and conversations. All the basic things were in place. But I couldn't quite accept what was happening.

She smiles: That's what it was like for me too. It seemed totally real, like any other place I've been. But I couldn't get myself to accept that I was there, even though I designed the thing and knew what to expect, at least theoretically. I think it might take some getting used to.

Jeff says: How did you pull me out of there?

She nods at the keyboard: By pressing command keys.

He shakes his head: But you were in there earlier. How did *you* get out? Who pressed the command keys?

She says: I did. I took the keyboard with me.

He laughs: Very clever. But what would have happened if you'd forgotten it.

She shrugs: I guess I would have been stuck in that *Royal Scam* space forever.

He says: What would you have eaten?

She looks surprised: You didn't notice there were restaurants open on some of the streets? I had eggs Benedict in an outdoor café.

He says: Real food?

She nods: It was delicious. It had some kind of incredible seasoning on it, something I've never tasted before. But the snarling heads were getting on my nerves—it must have bothered you too, all that growling and snapping and frothing—so I picked up my plate and my coffee cup and finished the meal inside.

He says: Inside?

She says: Sure. You should have gone inside. The buildings had interiors. Even though you can't see interiors on the album cover, they're implied. When you look at the album, the skyscrapers seem real enough to lead your imagination to assume the existence of inner spaces, even though you can't see them and probably don't actually picture them strongly enough to make a visual impression, but—

He says: Was there a waiter? Who was he?

She shrugs: There was, but I don't know who he was. Just a guy who worked there. Probably an out-of-work soap opera actor. Cute guy!

Jeff laughs nervously: You were attracted to him?

Betty shrugs again: Physically, yes. And he was definitely flirting with me. I left him a really nice tip. But he wasn't my type. He was dumb as hell, and you know I can't stand stupid men.

Jeff makes a face and says: I'm glad I'm smart enough for you!

She smiles and says: Just barely.

He says: But since you're such a genius, I'm wondering if you've had any brilliant thoughts about what you're going to do with this innovation you've come up with. Aren't there corporations that would give you lots of money for it?

Betty: No doubt. I'm sure I could get a nice deal with Apple. But I don't even want to think about the horrible things that would happen if Apple had control of this program. And I'm pretty sure they already know about it.

Jeff says: How would they know?

Betty says: If you own an Apple computer, they know what you've got, no matter what they say about respecting your privacy.

I could design a special firewall, but then I'd start catching shit from the NSA. They don't appreciate the kinds of barriers I'd probably come up with.

Jeff says: The National Security Agency? They're watching your computer? You're not just being paranoid?

She says: I wish I were. But I've set up my computer so I can tell when I'm being watched, and they've been on my tail for at least a year, along with the CIA and the usual market research groups. Something like *The Royal Scam* is bound to make them all watch me even more closely. By the way, that's what I'm calling it: *The Royal Scam*.

Jeff says: Even though there might be copyright issues? Wouldn't something like Brave New Worlds work better? If you used that name, you probably couldn't get sued, since Aldous Huxley borrowed the phrase from Shakespeare.

Betty says: But the worlds *The Royal Scam* can generate aren't really new. They're derived from existing images. I can see your point about legal issues, but I want a more contemporary point of reference, in case I decide to market the thing on my own, and—

Jeff says: Steely Dan isn't really contemporary. Or at least, *The Royal Scam* isn't. It came out in 1976, and even though they put out two new albums in the early twenty-first century, most people think of them as a seventies group, so I don't think—

Betty makes a face and says: Whatever. Look, I don't feel like arguing. We've never had an argument before, and there's no reason to start now. I can easily think of better ways to spend our time.

He laughs: I can too.

They tear off each other's clothes so quickly that they don't have time to get to Betty's bedroom. It's not the first time they've done it on her living room floor. They've always been hot for each other. But it's more complex than it looks. Jeff suspects that she's imagining someone else the whole time, and he doesn't mind because he's fantasizing too, though the other woman is often Betty, or rather a modified version of Betty, doing sexy things in his mind, though not exactly the same sexy things that the flesh-and-blood Betty is doing. Jeff grew up in the sixties, back when people were supposed to be doing it in the road and deeply in touch with their bodies, which led him to think that erotic pleasure was meant to be mainly physical, not mental. So he often feels wrong about his tendency to fantasize while fucking, using physical contact as a take-off point for a theater of images. He's pleased that his sex with Betty would pass for good sex in a movie. But he can't help telling himself that it's also good sex in quotation marks, and he figures that Betty probably feels the same way, even if she always looks like she's fully caught up in the passion.

When they finish, they fall half-asleep in each other's arms, relaxing deeply, one of Jeff's favorite things about their sex life, the post-orgasmic tranquility, his equivalent of a mystical trance. He never felt so calm with previous lovers. With most of them, he wanted to get up and leave as quickly as possible. But now on Betty's hardwood floor there's nowhere else he'd rather be, even without the comfort of a mattress.

It's clouding up outside, but then there's a burst of sunlight through the dusty venetian blinds, making bars of light and shade on a landscape painting framed above her computer, a pastoral scene with a barn, cows in a fenced pasture, a dirt road curving past a windmill into a forest. He's looked at it many times before without thinking much about it, except to assume that since it looks like a Dutch landscape, it's got to be a copy and not an original. After all, the real thing would be worth much more than

Betty could afford, and would no doubt be in a famous museum, giving people observing it the privileged feeling of being in the presence of a certified masterpiece. But now he sees that it's not a normal reproduction. There's a flying saucer above the windmill, caught in the dusty light coming in through the window. He quickly decides that the painting is a joke, like Duchamp's Mona Lisa with a mustache, something that would fit Betty's personality better than a real Dutch landscape would. But he's surprised that he never noticed the flying saucer before.

He wants to ask her about it, but she's fallen asleep and his gentle attempts to wake her up have no effect. He gets up and takes a closer look at the painting. He thinks he can hear the flying saucer humming. It might even be spinning, preparing to fly out the window, spreading terror throughout the city. Maybe it would be too small to scare anyone, but then people might think it was a drone attack of some kind, releasing tiny weapons of mass destruction, terrorism tailor-made for the second decade of the twenty-first century.

He tries again to shake Betty awake, this time not so gently. She tells him in a groggy voice to leave her the fuck alone, and she's been nasty in the past when he's forced her to wake up. So he leaves her a nice note signed with smiling faces, drives home and eats more popcorn, then feels bloated. He hates feeling bloated. It makes him want to swear off popcorn forever, but he's sworn it off many times in the past and he knows it won't help to do it again. He looks outside at the cool sky filled with clouds, his favorite weather, and decides that it's a good time for a walk. He lives in a great neighborhood for walks, tree-lined streets and nineteenth-century brownstones. He knows each block by heart, the carved stone doorways and bay windows. But as soon as he steps outside, his body starts tingling, like he's in Betty's vibrating chair, *The Royal Scam* version of Brooklyn Heights, a space that only seems to exist, something someone else can change or destroy by pushing buttons. He feels unsafe, like he did on the Brooklyn Bridge when the towers collapsed. He can still feel panic spreading all over his body. After fifteen minutes, he ends his walk, goes home and wants more popcorn, but the bloated feeling hasn't quite gone away. He starts to scan the titles on his floor-to-ceiling bookshelves. But he already knows that he doesn't want to turn pages filled with language.

He's not sure what to do, so he tries the Princip DVD again. He's not surprised that it continues to annoy him, this time by claiming that a Black Hand official nicknamed Apis was responsible for planning the assassination, without mentioning that Apis was legally exonerated a few decades later, once classified Serbian documents were made public. The voice-over says that Apis recruited Princip and trained him as an assassin, though all the accounts Jeff has read clearly indicate that Princip had no direct contact with Apis. Princip got in touch with Black Hand agents not because they were trying to recruit him, but because he needed weapons to carry out plans he and Cabrinovic had developed on their own. The documentary shows Apis wearing a fez in a darkened room in Belgrade, waiting for information from Sarajevo, while the hard rock soundtrack starts up again, quiet at first, getting louder and louder, reaching the point where it sounds like someone has set a guitar on fire. Jeff knows that this music is meant to trigger an emotional reaction and get viewers to suspend their critical intelligence. He's been around the advertising world for too many years to miss the crude manipulation techniques. He quickly concludes that the image of a shadowy mastermind secretly directing grim and fanatical hit men is an attempt by the director (who made the film in 2003) to suggest similarities between Apis and Osama bin Laden, as if to say that all terrorist actions are equally sinister and delusional, though anyone thinking carefully would see obvious differences between the Black Hand and Al-Qaeda, and even more obvious differences between Gavrilo Princip's pistol and the hijacked planes of 9/11, not to mention the radically different historical situations.

On trial Princip testified that Apis and the Black Hand weren't directly involved with the assassination, had nothing to do with planning it, that he and the rest of his "gang" were acting on their own. The other assassins agreed with this, and two of them explained that they'd gotten involved in the plot only two days before the shooting, had no contact with the Black Hand, and weren't even sure what the Black Hand was. None of this is mentioned in the BBC film. Jeff assumes that a few informed viewers will be disturbed by the crucial omissions and distortions. But most viewers won't notice anything. For millions of people, the schlock version will become the definitive version. He wonders how much of what people call historical knowledge is really kitsch entertainment.

Again, he pops the disk out of the DVD player and tries to get beyond the stick figure version of Princip he's been watching. He imagines the assassin waking up in a borrowed little room on the morning of June 28, trying to fully grasp what he's about to do. He sees Princip clearly, looking tired and hungry, oppressed by the summer sunlight forcing its way through dusty venetian blinds. Princip stares at the political pamphlets and books on the floor beside his bed. He's read them all carefully, some of them several times, and they've had a crucial impact on his thinking. Without them, he wouldn't be where he is now. He takes his gun from the Gladstone bag beneath his bed and imagines pulling the trigger.

Three days before, he'd been at the city market when the archduke made a surprise visit, shopping with his wife Sophie and members of their royal entourage. The two men looked at each other, looked away, then looked back and stared at each other. Though the crown prince couldn't have known who he was looking at, Princip could sense that the great man was uneasy with the moment, as if he knew that murder was in the air. Jeff puts the moment on mental freeze frame, making the contrast as stark as possible: a man without a single room to call his own facing a man with a mansion in Vienna and two famous country palaces. Princip wants to pull out his gun and accomplish his mission, but the archduke is surrounded by people in uniform, and Princip knows that if he gets caught now the whole plot might be exposed. Then he remembers that his gun is back in his room beneath his bed, since he had no way of knowing that he'd be meeting the archduke today. The great man's visit to the market square wasn't on the posted schedule. So Princip has to content himself with the pleasure of winning a staring contest, using his eyes to induce a cold sweat and make a famous person squirm. It's a look Princip has mastered over the years. He's been told more than once that he's got a talent for making others uneasy.

He still can't believe that the archduke came to Sarajevo despite the clear warnings he received back in Vienna. Surely he suspects that people are tracking him with weapons, that he's being hunted. Princip has heard stories about the heir apparent's hunting techniques. He likes to shoot animals but doesn't do the hunting himself. Rather, his servants function as beaters to drive the animals toward his waiting gun, or they pen the animals in enclosures where Franz Ferdinand can shoot them one by one. Jeff likes the idea that when Princip shoots the crown prince he'll be avenging helpless animals. He wonders what Princip's reaction

169

would be if he saw a now-widely-circulated photograph of the archduke, posing in his uniform with all his decorations, holding a rifle with heaps of dead deer at his feet. The great man has a victorious look on his face, as if he's accomplished something of monumental significance. The image makes Jeff so mad that he wants to use *The Royal Scam* to enter the picture, confront the crown prince and beat the shit out of him.

But Jeff isn't the type of guy who beats the shit out of people, even in moments of extreme rage. He isn't even the type who uses brutally clever language to shoot down people who piss him off. He quickly feels silly about the idea of going back in time to confront Prince Ferdinand, since he probably wouldn't know what to say, and the heir apparent would quickly dismiss him with the regal disdain he was known for. Still, the time-travel idea makes him wonder if *The Royal Scam* could be used to arrange a direct meeting with Princip. He imagines what Princip would think if someone from the twenty-first century suddenly stopped him on the street and offered to buy him a sandwich. Jeff is realistic enough to suspect that they wouldn't have much to talk about. After all, he's forty years older than Princip was at the time, and he can't imagine himself as a martyr, sacrificing himself to a cause or belief the way Princip did. But there's a younger version of Jeff that sometimes governs what he does and thinks, and it's this part of him that's eager to meet history's most infamous teenager. All Jeff needs is a good picture of the assassin. Then he can ask Betty to scan it into her computer and run *The Royal Scam*.

When he calls Betty's cell, he gets her voicemail, so he decides to show up unannounced, which turns out to be a mistake. He arrives to the sounds of intense sex on the other side of her door. He feels betrayed, then wonders if he's been going out with her long enough to justify the feeling. They haven't established the rules of their relationship—in fact, they've both been clear that they don't want rules—but Jeff still feels funny about Betty fucking someone else only a few hours after having good sex or least "good sex" with him. He decides to break down the door, something he's never done before, and though he's seen it many times in movies, it's more difficult than it looks on screen. He smashes into Betty's old wooden door several times before giving up. Then it occurs to him that the door might not be locked, and sure enough, when he turns the knob the door opens with no resistance, and he walks in feeling sheepish in addition to feeling betrayed, only to find the apartment empty and a porno film playing on Betty's computer.

At first he's glad that she isn't cheating on him. But when he looks closely at the screen he sees that Betty is there in the film, in bed with another woman, both of them ecstatic in a beau tifully furnished room with an unobstructed view of the One World tower. He doesn't know how to enter the film through the screen without Betty at the keyboard, and he's even less clear about whether it still makes sense to accuse her of cheating on him, since technically she's in bed with an image and not a real person. In fact, as he looks more closely, he decides that the other woman looks very much like Betty, only ten years younger. Is it possible that Betty is in bed with a younger version of herself? Could she really be so stuck on herself, so stuck in her past? Or is he just misreading what's happening on the screen?

There's no keyboard in front of her computer. He looks closely at the screen, and he sees that she's taken the keyboard with her into the room of passion. It's on the glass coffee table across the room from the four-poster bed. He concludes that Betty's lover is definitely Betty at an earlier stage of her life, wearing a spiked leather collar and nothing else. It's all too much for him, so he decides to go home and try to hook up with her later.

Back in his apartment, he's again not sure what to do with himself. He tries to return to the promotional projects he avoided earlier, but when he sits down at his computer and starts typing, the screen goes blank. He types in several commands but nothing happens. He tries the restart button but nothing happens. Then a hairy hand slides up into the screen and gives him the finger. It stays there motionless, even after he shuts off the computer. He was hoping to avoid calling Betty until he calmed down, but now he's dialing her number, since she's the one he relies on to solve his computer problems. In fact, they initially met when she fixed his computer for him at the public library.

Betty answers the phone this time and tells him to come right over with his laptop, but Jeff decides to bring more than that. He finds a photo of Princip in a book he's been reading, a shot taken in Belgrade in the spring of 1914, a few months before the shooting. Jeff cuts out the picture and puts it unfolded into a large manilla envelope. He's careful to protect the photo with pieces of cardboard. He doesn't want it to be damaged in any way, since he's nervous about being transported into a torn, creased, or wrinkled world.

But on his way back to Betty's apartment, the world already feels creased and wrinkled, especially since the windows of his 1995 Honda Civic haven't been cleaned in a long time. Then one of the streets he normally takes to Betty's neighborhood looks too congested. It's been taken over by a film production team, with cameras and cables and trucks and huge glaring lights and reflecting screens, so he turns off onto a side street, figuring he can easily recalculate his route. But after making several turns he

172

feels lost. He stops and goes back a few blocks, thinks that he sees a street he should have taken, turns and drives a few blocks, then decides again that he's on the wrong street. He does a three-point turn. Soon he comes back to the street where the movie people are working. It's even more filled with cameras and lights and production trucks than it was before. He goes back down the same side street he took a few minutes ago. But the sun has broken through the clouds, and it's making the buildings look different, much older than they looked before, like they're on a page that's been torn and taped back together, and again it feels like he's on the wrong street.

He's not the kind of person who gets lost. He's always laughed at people who need the GPS on their phones to tell them where to go. He tells himself that there must have been a *Twilight Zone* episode in which someone kept getting lost on familiar streets and never found his way back. Then he remembers *Days That Shook the World*, the schlockumentary, which mentioned only in passing what other sources describe as a crucial mistake, the most fateful wrong turn in Western history. Right after Nedjo Cabrinovic, the so-called suicide bomber, failed to kill the archduke, the Austrian generals decided that the situation was too dangerous, that the royal motorcade should change its scheduled course, taking streets that would get them out of Sarajevo as quickly as possible, while preserving the appearance of calmly making a royal tour. But apparently no one told the archduke's driver, who followed the original route, turning down a street named after the archduke's uncle, Habsburg Emperor Franz Joseph. The mistake was quickly noticed and the driver was told to put the car in reverse, but the gears jammed when he tried to back up. The car stalled right in front of a café where Gavrilo Princip was waiting, eating a sandwich, hoping that the heir apparent would pretend to be unfazed by Cabrinovic's bomb and follow the original plan, published in the papers a few days before. The crown prince was suddenly an easy target.

Jeff remembers laughing in disbelief when he first encountered the story. How could World War I, a major turning point in Western history, have been the result of a wrong turn, a simple mistake? How could supposedly trained and competent people, high ranking military men accustomed to giving orders, forget to tell their driver where to go? Jeff is briefly annoyed that such a crucial part of the assassination narrative was only mentioned briefly in the BBC presentation, probably because a more careful examination would have disrupted the show's dramatic momentum, making history seem more like a slapstick comedy than a coherent narrative. Jeff thinks of a class he took at UC Berkeley, a seminar that might have been called "The History of Mistakes," or "The Mistakes of History" or "The Accidents of History." He can't recall exactly. But now he remembers a class session focused on the wrong turn in Sarajevo. He can almost hear the professor talking, a grim smile on his bearded face, a class of long-haired students laughing in stoned horror. He wants to go back in time and sit through the class all over again, recapture it like an hour-long YouTube video, putting selected moments on mental freeze-frame. But he needs to focus now on his own mistake. He hates the feeling of being lost, doesn't like being stuck in the twilight zone, so he pulls out his smart phone and Googles for directions, only to find that he isn't lost, that he's right where he's supposed to be, a few blocks from a familiar destination. He's relieved when the rest of his drive is unproblematic.

But confusion returns when he gets to Betty's apartment, and she greets him smiling at the door he tried to break down a few hours before. Is it the real Betty, or the younger version of her?

She looks great, somehow even more attractive than before, and for a second he assumes that the younger Betty has exchanged places with the older one, that she's not past her prime anymore, that she's become what she used to be. But there's no time to figure out what's going on because she pulls him into bed so quickly that he doesn't even get a chance to make basic small talk. The younger Betty—if that's who she is—doesn't seem as capable as the older Betty in bed, like she hasn't had as much experience and hasn't yet mastered the moves. But it feels like she's in better shape, has more energy, and she comes twice and wants to keep going. With a burst of strength she throws him onto his back and reaches down to pull him inside her again, but he's worn out, too tired to continue, begging her to let him relax for a while.

It's only when they're resting under the sheets that he gets worried that he and the younger Betty don't actually know each other, and that she might not know anything about *The Royal Scam*. But when they start talking it's clear that she knows everything, and he wonders if the younger and older versions of Betty, since they're not really separate people, are both in bed with him now, in the same body, even though they looked like two distinct women earlier, making love on screen. Is it possible that by going to bed with her younger self, Betty is making her body younger while preserving her mind in its current state? If so, then *The Royal Scam* will make her lots of money if she ever puts it on the market, offering anyone who can afford it a chance to recapture their youth. Jeff can already picture himself as her marketing director. He's dying to ask her about her cybersex adventure, but decides not to mention it yet, since his real reason for being there is Gavrilo Princip.

He shows her the picture of Princip. He's wearing a dark suit and fedora, sitting on a park bench in Belgrade. On the other end of the bench is his good friend Nedjo Cabrinovic, wearing exactly the same outfit. Between them is Milan Ciganovic, a veteran of the Balkan Wars, wearing a three-piece suit but no fedora. Ciganovic is the Black Hand agent who gave Princip and Cabrinovic the weapons they used a few months later in Sarajevo. It's not clear in the faded photograph whether he's already given them the guns and bombs, or if he's just planning to. The expression on his face reveals nothing, except that he's facing a camera that's going to shoot him.

Jeff quickly explains the picture's significance, telling Betty what he knows about the Black Hand. He also mentions Young Bosnia, a subversive network of students who met in cafés in Belgrade and Sarajevo. He expects her to ask for more historical information, but instead she laughs and asks: Did all the Young Bosnians wear dark suits and hats? Were they trying to look like Hollywood gangsters?

Jeff says: It was 1914, and I don't think there were Hollywood gangster movies yet, especially not in places like Belgrade and Sarajevo, where there probably weren't many cinemas. But I guess the Young Bosnians thought the look was cool, like hippies with flowers in their hair or punks with mohawks. You can't—

Betty says: Actually, they do look kind of cool. I like Princip and Cabrinovic more than the older guy.

Jeff says: Even though the older guy's nickname was Handsome Cigo?

Betty says: I'd go to bed with Princip any day.

Jeff says: Then you'd be taking his virginity.

She says: He died a virgin?

Jeff says: Supposedly. Of course, no one knows for sure. I read somewhere that he was with a woman a few nights before the assassination, but had performance anxiety problems.

Another article connected Princip's desire to shoot the archduke with his lack of sexual satisfaction.

She makes a face and says: Sometimes a gun is just a gun, as Freud might have said. But, whatever. I think the suits look cool.

Jeff says: You can't really tell from the picture, but they were all desperately poor. Their suits were old and smelly. They couldn't afford to clean them. Handsome Cigo had been thrown out of a café a few weeks before because his suit was infested with lice. He was—

Betty says: Why are you showing me this picture?

Jeff says: What would happen if you scanned it into your computer and then let me enter it through *The Royal Scam* program?

Betty says: You'd be in the world of the picture.

Jeff says: In the spring of 1914?

She nods but then stops and laughs tensely: Actually, I'm not sure.

Jeff says: When I entered the picture, would Princip and his friends be in black and white, like they are in the picture?

Betty shrugs: I don't know. I don't fully understand how the program works—

Jeff makes a face: Even though you created it?

Betty nods: Even though I created it. I'm pretty sure the program does more than I intended.

Jeff looks doubtful, so Betty says: It's called wet programing. You make a design that includes potential operations, which lead to more potential operations, pathways that branch out from each other, enhancing and modifying each other, sometimes in ways that are impossible to predict. It's the same with any signifying system. You can only control language by obeying it, respecting its autonomy. So it's possible that you'd just be in a black and white world with those with three guys and whoever else

177

happened to be in the park at the time. It would be the spring of 1914, but it also wouldn't be. It would be a kind of stopped moment stolen from 1914 and framed on a flat piece of paper. I'm not sure what to call it: Picture time? It's complicated. With the Steely Dan image, you weren't entering a place that existed outside the album cover. But this Princip picture was taken in a place that existed before and after the picture was taken. That Belgrade park was a place with an independent existence, and maybe it still is. But like I said, this is all pretty new to me. I don't really know. Maybe you'd actually be back in 1914.

Jeff is dying to ask about her cybersex episode, and what kind of past world she entered when she went to bed with the woman she used to be, but again he doesn't want to create conflicts that shift the focus away from the Princip photo. He says: So if I was really back in 1914, and I was able to talk them out of their assassination plans, and World War I never happened, then what?

She says: You're familiar with the time-travel novels and movies. If you talked them out of the assassination and World War I didn't happen, then the rest of the century would probably happen differently than it did, and computers might not be invented, and we wouldn't have *The Royal Scam* to send you back in time to talk Princip out of his deadly plans, and he'd go ahead and kill the archduke, and the twentieth century would happen the way we know it did, and we'd have computers and *The Royal Scam*, and I'd send you back to talk Princip out of his deadly plans again. You'd be creating a loop in which two different versions of the twentieth century happened and didn't happen. But that's only if your appearance in the photograph was an authentic time-travel episode.

Jeff says: There's no way to know for sure?

She says: The only way to find out is to give it a try.

Jeff expects her to start cackling like a witch. But instead she looks at him like she's trying to convince him that she's really who she is and not who she was ten years ago. Or at least that's what Jeff is reading into her expression. He knows her well enough to know that she's always thinking of several things at once while trying to look like she's focused only on the person she's with. He gives her a look designed to let her know that he knows that she's trying to convince him of something but he's not being fooled and he's just going along with it to be a nice guy or because it's more convenient. He suspects that she can read the look, but she's being careful to not look like she's reading it.

He takes her hand and says: Okay, let's give it a try.

She smiles: But first, you better get dressed. If you really end up in a park in 1914 Belgrade, I don't think you want to be walking around wearing nothing. You're sure you really want to try this?

He starts getting dressed and says: No, but I don't want to keep thinking about it. I spend way too much time thinking about things instead of doing them. The time to hesitate is through.

She hesitates, then says: What song is that from?

He says: I don't remember. It's not Steely Dan. The Doors maybe.

She says: I hate The Doors. They're so overrated.

He says: You're too young to remember the feeling of first hearing their music back in the summer of 67. But there's a younger version of me that's still back there and still hasn't grown tired of hearing The Doors, especially the long version of "Light My Fire" and not the edited version that became a big hit.

She says: The only version I've heard is the shorter one. You're lucky you actually lived through the mythical Summer of Love and haven't just heard about it, like people from my generation. I mean, we grew up watching silly black and white footage of people with long hair and beads, stick figure hippies. It's obviously different for an ex-hippie like you. You were really there, back when doing drugs was cool and revolution didn't sound like a bad joke or an advertising buzz word, and people talked about being in touch with their bodies and doing it in the road and thought it was cool to look like very stoned caucasian versions of Jesus. But it's weird the way you talk about the younger version of you as if it were a separate person that still exists and not just a collection of memories.

He says: You should know.

She says: What?

He says: Never mind. Let's run *The Royal Scam.*

She picks up the picture and does the royal scan. The photo appears on her screen. When Jeff, at first, doesn't sit in the computer chair, she guides him down into it and says: You have to sit in the chair. *The Royal Scam* won't work unless you're in the chair. Remember?

Jeff stands up and looks puzzled.

She says: No really, sit back down. It's a special chair. It's upholstered with smart foam, which is a crucial part of the application.

Jeff sits and says: Smart foam? Like they use in orthopedic beds and football helmets?

She says: Smarter. Much smarter. I'll have to come up with a different name.

She types the commands. The screen turns orange with a smiling blue sun that opens its mouth to reveal a small version of Jeff inside. There's a pop like a flashbulb going off, a burnt popcorn smell, and suddenly he's in a park, standing beside a tripod camera pointed at three men sitting on a bench, looking exactly the way they did in the picture. Jeff glances quickly around the park, which is filled with trees and grass and light and shade and people walking and talking. The three men look at him expectantly. Jeff understands that they're waiting for him to take their picture, so he puts his head under the camera's black hood and looks through the aperture. Again, they look exactly like they did in the picture, except that they're in color, not black and white, and the photographic silence has been replaced by sounds coming from other parts of the park, voices and footsteps approaching and receding, the brief rustling of trees as the wind comes up and dies down. He's never used a wooden tripod camera, but it's clear what he has to do. He pulls a cord, the camera flashes, then something is pulling him through an orange transparent membrane, and he's back in Betty's room, staring at the picture on her screen.

She looks at him with obvious relief, then smiles: So?

He says: How long was I gone?

She says: Maybe ten minutes. What happened?

He says: I took their picture.

She says: That's all?

He says: That's all.

She says: You didn't try to talk to them?

He says: I thought about it, then realized that they probably didn't speak English.

She says: I was wondering how that was going to work out, since I know you don't speak Serbian.

He says: Not a word. But the park and the people were there in full color, doing all the normal things.

She says: What did you look like? Were you wearing what you're wearing now?

He says: I don't know. I was so stunned I didn't notice. But the men in the picture didn't act like I was wearing strange clothing, so I guess I looked like a 1914 Serbian photographer. But I wasn't

181

sure why they'd arranged to have their picture taken. Why would people conducting a secret transaction want to be photographed?

She says: Maybe the Black Hand wanted photographic records of all their secret transactions?

Jeff says: Yeah, maybe. I don't know that much about how the Black Hand did things. No one does, because they were a secret organization, and all their members were sworn to secrecy. But I did read somewhere that all the Sarajevo assassins were under oath to kill themselves afterwards because if they lived and got captured they could be tortured into revealing Black Hand secrets. So it's possible that right before I took the picture Handsome Cigo had just told Princip and Cabrinovic that they would have to take poison after killing the archduke. In fact, it's even possible that they had cyanide packets in their pockets.

She looks confused and says: Wait a minute. I just realized something weird. The names you've been using: Cabrinovic, and Handsome Cigo, what was his real name again?

Jeff says: Milan Ciganovic. Why?

She says: You were gone ten minutes, which isn't really a long time, except that I was thinking about the picture time issues we talked about earlier, and I started to worry about the bad quality of the photo you brought over. I mean, with such a faded image, you might have entered a faded world that didn't have enough definition to fully exist, which might have meant that you yourself couldn't fully exist and I might not be able to bring you back. So I did a quick Internet search and found a better copy of the picture, thinking I could substitute it for the one we used.

Jeff says: Would that have worked?

She says: I'm not sure. But I thought it might be worth a try, in case you didn't come back. I mean, with the Steely Dan image I could see you on screen. This time I couldn't.

Jeff says: That's pretty scary. I mean—

Betty nods: But wait. When I looked at the new picture, I noticed that the caption gave the name Gavrilo Princip, but the other two men are identified as Trifko Grabez and Djuro Sarac. They're the same guys, but the names are different.

She points to the screen, where the new picture sits in a small window beside the faded version. Jeff reads the names and says: Some editor somewhere must have made a mistake.

Betty says: Who were Trifko Grabez and Djuro Sarac?

Jeff says: Other guys involved in the assassination plot. Grabez helped Princip smuggle guns from Belgrade across the border into Bosnia. He was convinced that the archduke's plan to inspect the Austrian troops in Sarajevo, which was one of his published reasons for making his visit, was just a pretext, the prelude to a military invasion of Serbia. That's why he was eager to join Princip and Cabrinovic when they told him about their plan. Sarac helped them get the guns from Ciganovic. Sarac was the founder of a secret society known as the Avengers of Kosovo, which conducted secret induction ceremonies in dark basements. Princip and Grabez were in the society, but not Cabrinovic or Ciganovic. They were in a different secret society that conducted ceremonies in basements. It gets confusing. I can see why their testimony was so garbled when they were put on trial after the assassination. Think about it: They insisted that the Black Hand had nothing to do with the assassination plot. Yet they also said that people from the Black Hand had given them weapons and helped them carry bombs and guns across the Serbian border. At one point in the trial Princip and Cabrinovic led the judge and the attorneys to believe that the Freemasons were involved, but later in the trial, when the judge referred to them as Masons, they laughed at the idea. Were they making deliberately misleading statements? Or were they just confused?

Betty shakes her head: There's no way of knowing. Maybe both.

Jeff says: If I'd actually gotten stuck in 1914, I'm sure I would have been confused too. I mean, the situation was bad if you were a Serb. The Habsburgs had annexed Bosnia-Herzegovina several years earlier. People in Sarajevo woke one morning to find announcements posted all over the city, declaring their country a province of the Austro-Hungarian Empire. That's when the student resistance movement began. Princip and Grabez got thrown out of school for organizing campus protest actions. Djuro Sarac got thrown in jail for comparing the annexation to property theft.

Betty says: Doesn't sound all that different from Bush and Cheney invading Iraq, a free enterprise bonanza, and now you've got journalists over there getting their heads chopped off.

Jeff nods: I was thinking more or less the same thing, though of course there are significant historical differences, so the parallels might not be obvious at first—

Betty says: They seem pretty obvious to me, and I haven't even done the kind of research that you've obviously been doing. I didn't know you were such a history buff.

Jeff says: I really wasn't, until I re-read *All Quiet on the Western Front*, and then read a few books about the nationalist insanity that led to World War I. Then this morning I saw this schlockumentary about the assassination, and—

Betty shrugs: I guess the important thing is that you're back. I was starting to think you'd gotten stuck in a virtual 1914 Belgrade.

Jeff says: It didn't seem virtual. It was just like being in a real urban park, and the three men—whoever they were—were three-dimensional flesh and blood human beings. If I'd been trapped in that world, it might not have been so bad. The park was beautiful, and the people I saw there looked a lot happier than the people you normally see in Central Park.

Betty looks disturbed: That's not saying much. But now I'm wondering about the photographer. There's no photo credit on the version I found on the Internet. It just says "Muzej Sarajeva," without naming the photographer. I'm wondering who really took the picture. Was it you? Did *The Royal Scam* project you into a picture that didn't exist until you went back in time and took it?

Jeff says: Before I got there, someone had already set up the camera and arranged the shot. For a second, right after I arrived, I thought the guys on the bench were laughing at me, like they thought I looked weird in my twenty-first century clothing. But they also clearly thought I was the photographer, so I must have looked like him. Or maybe they saw some kind of double exposure, right before *The Royal Scam* transported me into the photographer's body, and from then on I was literally seeing things through his eyes. That might explain why you couldn't see me on screen.

Betty nods: Right, and for that Belgrade photographer your presence in his body and mind was just a momentary strange feeling. Or maybe your intervention made him briefly aware of things he couldn't have known at the time, things that are normal parts of our lives a century later. Like what's happened to photography, for instance, all the digital images. When I was looking for a good copy of your picture, I found other shots of Princip, and so many people have had fun playing around with his image.

Jeff knows exactly what she's talking about. In the online research that he's been doing, he's found pictures of Princip everywhere, images modified for almost every conceivable purpose: Princip wearing glasses in a short-sleeve Superman shirt, Princip in a dashiki playing tenor sax in a jazz café, Princip looking like

185

Einstein facing a blackboard filled with equations, Princip in a cave man outfit clubbing a sabre-tooth tiger, Princip in a Che beret on a hammer and sickle poster, Princip giving the peace sign from a day-glo bus at Woodstock, Princip in a string quartet on the deck of the *Titanic*, Princip drinking with Bogart in a scene from *Casablanca*, Princip in a game of cards with Darwin, Freud and Marx, Princip in a hospital gown with electrodes attached to his head, Princip on the cross with a crown of thorns in a black light poster. Jeff is briefly amused by the idea of Princip doing an Internet search, finding himself so widely reproduced and reinvented.

Betty says: And now you've taken a picture someone else had already taken. It's funny, isn't it, how the word "taken" gets used in the photographic process. I can see why the Native Americans didn't like it. It's—

Jeff says: Can I ask you something?

Betty pauses and narrows her eyes: No.

Jeff says: I can't?

Betty says: No, you can't.

Jeff says: Really?

Betty says: Normally, when people say "Can I ask you something" they're preparing to say something disturbing and their question isn't really a question. It's a rhetorical device that means "What I'm about to say will probably upset you." And my answer is "No, I don't want you to upset me."

Jeff is now convinced that she knows he knows about her virtual infidelity. Why else would she be cropping his question out of the conversation? He says: Really? I'm not allowed to ask—

Betty says: Wait a second!

She's squinting at the photographs on the computer. She says: Check to see if you have your phone.

Jeff puts his hands in his pockets, quickly looks around the room, then shrugs and says: I don't have it.

She points to both copies of the picture, a small white shape in the grass near Princip's foot. She says: I think you left your phone in 1914. It must have fallen out by mistake.

She quickly enlarges part of the picture, making it clear that the white shape is an iPhone. Even the Apple logo is partially visible. She says: I wonder if it was in the picture before you took your little trip.

Jeff shrugs: I don't remember. When I looked at the picture before, I didn't notice anything unusual. But now it's in both copies of the picture on your screen. Why don't we find other copies of the picture on the Internet, and see if the phone is in all of them? And now I'm wondering what happened when Princip found the phone and tried to figure out what it was, assuming he noticed it. Do you think—

Betty says: We can do the Internet search later. Right now, we've got some unfinished business. We never really finished fucking.

She gets up from her desk, walks across the room, lies down on her bed. She looks at Jeff with laughter in her eyes. She says: You pooped out, remember? But now that you've refreshed yourself in 1914, let's get back to the task at hand.

Jeff wants to keep talking about his phone. He wants to think about Princip tinkering with it, tapping the screen, amazed by the sudden changes, looking at full-color digital pictures, listening to voicemail messages, trying to read text messages filled with emoticons and keyboard symbols, acronyms and weird abbreviations. But then Jeff looks at the landscape painting above the computer. There's no flying saucer, just a gap in the painted sky, revealing colors and parts of shapes that suggest the presence of another painting underneath, as if the pastoral scene were just a cover-up. For a second he's convinced that the secret painting is a photorealist picture of Betty's apartment, that he and Betty are there, painted versions of themselves in bed with each other. Again, Jeff wants to ask Betty where she got the painting, but she repeats her invitation, and she looks so good that he can't resist. He joins her in bed and the sex is great, not just great in quotation marks. They try new things that work amazingly well. His younger self is filling him with more energy than he normally has, like he's having all the good sex that Gavrilo Princip never had.

WRITING THINGS DOWN

Three days before the planned assassination, Gavrilo Princip is looking for a meal at the city market. He doesn't have any money. He never has any money. But he knows that at the market you can usually get free samples of food, and if you can get them from three or four vendors, you might feel like you've almost had a light lunch. This is the only reason he's here. He'd rather be reading quietly in his room. He strongly prefers good prose to the physical presence of other people. The market is swarming with festive faces, bursts of aggressive laughter, shouted words and phrases, prices on signs, obnoxious odors, bodies rushing past each other, bumping into each other, standing beside and behind and in front of each other.

Then it's all replaced by surprise, everyone pointing and whispering. Princip scans the crowd, quickly sees what's going on: Archduke Franz Ferdinand has arrived, an appearance that wasn't on the official schedule, posted throughout the city the week before, published on the front pages of yesterday's papers. Is it really the heir apparent? Princip looks again. There's no doubt about it. He's seen the great man's picture so many times that he'd know him anywhere: the cold unfocused eyes, the waxed impeccably upturned mustache. Beside him is his wife, Countess Sophie, the one his terribly noble Habsburg relatives won't acknowledge, insisting that she's socially beneath them, even though she's from an old aristocratic family. Princip is annoyed by her floral hat, and even more annoyed by her facial expression, the lively eyes that look like they want to like whatever they're looking at. He doesn't want to like whatever he's looking at. When he looks at Sarajevo, he sees a place that's been replaced, an awkward combination of foreign cultures, the clash of Turkish and Austrian buildings and customs, faces of people that don't even know how much they're just pretending, how much they don't like what they don't have the strength to oppose, the all-consuming presence of one of Europe's most powerful empires, though everyone suspects that its days are numbered.

The archduke and the countess are surrounded by people in uniform, but the crown prince drifts away from his protection, apparently drawn by the unfamiliar merchandise, or maybe it's just that he doesn't like having bodyguards. Soon he and Princip are standing side by side, facing a table heaped with Asian fabrics. The archduke is trying to smile, making small talk with the vendor. Princip doesn't try to smile or make small talk. He's a man with the big dreams of someone versed in radical writing, but he's physically small, and small talk makes him feel like he's getting smaller.

He's mad that he doesn't have his pistol with him. But he wasn't expecting to fire the fatal shots until Sunday morning. It's a moment he's pictured many times, the royal motorcade moving down an avenue lined with assassins, the archduke and the countess waving and smiling, thousands of people cheering and shouting slogans. He waits until the great man's car is only fifteen feet away. Then he pulls out a gun from his inner coat pocket and everything is different. The archduke is dead and people are shouting and screaming. He quickly drinks poison, shoots himself in the head.

But the moment is three days away. For now there's no gun, no poison to swallow. For now he wants nothing more than samples of food that he won't have to pay for. Then Princip recognizes someone else, a plump young man with short blond hair and a brown suit, a former high school classmate. For a second, Princip wants to wave and smile like a normal person. But he can't put a name on the face, though at one point they were going through the motions of friendship, back when both were unfamiliar with Sarajevo, having just arrived from distant villages. The man is yawning and stroking his chin, scanning the crowd, apparently not intent on buying anything, like he's at the market only because he doesn't want to be somewhere else. Then Princip almost remembers the name, Heinz or maybe Viktor, then clearly remembers why they parted ways. Heinz or maybe Viktor joined the police force, became a detective, while Princip began visiting cheap cafés in dubious neighborhoods, places filled with students eagerly talking about revolution, loudly proclaiming the need to shed the blood of foreign tyrants, to sacrifice themselves in a struggle to form a new Yugoslavian state, becoming the martyrs that future generations would be inspired by.

The detective keeps yawning and stroking his chin, scratching his head and looking up at the sky, playing with the awkward knot in his tie, never quite paying attention to the aggressive displays of merchandise. Princip assumes that he's on the job right now, watching for dangerous people. Heinz or maybe Viktor reaches into his inner coat pocket. Princip thinks that his ex-friend might be getting ready to pull out a gun. But instead he pulls out a small black notebook, turns the pages until he finds what he's looking for, pulls out a pencil and writes something down, pauses and looks at the sky like he's never seen it before, writes something down, looks at the opening door of a clothing store, frowns and writes something down, quickly puts the notebook away, shoots a concerned look in Princip's direction. They share a brief smile, a half-acknowledged moment of recognition, though Princip can detect a trace of suspicion, mixed with a trace of embarrassment in Heinz or maybe Viktor's face, tension cramping the corners of his mouth. Then he's yawning again.

Princip returns the yawn and turns away, gazing over the minarets on the western side of the market square. A huge flock of blackbirds passes in front of the sun, turns and passes in front of the sun again, turns and does it again, again and again, over and over again, as if they were trying to flash a coded message down from the afternoon sky. Princip thinks of blackbirds on a battlefield feasting on corpses: June 28, 1389 on the Field of Blackbirds, thousands of young men slaughtered at the Battle of Kosovo, fighting to free their homeland from Ottoman domination. He wonders what all those men would think if they saw their country today, so many people accepting the rule of another foreign power, pleased to think of themselves as provincial Austrians, seduced by the modernization projects coming down from Vienna, new miles of roads and railroad tracks, new plumbing and heating and lighting. He looks with disgust at all the people around him happily shopping, excited now that they're getting to share the space with a royal being.

He sees that the archduke is also watching the blackbirds, as if he, too, were thinking of dead soldiers. But Princip knows that the great man has never been in combat, never seen dead soldiers on a battlefield, that instead he's probably just enjoying the view, thinking of blackbirds circling the turrets and spires of his countryside palaces, or perched on the gabled housetop of his mansion in Vienna. Princip thinks of his own current home, a borrowed room on the outskirts of Sarajevo, and then of the place where he spent his first thirteen years, a one-room house with a dirt floor and no windows, a rented scrap of land where blackbirds weren't afraid of scarecrows. Then he thinks of a childhood song, blackbirds baked in a pie, a dainty dish to set before a king, or an heir apparent.

He knows he needs to be careful. He's almost always careful. But he can't resist what the moment seems to be offering, the chance to put the pompous man in his place. He shoves his way in front of him, knocking him back. He looks him in the eye and sneers an apology. The crown prince looks annoyed, then tries to pretend that nothing has happened. But Princip is right in front of him now, and the archduke can't avoid his aggressive eyes. Princip repeats the apology with even more disdain than before. He knows how to stare people down, how to make big people nervous. He's been doing it all his life. It's an ongoing part of who he thinks he is. He's dying to spit in the archduke's face, but he doesn't want to go too far, so he settles for a look of blunt contempt, a look that says that there's no such thing as an archduke, that the very concept of royalty has long been obsolete, that the archduke is nothing more than a bag of chemicals, an ape that somehow learned to speak a million years ago, a mammal that would have been walking on all fours ten million years ago, someone who has no business telling others what to do, someone who could learn a great deal if he actually had to work, perform well enough to find and keep a job, earn the respect of others by treating them with respect, even if respect will always remain an elusive concept, especially since respect will always remain an elusive concept.

Princip knows that openly saying these things would be a mistake. The archduke would write him off as a raving derelict.

195

Heinz or maybe Viktor would intervene with dangerous questions. But Princip likes the way the prince is trying not to back away, trying and failing not to look weak, like he's just about to pee in his pants. Princip would love to see the heir apparent pee in his pants, unable to control or conceal the mess he was making in public. Making the great man embarrass himself would almost be better than shooting him.

The archduke nervously pulls an old gold watch from his inner coat pocket. Princip shoots a startled glance at the sky. The archduke looks at the sky and Princip slides the gold watch out of his hand, quickly slipping it into his inner coat pocket, pulling out a pencil and slipping it into the archduke's hand. The substitution goes unnoticed at first. Heinz or maybe Viktor is turning the pages of his book. Countess Sophie is running her hands through dazzling Asian fabrics. But the crown prince suddenly sees that he's holding a pencil and not his watch. He looks baffled, looks at Princip, looks at the pencil, clears his throat, looks at the pencil again, looks like he wants an explanation.

Princip says: What you're holding is called a pencil. It's used when you need to write things down. The sharp end makes marks on a piece of paper. The pink thing on the other end is an eraser. It's used to change or eliminate things that you might have written down.

The archduke stares at the pencil, touches the sharp end, then the eraser, then slowly nods and slides the pencil into his inner coat pocket.

The blackbirds continue their motion, weaving a web around the sun, a web turning into a cage. The sun is in jail. Its crime? The passage of time, the way it's always making things later and later, even when it first comes up, even when it's behind the clouds. Princip hates the sun, just like he's always hated the circus, things that make people happy in ways that he's never been able to share. He finds the clowns especially depressing. He doesn't like it when people try to put a smile on his face. He doesn't like performances or performers.

But then he sees that the archduke is looking at someone, a man with an aggressive smile and a wooden box in his hands. His long black hair and sandals make Princip think of Jesus, though Princip isn't religious and normally doesn't think about Jesus. Looking more closely Princip sees that the box is really a camera.

The photographer clears his throat and says: Gentlemen, prepare yourselves to be happy.

Princip says: Happy?

The photographer says: Yes! Happy!

Princip says: Happy? What the fuck are you talking about?

The photographer's teeth look sharp, like he's thinking of putting Princip's head in his mouth. Heinz or maybe Viktor is watching carefully, writing things down. Princip assumes that whatever he says at this point will end up in the little black book.

The photographer says: The person who doesn't know what it means to be happy needs to find out, and there's no better time to find out than the present moment.

The archduke clears his throat and opens his mouth, but it's not his own voice that speaks: Your message is important to us. Please wait for the next available representative. We appreciate your patience. Press one to hear this message again. Press two to suck my royal dick. Press three to return to the main menu. Your message is important to us. Please wait. We appreciate—

The photographer says: Wait? Why wait? It's time to meet the future, the future belongs to the camera, the camera belongs in every home, and the camera wants you to smile. People today think the camera wants them to put on a serious face. But the future will be a time of smiles in billions and billions of cameras. Everyone will be terribly busy taking pictures of everyone else, terribly terribly busy taking pictures of themselves. So gentlemen, don't hesitate. Prepare yourselves to be happy!

Princip says: Happy? The word doesn't mean a goddamn thing if you haven't had a good meal.

Heinz or maybe Viktor looks confused. He stares at Princip, starts to write something down, stops and stares at the page, looks confused and shuts his book, opens and shuts it again, then moves it back toward his inner coat pocket. For a second he doesn't seem focused on what's in front of him. He looks like he needs to make sure that all of his physical organs are working, convinced that he's got to keep track, make them perform by thinking about them, that if he stops controlling every motion that they make, they won't continue to function, and he'll collapse in a shapeless heap, something that needs to be taken away by the sanitation department. He starts to yawn but stops and looks confused, as if he can't remember how to do it, as if he hasn't practiced enough to yawn without thinking about it.

The photographer says: People in photographs don't need food. They don't need to talk. They don't need to breathe.

There's a flash. The market becomes a black and white photograph, a small flat square. The blackbirds freeze into place like notes on a musical score, or words on a page. The sky looks like it might get folded up or torn in half. One of the Heinz or maybe Viktor's hands are trapped in his inner coat pocket. His mouth is trapped in a yawn it can't complete. Countess Sophie's mouth is trapped in a word she was starting to say. Her eyes look like they're being told a secret. The noise of the market is gone. It's like all sound has been suspended, or maybe put on trial for disturbing the peace.

The photographer isn't there anymore. The space he occupied looks like it's been removed, cut out with scissors, a hole in a page whose other side is darkness.

The archduke and the assassin are facing that darkness, so motionless that they might be mistaken for figures in a wax museum, except that they wouldn't make much of an exhibit, since they haven't been caught in dramatic poses, the positions they'll be assuming three days later, the assassin with his gun drawn looking fierce, the archduke slumped in the back of a black Double Phaeton, bleeding from a bullet hole in his neck. Instead, they're trapped in inconclusive postures and facial expressions, like people who can't figure out how to follow instructions, like people not getting a very obvious joke.

The moment waits, as if it can't figure out how to be the next moment, how to be more than a snapshot of itself, a photograph in a studio dark room slowly revealing a fragment of time, a bordered black and white space without sound and motion, later printed and published in a book, which turns up a hundred years later in a thrift shop thousands of miles away, having been translated several times and then gone out of print. It's covered with dust and you get it for almost nothing. You're eager to read a book that you've been trying to find for years.

But once you're home and turning the pages you're not sure what to think. The writing seems to be covering something up, like a painting painted only to conceal another painting. When the text is focused on martyrdom, it might be describing an afternoon made of aluminum. When the text is focused on war as a way of reviving failed economies, it might be describing robots whispering prayers to a robot Christ, failing to find the missing parts that might bring him back to life. When the text is focused on labor camps for people with subprime credit scores, it might be describing an ashtray in Bohemia, made from a massacred elephant's foot, a conversation piece. When the text is focused on subdivisions turning into ghost towns, it might be describing music made of stars, a composition that's also a new constellation. It's like you're trying to read a double exposure, and you can't help having doubts about the translation, or wondering if there was something wrong with the author's original prose, or if the past was simply too confusing to put into words.

Then you come to a fuzzy picture of Princip and the archduke. Both men look disturbed, like they never learned how to smile for a camera, like they don't understand why they're in a picture together. Knowing what you know about the fateful assassination, you can't imagine how such a picture was taken. The caption gives you nothing but the names, not the situation—what they were doing at the time, why and where they were standing side by side. So you start to think that the picture might be fake, an example of what used to be called trick photography, and you're not sure why such nonsense would appear in a serious book, especially since the book isn't really about the assassination. It's hard to know what the book is about. It reads like it might be a joke, but not kind of joke that people laugh at. You wanted the book because it's mentioned in many other books you've read, praised as the missing part of one of the world's most difficult puzzles. But now you're not even sure what the puzzle is, let alone how to solve it.

The confusion is making you mad. You want to throw the book out the window. But since you don't like leaving things unfinished, you keep going, though now the text itself seems less important than it did before, and you're mainly concerned with writing things down in the margins. When you finish a few days later and find a place for the book on your shelf, you tell yourself you'll read it again at some point, return to your scribbled notes and think about them at greater length. But you know you probably won't, that other things and books will get in the way. The book will sit on your shelf with all the other books that you won't read again, even though you've always thought of yourself as a careful reader, the kind of person who tries to learn from every book he opens, a throwback to a time when it wasn't easy to find things to read, when printed words were so rare that they had an almost magical status, and reading even a page from a book was a rare and wonderful privilege, conditions radically different from what you take for granted now, the endless circulation of mass produced images and language, a concern that will soon be staring you in the face, taking the form of a letter you'll be taking out of your mailbox. You'll know that somewhere someone's job is to send such letters out. You won't know that this person's name is Linda. But you will know without even reading the letter that Linda doesn't know or care what it says. But she can't afford to get fired so she does her work as well as she can.

Each afternoon, a one-page letter gets printed out a thousand times. She stuffs them all into envelopes she labeled in the morning, drops them into a large gray bag, which goes to the mailroom when it's full. By the end of the day, Linda wants to forget what she's done for the past eight hours. She wants to forget that junk mail even exists. But she knows that her mailbox at home will be filled with junk mail. She'll take it out and throw it away and more will arrive the next day.

Tonight she'll be meeting friends at a club to hear music. But she wants to go home and relax before going out. She makes a five-minute drive through the town that's been her home for the past eight months. A gauntlet of billboards blocks her view of the summer sun going down, the brilliant colors it spreads over desert mountains in the distance. Things in her one-bedroom apartment look normal at first, but then she's surprised to find a piece of paper on her kitchen table. She doesn't remember leaving it there before going to work in the morning, and the writing on it clearly isn't hers. It looks like someone was trying to solve an equation, or working out some other kind of computational problem, something that takes up most of the page, so apparently it's quite complex, but she can't be sure because she doesn't know anything about math. For all she knows, it might not even be math, since there aren't any numbers.

The figures on the page appear to be spoons and feathered arrows, crescent moons and footprints, greater-than signs, less-than signs, ampersands and lightbulbs, broken ladders, pitchforks, telephone poles and lightning bolts, combined in patterns that make no immediate sense. Yet it looks like someone knew what they were doing. The signs appear to be carefully arranged, leading up to what might be a result, something an expert could translate if he studied it long enough.

Linda thinks about throwing it out. But she can't avoid the disturbing questions: Who did the writing? Why did they leave it on her table? She feels uneasy, that a dangerous man might have been in her apartment, might still be hiding in a closet or under the bed. She quickly checks, trying hard not to panic. There's no one there. She thinks briefly that one of her friends might be playing a joke on her. But if so it's a bizarre joke, almost menacing, unfriendly, not the kind of thing the people she knows would likely do.

She doesn't want to stay in her apartment, afraid that whoever left the page might come back, so she drives a few miles west of town to the club where she'll be meeting her friends, tries to relax by nursing a Bloody Mary. The place is called The Other

Side, a phrase from a song by The Doors, lyrics her favorite uncle was always reciting, though she can't remember them clearly anymore. She's never been here before, but she likes what she sees, a circular room dominated by one huge photograph, spiral galaxies drifting through space, spread across the walls and floor and ceiling. There's a large group of circular tables, each with a scented candle, filling the room and the stage with pale blue light, which dimly reveals a drum kit, an upright bass propped against the back wall, a saxophone on a chair beside a cluster of keyboards. One of the keyboards looks like it's plugged into something. Aside from that there's nothing electronic, no microphones or jumble of cords or stack of amplifiers, a reminder of what her friend Amy told her on the phone a few weeks ago, inviting her to the concert.

Amy had seen the band play a month before when her boyfriend insisted, even though they had to drive more than a hundred miles, an outdoor performance in a small town near Death Valley. She'd called the music stunning, overwhelming, yet emphasized that the group had performed without theatrical displays, no rock star affectations, no massive amplification. But it wasn't mellow folk or country music. There was something wild and expansive about it, connected to a light show in the sky, which Amy insisted came from the music itself, not from special machines or laser devices, an impossible situation she admitted she couldn't explain.

She seemed like a changed person when she came back. She and her boyfriend quickly got involved with an online eco-terrorist group, and made important contributions to the group's most recent cybertage project, which shut down SUV dealerships throughout the Mohave Desert. Though Amy had never considered herself an activist before, now she was eager for aggressive interventions, even if there might be fierce confrontations with legal consequences. At first Linda thought of the hard core punk bands her older cousins had grown up listening to, groups violently involved with radical politics. But Amy emphasized that the music itself was anything but violent. The members of the band weren't openly promoting revolutionary agendas. If their music had a subversive effect, it was mainly because it was so unexpected. Even with her extensive training as a jazz and classical pianist, Amy couldn't come up with a clear description. She was also confused by the tour the band had arranged, with concerts only in desert towns of less than a hundred people, as if they wanted to share their sound but also keep it a secret, keep it from becoming a mass phenomenon. Linda was intrigued and did an extensive Internet search. She found almost nothing, no website, no YouTube clips, no Facebook page, no Wikipedia coverage, though she did find compelling comments on various blogs, people profoundly affected by the music without knowing why, all of them insisting that the sound was beyond description.

The band is called Assassination Sandwich. The name alone would have made Linda want to come out and hear them play. It makes her want to laugh, even though it has sinister implications. But the intergalactic atmosphere of the club doesn't feel at all sinister. There's nothing that would suggest political murders. Two long-haired guys who look like they're probably members of the band, with pictures of sandwiches printed on their t-shirts, are on stage sitting on stools, caught up in a lively conversation. They're holding what Linda thinks are sheets of music, though she's too far away to be sure of what's on the pages.

She gets a weird thought. What if the scores are like the page on her kitchen table? What if one of the guys in the band was the one who was in her apartment? She could have forgotten to lock her door when she left for work in the morning, and he could have been visiting someone in her building, could have entered her apartment by mistake, not figured out right away that he was in the wrong place, then gotten an emergency call on his cell, rushed out in a panic, left the musical score by mistake on her table. She knows it's an unlikely scenario, but it's better than no explanation at all, and it seems consistent with Amy's account of the band's unusual sound, which might require a new kind of musical notation.

She tells herself to do something she's never done before: Work up the courage to start a conversation with men she doesn't know. She quickly drinks the rest of her Bloody Mary, sits for a minute and lets a buzz develop, then walks to the stage and tells the men that she's heard amazing things about their music. One of them looks alarmed, quickly folds up the scores, excuses himself and hurries off stage. But the other one smiles and says it's great that she's eager to hear them play.

He says: How did you hear about us?

She says: A friend of mine heard you guys play and raved about your music, something she almost never does, since she's a really tough critic. Then I saw this great poster someone put up at the grocery store. I loved how weird it looked, the sandwiches with the faces on the bread. What a bizarre concept: Assassination Sandwich! Where did you get that name?

He says: We were in a small town gallery somewhere north of Vancouver, and we saw an exhibit of plastic sandwiches, and each one had an assassin's face on one piece of bread and the victim's face on the other.

She says: But your music isn't about death, is it?

He laughs and says: Our music isn't about anything. There aren't any lyrics. But our keyboard player is from Sarajevo, and his grandmother knew one of the people responsible for assassinating Archduke Ferdinand back in 1914.

She hesitates, then says: I think I remember something about that from history class. Was the guy you were just talking to the keyboard player?

He nods: Yeah. That's Gabriel. But that's not his real name.

She says: What's his real name?

He shrugs: He's never told us.

She says: Really? He won't tell you his real name?

He says: He stopped giving out his real name a few months after he moved here from Bosnia ten years ago. He got tired of hearing people mispronounce it, no matter how many times he tried to correct them. And then people were always asking him about being in Sarajevo back in the nineties, during the siege, like they thought it was just a TV show he could tell them about.

She nods and says: I had a friend who was on the Brooklyn Bridge on 9/11 when the Towers collapsed, and he told me how he got tired of people asking him what it was like, and how they talked about the footage they'd seen as if it was just another action movie.

The drummer nods: I remember how that footage kept showing up on all the news programs, over and over again. It's one of the reasons I almost never watch the news anymore. And it made me want to avoid New York City, even though it's the place to be if you want to make music. And Gabriel told me that he avoided New York for the same reason, back when he first arrived in the States. He didn't want to be in a battle zone again, so he decided to try the West Coast, and ended up in San Diego for a while, and—

Linda says: San Diego? Why San Diego?

He says: Because it rhymes with Sarajevo and has the same number of syllables—or at least that's what he told me, but I think he was joking. It's hard to tell with him. Everything seems to be a joke, even when he's serious. But he figured out pretty quickly that San Diego was the opposite of Sarajevo. I think he'd heard that San Diego is one of those places where people are nice all the time, but when he got there he found out that they weren't really nice; they were *too* nice. And they spent all their time texting each other, taking pictures of themselves with their phones, or putting on suntan lotion. But he stayed there because he got hooked on the pleasant weather—no humidity, no freezing temperatures—and he might still be there, except that we were looking for a keyboard player and he saw an ad we placed in *Downbeat*. So he's been through some weird changes over the years, and he's not that good in social situations. But he's a damn good keyboard player.

She says: I've got an old friend who lives in San Diego. She's got advanced degrees in history from Stanford, published articles, and she's always complaining that the people in San Diego act as if history never happened—

He says: Right. And Gabriel talks about Sarajevo like it's suffocating under the weight of too much history. But what's up with your friend? If she thinks San Diego is such a silly place, why is she still there?

Linda shrugs: I'm not sure. Probably not because of the weather. She's not a sunny weather kind of person, and apparently it's outrageously expensive there, not a great place for someone stuck in a series of part-time jobs. But anyway, what do *you* play?

He points to the drum kit.

She says: You're the drummer? Wow! Amy told me that when she heard you guys play the drumming was amazing. Like you weren't just keeping the beat.

He says: Most people think that drums are just rhythm instruments. But that puts limits on their expressive potential. We all play whatever we want.

She says: Really? But just a minute ago it looked like you and Gabriel were holding musical scores of some kind. Aren't sheets of music supposed to dictate what you play?

He shrugs: Ours don't. I mean, sure, they're guidelines, points of departure. But they're also visual music, things your eyes can listen to, once you learn how to read them. Every time we play, we read them differently. And they change in response to the way we read and play them.

She says: That reminds me of something my friend Amy was telling me a few months ago when she got back from New York City, where everyone was talking about that weird wall that suddenly appeared in Central Park. You've heard about that, haven't you?

The drummer nods: Like I said, I almost never watch the news anymore. But one night I was in a club with Gabriel and the ten o'clock news was on the tube and there was some expert claiming that the thing in Central Park might not really be a wall, but maybe a huge book sent here from another planet, or another dimension. Is that what you're talking about?

Linda nods: I heard that if you look at the wall in the right state of mind you can read it like a book, but not a normal book. You can see pictures that might be a language of some kind, like in ancient Egypt, but instead of moving in sequence, the pictures are stacked on top of each other, and you read downward from the top and upward from the bottom at the same time. I guess it takes practice.

He smiles: I'm sure it does! I'm sure if I watched the news more often I'd hear all sorts of stories about that wall. Maybe it's here so that people can make up stories about it. When you create a situation that seems to require an explanation, there's no end to the things that people will come up with. But I haven't really thought about it much. Like I said, I haven't been keeping up with current events. I probably should, but the band is taking up all my time right now.

Linda badly wants to take a look at the sheets of music, to see if they're filled with lightning bolts, crescent moons and pitchforks. But the drummer politely says that he's got to go backstage, that the band still has some details they need to work out before they begin.

The club fills up quickly. At least half of the town's ninety people seem to be present. Everyone looks excited by what they've heard about the band. Her friends arrive just before the music is scheduled to start, so there's no time to talk, which normally wouldn't be a problem at a concert, but Linda was hoping she could tell Amy about the mysterious page, since Amy majored in math in college and knows a lot about music.

When Assassination Sandwich takes the stage, all conversations instantly stop. But there's no introduction, and the band doesn't seem to begin. They just make random sounds on their instruments, apparently unaware that they're supposed to be performing. In fact, they look like they're fooling around, sharing a private joke, barely keeping themselves from laughing. Linda looks at her friends and the other people in the club. They've all got their eyes closed, listening carefully, some of them swaying, others nodding their heads. Finally Linda figures out that the concert is already happening, that the disconnected sounds are a composition. They're pleasant enough in themselves, eerie yet somehow soothing, making her feel like she's relaxing on a couch watching tropical fish swimming in a huge aquarium. But at first she doesn't know if what she's listening to is music. She starts to think that she might be slightly drunk, that the Bloody Mary is keeping her from appreciating what's happening. But if the drink had any real effect on her, it seems to have worn off. Her mind is clear. Her perceptions don't seem distorted. Instead, she's slowly becoming aware of an unfamiliar clarity, the careful adjustments her mind has been making, learning to follow the moves the music is making. Soon she feels so calm that she's not sure where she is anymore, and doesn't care.

Then there's an explosion of drumming, a crashing of dark piano chords, heightened pulsing from the bass, sheets of sound from the tenor sax, and the room feels like it's traveling through space, moving through the galaxies on the walls and floor and ceiling, light years passing in a matter of seconds, distances taking form in a series of disconnected phrases, a narrative that develops by moving in unforeseen directions, words that might have been stars in a previous lifetime, stars that might have been words in a previous lifetime, released from the burden to mean the things that meaning normally makes them mean, releasing themselves from the scripted play of nouns and verbs and connecting words, no longer forced to function as background elements, in against until beside above behind inside before unlike between outside below within about across, an ongoing series of shuffled prepositions, finally clear of the need to play supporting roles for other words, no longer made to behave themselves and act like parts of speech, time and space dissolving into a purely syllabic process, where everything is possible and nothing needs to exist, leading to the birth of a new constellation, stars in a pattern that's not the result of human observation, a picture of something that's changing into a picture of something else, a picture of something that can't be contained by a picture. The music keeps changing and making things change, and now she's so caught up in it that she can't imagine anything else, can't remember what music used to sound like. She's mesmerized especially by Gabriel's keyboard playing, the almost casual way that he's filling the room with bizarre combinations of sound, making her think of the violence he must have endured in Sarajevo, his connection to the assassination that led to World War I, and it occurs to her that the music is both a reflection and a rejection of his past, though it also feels like the sound has nothing to do with anyone's past.

Now the room is slowly spinning back down through the stars. The earth appears like a dot, then like a tennis ball painted blue and green, then a turning globe with continents and oceans, and finally the building drops into place a few miles west of town, right where it was before the music began, setting down so gracefully that the drinks on the tables don't get spilled. Linda isn't aware at first that the band is no longer playing. She's lost in the motion her candle is making, the motions of all the candles on other tables, shadows darting and dancing over the galaxies on the walls, shaping the floor and ceiling until they seem to be the same thing. Everyone looks amazed, like they've had the experience of a lifetime, music that will live in their bodies forever, beyond anything they might want to say about it, beyond the need to start writing things down, to stage things on a page. There's no applause. It's clear that noise of any kind would be out of place. What's happened has almost nothing to do with what's normally called a performance. The guys in the band look amused and slightly sleepy. They start joking with each other, smile at the audience, wave goodbye, then walk off the stage like nothing important has happened, as if words like important were missing the point, as if the very notion of a point were missing the point.

Linda feels deeply relaxed. She's barely aware that she's leaving the club, barely aware that she's driving home, so pleasantly entranced that she almost forgets that she's almost out of gas. She hates the glare of the ExxonMobil sign approaching down the street, the flying horse that hatched from the head of Medusa, but she knows that she better stop. The pumps at the station have TVs. It's time for the ten o'clock news, with guest astronomers raving about the birth of a new constellation. They don't know what to call it yet, since it seems to be a series of changing shapes, like an intergalactic amoeba looking for food among the stars. It sounds like an important event, but Linda can't fully absorb it. She doesn't want anything verbal to intrude on what she's feeling, and she's always hated the news, the oppressively scripted faces and voices.

The drive home seems to take much longer than usual, as if time had been redesigned. She remembers Amy describing the same sensation when she came back from Death Valley, the sense that the spaces between moments had been stretched out, so that more things seemed to be happening, but somehow happening more slowly than before, allowing her to more fully perceive what otherwise would have been rushing past, but also making her more offended by things that in the past wouldn't have bothered her nearly as much, the information sickness that everyone seemed to be suffering from, the atmosphere of noise that made careful thinking impossible. Linda thinks again about the wall in Central Park, a theory she heard people in her office discussing recently, that the wall existed only to resist and destroy information, making anything anyone said about it sound stupid, making anything anyone said about anything sound stupid.

When she gets home to the page of strange notation on the table, it doesn't seem so strange anymore. It looks like something she can read. She sits and looks at the page for maybe an hour, not focusing, just letting her eyes absorb the pattern of images, the same relaxed attention she gave the music at the club. The symbols change as soon as she starts to think she might know what they mean, but she likes the feeling, the sense of something slipping away, fading into something else, even if it means that reading just this page might take the rest of her life, even if it means that she won't have time to work anymore, no time to send out letters like the one that's in your hand right now, the letter you can't be bothered to read, the kind of letter no one ever reads, though thankfully it only takes one side, so the other side of the page can be recycled, joining the other blank sides of pages you like to keep around the house, just in case you need to write anything down.

THE NEARSIGHTED ASSASSIN

It was late Fall, 1968, and London was a great place to be a nineteen-year-old acid freak. I was living in a flat in Chelsea near King's Road, a small room on the top floor with an open view of the Thames and Battersea Park. The people on the first three floors were members of a psychedelic rock band. I got along with them like we were old friends, especially after I found out that their first album was *Music in a Doll's House*, which I'd heard for the first time several months before, back at UC Berkeley. Someone down the hall in my dorm kept playing it over and over again, a perfect backdrop for a wild sexual afternoon with a woman who'd just turned me on to the best hash in the Western Hemisphere.

The band was called Family, not in the mom and pop sense, but because early in their performing career they wore double-breasted suits on stage, and someone told them they looked like they were in the mafia. By the time I met them, they looked like what they'd become, hippies who got their clothes from the Salvation Army. In the Fall of 1968, they were finishing their second album, *Family Entertainment*, and we often talked about what was happening in the studio as they worked their new songs into final form. From what I could tell, their new record was going to be just as bizarre as the first one. They weren't consciously trying to make strange music, but most people who listened to *Music in a Doll's House* came away wondering what they'd been listening to—an impossible synthesis of Bob Dylan, James Brown, Charles Ives, and Stanley Turrentine, refracted by studio electronics. This weird combination had led to mixed reviews, but their strongest supporters praised them for making songs that weren't easy to classify.

At first, I was almost afraid of them. Back then, I was easily overimpressed by artistic achievement. But they were easy to talk to, showed no signs of suffering from the genius complex, and unlike many of the musician types I remembered from Berkeley and San Francisco, the guys in Family weren't only interested in themselves. We had long conversations about the other great psychedelic bands we went out to see: Pink Floyd, Soft Machine, King Crimson, Yes, Nice, Procol Harum, Strawbs, Traffic, Spooky Tooth, and so many others whose names I don't remember. It seemed like we were always dropping acid and listening to music.

I couldn't play anything myself, but Family's two main songwriters valued my opinions about their lyrics. They were impressed when I showed them the anti-Vietnam War diatribes I'd published in the UC Berkeley newspaper during my one year there as a history major, and they were even more impressed that I'd dropped out of school to concentrate on doing acid. This might not have been the smartest decision I ever made, but apparently it made me the ideal critic for the crazy songs they were writing, and an ideal tenant for the flat itself, with its worn-down turn of the century details and thrift shop furnishings. And I had a skill that soon became almost as enticing to the band as my so-called verbal abilities: I made fantastic popcorn. I knew just the right way to pop it, making sure that small portions of the final product were slightly burned, then smothering it with butter and salt. We were truly a happy family when I came around with big bowls of popcorn. We ate almost nothing else.

My lover and landlady, Tasha, was the only one who wasn't addicted to my cooking. She was on a macrobiotic diet designed for her by an older friend, a doctor named Ivo Jovanovic from Yugoslavia. I always thought the food was obnoxiously bland, and I couldn't see how Tasha got anywhere near it, but she insisted that the reason she looked so good was that she ate so carefully. I'd met her in a history course we were taking at the University of London. I was there because I wanted the credits in case I decided to return to Berkeley at some point. She was there because of the professor's reputation. I'm sure he was a fine teacher. He knew what he was talking about and had an amusing way of presenting ideas. But I had trouble paying attention to him because I couldn't stop looking at Tasha, even though I could see that she was probably more than twice my age.

Once we became lovers, I stayed with her for a few days in her Georgian row house. Then she told me she had an empty room in a flat she owned a few blocks away, and I could live there for nothing—a good thing, since I was running out of money. Sometimes I helped out at the art gallery she was managing with great success, but she didn't really expect me to do any work, which left us lots of time for sex, concerts, and long conversations. It was a perfect situation. She told me she liked being with a much younger man because it meant that she didn't have to act her age, though she knew how to act her age quite well when she needed to.

Her doctor, Ivo, was the weirdest guy I'd ever met. The first time I encountered him was when he knocked on the door while Tasha and I were climaxing together. We made him wait on the stoop for a few minutes, but it wasn't long enough. As I sat at

Tasha's kitchen table trying to make conversation, the afterglow of the shared orgasm was so intense that I felt like I was still having sex. What made it even worse was that Ivo wasn't the best talker in the world. In fact, he might have been the worst. He mostly just sat there staring at me. I tried to talk to him about Family and the other music I liked. He said it was all junk. When I asked him what kind of music he enjoyed, a fierce feeling took over his face and his upper body, and he looked like a snapping turtle wearing a trench coat. Tasha later explained to me that Ivo started hating all music when his wife had an affair with the famous avant-garde composer Arnold Schoenberg. I'd heard some of Schoenberg's music and didn't like it. To me, the term avant-garde meant Soft Machine and Pink Floyd.

When Ivo finally left, Tasha told me that he was suffering from something she called post-traumatic stress disorder, a term which wasn't as widely known then as it is now. He'd spent four years in jail because in his late teens he'd been part of the assassination plot that triggered World War I, and now he was suspicious of anything that sounded like revolution. Back then, I thought it was a radical action to even listen to progressive rock music, that simply by rejecting the musical formulas of top-40 radio you were liberating yourself from the assumption that the goal of life was to make money and buy products. Tasha loved to hear me talk this way, and though at times I got the impression that she thought the idea was a bit silly, I knew she liked the rebellious atmosphere that surrounded the music, the feeling that in the middle of a long guitar solo nothing else mattered.

But Ivo didn't want anything to do with the counterculture that had taken over London in the late sixties. I remember one time Tasha convinced him to go out with us to a Ravi Shankar concert at the Royal Albert Hall, right after flying saucers were installed in the ceiling, removing the echo. She'd told me that she thought he needed to get beyond the resentments that were limiting his enjoyment of life, and facing the music was a crucial way of doing this. But even though the renovated acoustics in the place were superb and Ravi Shankar didn't act anything like a hippie, Ivo sat through the concert as if someone had tied to him to a chair and pistol-whipped him.

We went out to a small club later, one of those basement places where the darkness was so thick you could imagine people in secret societies wearing hoods and robes and swearing to drink poison. I was raving about the sitar, how the Beatles, Procol Harum, Traffic, Family, and the Moody Blues had all used it on recent albums, an indication that Eastern and Western cultures were starting to find significant points of connection, something I remembered from the liner notes of one of Shankar's albums. Ivo glared at me. I got the feeling he was trying to shut me up, so I started talking faster and louder, refusing to let him set my agenda. Finally, he slammed his fist down on the table, snapped out something in a language I didn't recognize, then got up and stumbled toward the exit. I didn't want him around anyway and I would have just let him go, but Tasha looked alarmed and got him to sit back down and talk. It was the only time I ever heard him say more than a few terse phrases, and I was surprised at how fluent his English became. With his bald perspiring head and wire-rimmed glasses, he kept reminding me of Rod Steiger in *The Pawnbroker*, especially when his face broke out of its usual gloomy expression into something that looked like a smile, and he started laughing, then abruptly stopped.

He insisted that he didn't want to talk about World War I, but he kept coming back to it anyway. Even though my major was history, and one of my Berkeley professors had been an expert on the assassination in Sarajevo, I couldn't remember much about it at first, so some of the things Ivo said didn't make sense to me. But Tasha repeatedly nodded as if she knew exactly what he was talking about and wanted him to say as much as possible, like a therapist getting a patient to confront something painful. I kept hoping she would stop encouraging him because I wanted to get back to her flat and get stoned and make love. But I didn't want Tasha to think I was too immature to appreciate the pain of someone who'd obviously had to live through a difficult experience.

I gathered from what Ivo said that he'd been part of a revolutionary youth movement in Sarajevo, which was how he'd gotten involved in a plot to shoot the heir apparent to the Habsburg empire. I tried to picture him as a teenage radical, shouting angry slogans and storming government buildings. I started to think that we might have something in common. But he had a tedious way of talking, explaining the same things over and over again, and soon I was leaning back in my chair and closing my eyes, tuning everything out except my stoned memories of Ravi Shankar's music.

It was music that had brought me to London in the first place. I'd heard great stories about the UFO Club and the progressive rock scenes in London and Canterbury, so when a friend of a friend said he knew someone who ran a nice bed and breakfast place near Russell Square, I booked the first cheap flight I could find. I'd managed to save a chunk of the money I'd made off a stoned week of successful appearances on *Jeopardy* soon after I left the Berkeley campus, so I didn't have to think about finding work right away. I wandered all over the city, enjoying the parks and neighborhoods and music clubs. It was an acid head's wet dream. But I couldn't entirely escape the beliefs I'd been raised with, the lectures my parents had given me about the importance of a college education, so when I heard about a special month-long history class being offered through the university, I signed up for it.

But I really wanted music and not history, sitar and not Sarajevo, and I was only catching fragments of what Ivo was saying until I heard him mention a revolutionary pamphlet called *The Death of a Hero*. When I opened my eyes he was glaring at me, speaking as if he were drilling syllables into my forehead. I can still recall exactly what he said: We read this pamphlet at all our meetings. We knew whole passages by heart. They weren't just words. They were a program of action, and we were ready to do what had to be done. We were ready to kill the tyrant and set our country free.

Tasha was staring at him like he was some kind of god. She quickly explained to me that early in the twentieth century Ivo's country, Bosnia-Herzegovina, had been annexed by the Austro-Hungarian empire, which led to widespread resentment among the younger generation. A resistence movement quickly formed, composed largely of starving students. As soon as she mentioned students, I nodded eagerly, again assuming that Ivo and I might have important things to talk about, that he might approve of the student demonstrations I'd helped organize back in Berkeley or the things I'd written about Vietnam. But he couldn't seem to grasp the connection between revolution and progressive music. When I tried to explain it, he looked at me with disdain and said: You talk about your psychedelic music as if it were a program of action. It's nothing of the kind! It leads you to stare into space, as if going blank in your mind were a kind of achievement. But would you and your long-haired friends be willing to put a bullet in Mr. Nixon's head? Do you think your music will stop the Vietnam War?

He started laughing. I wanted to put a bag over his head, so I didn't have to see how weird he looked when his features became animated. I felt stupid. The only thing I could say was: Guns aren't the answer.

He stared at me for a while, began laughing again, then abruptly stopped and said: Of course guns aren't the answer; they're the method. Do you think Richard Nixon will care if you waste your time on that stupid music? Do you know what he thinks you and your friends are? Dirty little bastards who can't even butter a piece of bread! Do you really think a man like that will listen to your music?

I said: Our music isn't for him. It's for us. It's what we listen to instead of him. Why should we believe anything he says? We've just had four years of LBJ, promising peace and delivering war. Now that Nixon's been elected, things are going to get even worse. It doesn't matter who's in the White House, or who's in control on Capitol Hill. Democrats are bad; Republicans are worse. They might seem superficially different, but they all have one thing in common: They talk bullshit nonstop.

Tasha was smiling at me. I couldn't wait to go back to her flat and fuck.

Ivo said: That's right! And bullets are the only way to stop the bullshit. Bullets are the only language tyrants understand.

Somewhere in the blur of my thinking the name Gavrilo Princip emerged, and I remembered from a history class at Berkeley that Princip, and not Ivo Jovanovic, was the one who shot the heir apparent. The class was a special seminar called "The History of Mistakes," taught by a professor whose central belief was that mistakes had been crucial in shaping Western civilization. He'd used the assassination in Sarajevo as a primary example, carefully showing that Princip would have had no chance to fire the fateful shots if the driver of the archduke's car hadn't made a wrong turn. The memory made me wonder about Princip, what kind of person he was, so I decided to stop arguing with Ivo and ask him how well they knew each other.

My question had a strange effect. He nodded slowly, but there was no creepy smile this time. When Tasha put her hand on his and tried to make eye contact, he wouldn't look at her. He was staring at the table, as if it contained a speech he'd been waiting to make. When he started talking again, his voice was different, like a younger version of him was there in the club with us. Some of what he said was in a language I couldn't understand. But what I remember clearly was that someone had taken Ivo to a park and given him a gun and a bomb and quickly shown him how they were used. The next day, the man took him to a place on the Appel Quay, a broad avenue which followed the Miljacka River through the center of Sarajevo. He waited there in the hot morning sun, knowing that there were at least six other assassins lined up along the avenue, but not knowing who they were. The crowd grew more and more agitated, shouting things that made it sound like they were glad to see Archduke Franz Ferdinand approaching in his Double Phaeton. Ivo stepped back from the excitement, leaning against the wall of a tobacco shop, because he'd been told that to prepare the bomb he needed to strike it against a solid surface—a wall or maybe a lamppost—and wait ten seconds before throwing it.

I tried to picture the scene that his words were struggling to assemble—Ivo Jovanovic as a young man standing there, taking a vial of poison out of his pocket and drinking it, reaching under his cape and gripping his gun, the crowd shouting wildly: *He's coming, he's coming!* and *Long Live the Crown Prince!* And then, an explosion, a young man across the street leaping onto the wall of a bridge and jumping into the river, chaos on the sidewalks, everyone shouting and shoving, the archduke and his wife looking terrified in their car, and Ivo Jovanovic standing there, only thirty feet away, unable to pull out the gun or the bomb and send the tyrant to his grave.

Ivo was trembling. Tasha put her arm around him but looked like she wasn't sure what to say. I wanted her to take control of the situation, or at least to put an end to a silence that soon began to feel way too long, even though the club was filled with loud music and silence was out of the question. Ivo finally said: I had no courage. I don't know what happened to me.

I closed my eyes and pictured the scene again. Pink Floyd's "Careful With That Axe, Eugene" was playing from invisible speakers planted all over the room. The tribal drumbeat, the deceptively calm electric organ, slowly building toward a climax of primal screams and a savage guitar solo, began to function like an assassination soundtrack, distorting the story and breaking it into fragments. I kept thinking about the guy jumping into the river. Who was he? Why was he jumping? When I asked about it, Ivo just gave me his dead fish look, but Tasha quickly explained that the man was one of the other assassins and that he'd just tried to kill the archduke with a bomb, but it hadn't worked and he'd tried to kill himself by jumping into the river, but that hadn't worked either since the river was only three inches deep.

At first I was surprised that she knew the story so well, but I figured that Ivo must have shared it with her at least once before, probably because she'd encouraged him to, for therapeutic reasons. Though I'd only known her for two months, I could tell she was the kind of person who liked it when people told her about traumatic events that had changed them forever. But the story itself was confusing. Even though I was starting to remember things from my seminar at Berkeley, realizing that I knew more about the summer of 1914 than I thought I did at first, I didn't understand why the river was only three inches deep, and why the assassin hadn't noticed how shallow it was before jumping. After all, if you're preparing to kill a world leader, don't you think out everything in advance, mapping out all the possibilities? And if you're thinking you might kill yourself by jumping into a river, wouldn't you first make sure that the river was deep enough? Or would it be the kind of thing you'd take for granted, since other details would seem more important? I tried again to picture the situation, the young man scrambling up onto the wall of the bridge, looking back one last time before jumping, a pause which gave me a full view of his face, which briefly filled with signs of deep confusion, as if he could hear the music I was hearing, the sudden drums, the primal screams, the fierce guitar solo. Somehow I knew exactly what he looked like, crouched on the bridge, facing the tumult he'd caused on the street. But when I tried to picture Ivo Jovanovic standing thirty feet away, leaning against a brick wall, unable to take action, talking to himself without knowing what he was saying, all I could see was a sky of circling blackbirds.

Someone turned up the music, a change that triggered an obvious question: Why wasn't Ivo Jovanovic dead? Hadn't he swallowed cyanide right before failing to pull out his gun? I had to shout above the music: Didn't you drink poison? What happened?

He said something I couldn't hear so I asked him again. He didn't answer. The primal screams got louder and louder. I kept expecting the speakers to blow. Tasha finally leaned over and yelled in my ear: The poison wasn't any good! It was past the expiration date. It didn't work for the other assassins either!

I looked back at Ivo sitting there in the outfit he always wore: an old gray trenchcoat, button-down shirt, thin black tie, and baggy dark wool pants. He looked tensely around the room as if people were listening in, though the music was too loud for something like that, even after someone turned it back down. He suddenly said: I couldn't see anything. It was all a blur. I've always been near-sighted.

Tasha looked surprised, as if she hadn't heard this part of the story before. She said: You weren't wearing your glasses?

Ivo shook his head and said: I didn't have glasses back then. I couldn't afford them. A friend who knew about the plot offered to lend me his. But I thought they would make me look too conspicuous.

She said: Why would glasses have made you look too conspicuous?

He said: I never wore glasses. If someone who knew me saw me with glasses, they might have wondered why, and said something to me.

She said: And then what?

He said: The streets were filled with cops and undercover detectives. Anything unusual would have been noticed.

She said: How nearsighted were you?

He said: Anything more than ten feet away was a blur.

Tasha was trying to be a good listener, but I could see that she was struggling not to smile. She finally said: The nearsighted assassin sounds like the title of a surrealist painting.

I was surprised by her flip tone. It was the first time I'd heard her say anything even remotely offensive to anyone.

Ivo said: The surrealists were full of shit.

I couldn't keep myself from trying to tease him: I suppose you think they were all dirty little bastards who couldn't butter a piece of bread.

He nodded slowly, and again I could see Tasha trying not to smile. But then I was distracted by a surprising change in the

228

music. "Careful With That Axe, Eugene" was followed by Family's "Summer 67," a live bootleg version of a psychedelic instrumental that I knew would be included, in more polished form, on the band's next album. The song had special significance for me, since I'd helped the band rework the studio version. It also reminded me of my own Summer 67, reading Timothy Leary's book on psychedelic experience, taking acid for the first time a few days after I graduated from high school, my friend Carl playing me Procol Harum's "Homburg," a beautifully strange song that somehow never became as successful as their famous "Whiter Shade of Pale." The lyrics were focused on a clock with its hands turning backwards and devouring both themselves and also any fool who dared to tell the time. The image took me by surprise. I knew I should have been disturbed, but I was laughing, then laughing because I couldn't say why I was laughing, then laughing harder because I was laughing because I couldn't say why, then laughing even harder. The laughter could have gone on forever, and though it felt good to be caught up in it, like I might have been surfing and riding a monster wave, it also felt like a one-way trip to a nut house, so I grabbed Carl's arm and asked what time it was and he said 7:34, and I got lost in the song's haunting organ solo for at least fifteen minutes, then grabbed Carl's arm and asked what time it was and he said 7:34, and I got lost in the song's haunting organ solo for at least fifteen minutes, then grabbed Carl's arm and asked what time it was and he said 7:34, and I got lost in the song's haunting organ solo for at least fifteen minutes, then grabbed Carl's arm and asked what time it was and he said 7:34, and I got lost in the song's haunting organ solo for at least fifteen minutes, then grabbed Carl's arm and asked what time it was and he said 7:34. The next day Carl told me that I'd kept asking him what time is it what time is it what time is it what time is it what time is it, over and over again with only short pauses, and after the first three times it wasn't funny. When he played the song for me again, I was surprised that there was no organ solo, haunting or otherwise.

Carl was the only high school friend I was still in touch with. High school hadn't been much fun, since most of my classmates were middle class suburban kids who saw nothing wrong with being middle class or suburban, and I felt so self-conscious around them that frequently I didn't wear my glasses. I didn't want to see them looking at me. The blur was better. This might have had something to do with the low grades I kept getting, and how I'd only been accepted at Berkeley because my uncle was the Chair of the History Department. But now that I'd heard Ivo's story I was glad that I'd been a nearsighted underachiever and not a nearsighted assassin. After all, my bad high school grades hadn't led to prison time and post-traumatic stress disorder. Still, I had to admit that no matter how unpleasant Ivo was, I admired him for having the courage to get involved in an assassination plot, knowing that he might be shooting into a blur.

I don't remember him leaving, but he kept looking at his watch, and at some point he wasn't there anymore and I was relieved. The situation must have been frustrating for him. It was clear that he just wanted to be with Tasha. Even if he was too old to have sex with her I'm sure he still fantasized about it. After all, she was aging beautifully, with her long, black, curly hair and athletic figure. Instead he had to sit in a loud club listening to my hippie ideas knowing that I was the one who would be going to bed with her. But I figured he'd gotten used to the feeling over the years, since Tasha had always been an actively sexual woman, and never hesitated to talk about past and present lovers, not all of them men.

Soon it was closing time and we were outside walking. I'm not sure where in London we were, but I remember a waterfront of abandoned brick factories and warehouses filled with furious drumming, surging bass lines, crazed guitar solos, wild keyboard improvisations, as if the city of commerce had been replaced by a city of music. At some point, we stepped into a small club filled with a huge sound, the Soft Machine with their constantly smiling drummer and constantly scowling organist playing a forty-minute song based on one repeated phrase, "we did it again," chanted in a very deep voice by a guitarist who'd painted his face to look like a chessboard. Then we were outside walking again, and then we were in a huge industrial space that was totally dark, filled with whispered conversations and quiet laughter. Suddenly, there were lights on a wooden stage made of shipping pallets, and I was surprised to see my Family roommates up there playing "A Song for Me," possibly the craziest song ever made, with its church organ intro suddenly becoming a raunchy guitar-based rock song with weirdly disconnected lyrics, then dissolving into a lengthy instrumental passage filled with eerie violin and saxophone riffs, which sounded like whales calling to each other deep in an ocean filled with turbulent drumming, bursts of electric piano, and unpredictable shifts in volume and tempo. They'd been messing around with the song for weeks back in the flat, but I'd never heard the whole thing played from start to finish, and it left me feeling that my sense of time had been permanently altered, biochemically redesigned, no longer just a reflection of standard chronological patterns.

At some point Tasha and I were back outside, and she was kissing me against a brick wall and going down on me, and then we were walking again, and then I was kissing her against a brick wall and going down on her, and then we were walking again, and there was music everywhere, surging from open doors and windows, and we just kept walking until sunlight appeared very faintly over the buildings in the east and we knocked on a friend's door and she took us into her big bed and the three of us fucked our way through the day and into a wonderful stupor that lasted until the sun went back down and the music started up on the streets again.

I wanted to go right back out and see more bands in clubs. Tasha's friend, Barbara, gave us a special kind of blotter acid called Paper Sun, which was popular at the time because it got the trip started quickly. It was also the title of the opening song on the first Traffic album, a tune that introduced me to the sitar more than a year before I knew who Ravi Shankar was, the summer after my high school graduation. I saw that Barbara had the album so I played it, and by the end of the last song, "Mr. Fantasy," which featured a densely distorted Stevie Winwood guitar solo that seemed to last much longer than the song itself, the chemicals were starting to do their job. The walls and rugs and cabinets were throbbing with color.

Tasha was staring out into the twilight with a look so vivid I could see the hallucinations in her eyes. I remembered she had that same look the first time we'd gone out for coffee after class, when she told me what she remembered about the Blitz in World War II, listening in her basement to the bombs destroying her family's flat during the Battle of Britain. For a second, I remembered Ivo's face in the basement club, his claim that World War II had been the result of World War I. But I didn't want to think about war anymore. I'd heard too many stories about bad trips triggered by violent images. Certain subjects were off limits when people were doing LSD, war being right at the top of a lengthy list. There was also music you had to avoid on acid—the

Doors, Country Joe and the Fish, the Mothers of Invention. I wasn't sure why. I couldn't imagine good music being a bummer. But people I trusted were sure that these groups were dangerous, that their lyrics could take you to places you'd never come back from. I didn't want to take the chance, especially since there was lots of other music I liked more.

The twilight had gone almost completely dark when I noticed that no one had said anything for a long time, though I wasn't sure at the time what a long time was. I kept thinking we should have more three-way sex, since I was almost as attracted to Barbara as I was to Tasha. Barbara was a heavy-set woman with a bob of black hair, and though it was obvious that she didn't take the same kind of care to look trim and young as Tasha did, there was something appealing about the chemistry she and Tasha had between the sheets, and I wanted to see what else might happen if we all went to bed again. But the silence was so mesmerizing that I didn't want to break it.

Barbara finally looked at her watch and said: I've got to get going soon. Mary and I have tickets to see Dexter Gordon tonight.

I said: Who's Dexter Gordon?

Barbara and Tasha looked surprised that I didn't know. Tasha finally said: He's probably the greatest tenor saxophonist in the world.

Barbara nodded and said: Right. Along with Sonny Rollins and John Coltrane, except that Trane's no longer with us. You guys should come with us. I can call and see if tickets are still available.

Tasha said: I'd love to.

But I was nervous about tripping to music older people liked. Tasha could see I was hesitating, so she took my hand and said: Don't you think it'd be interesting to hear the music your favorite groups are trying to imitate.

233

Suddenly I felt betrayed, not a good way to feel on acid. I'd read so-called serious discussions of psychedelic music, and they always mentioned jazz or blues in relation to Family, the Soft Machine, King Crimson, Spooky Tooth, and Pink Floyd, or classical music in relation to the Moody Blues, Procol Harum, Yes, or the Nice. Such descriptions were often meant to be flattering, but they annoyed me. It seemed like the writers were saying that progressive rock was interesting mainly because it could be connected to well-known traditions, that when these young hippies grew up and finally learned how to play, they'd become jazz, blues, or classical musicians, if they were good enough.

But I was sure that psychedelic music indicated a radical break from traditions of any kind, a new form of consciousness that would leave behind the dismal world created by my parents, LBJ, and Tricky Dick. I took it for granted that Tasha felt this way too, except that when I'd tried to talk plainly about it, I got the feeling she was humoring me. When I told her how pleased I was to be living in a flat with one of my favorite psychedelic bands, I wasn't sure that she liked their music as much as I did. But she was so skilled at either changing the subject or trying to appreciate what other people liked that I didn't have time to wonder about her real opinion of the music revolution. It was clear what people like Ivo Jovanovic thought about progressive rock, but it was easy to write them off as the older generation. They were trapped in the tragedies history had created and couldn't embrace the future. But Tasha was different, or at least I thought she was. And I assumed Barbara was too. After all, she'd just had three-way sex with us, and had seemed comfortable with the wild positions Tasha had taught me.

But now I was confused, and the acid was making it worse. Suddenly Tasha and Barbara seemed a lot older. I said: *Trying* to imitate? Really?

Tasha laughed: Don't take it the wrong way. I just meant—

But I was hurt: *Trying* to imitate?

Barbara said: She just meant that all young artists are influenced by previous artistic traditions. They start off sounding a bit like the people they grew up listening to.

Tasha nodded and started rubbing my back: There's nothing wrong with being influenced by great musicians. It's a necessary part of maturing as artists and—

I said: Fuck that! I've seen jazz musicians. They wear coats and ties on stage and have music stands with musical scores. I remember my parents listening to Duke Ellington and Count Basie. There was nothing revolutionary about that music. Or Stan Getz and "The Girl from Ipanema," which was Top-40 bullshit, dumbass lounge music!

The room was silent except for the sound of chemicals popping and snapping behind my eyes. I wanted to find better insults than the ones I'd just dished out, but the acid wasn't making me clever. The best I could do was shrug Tasha's hand off my back and walk out of the room, down a dark hallway lined on either side with tall piles of books. The sound of my feet on the hardwood floor went on much longer than it should have, and I remember wondering why it was taking so long to walk fifteen feet, but at some point I was staring out over the darkened rooftops of London from the kitchen window, losing myself in the vast pattern of lights.

From what sounded like a long way off Barbara laughed and said: Somehow, Tasha, I don't think you'll be coming with us to hear Dex tonight.

Tasha said: Doesn't look like it. How long will he be in town? It's been years since I heard him live. I think the last time was when he had that nightly gig in Copenhagen, back when Graham and I were still getting along and—

I shouted down the hallway: Graham? Who's Graham?

I stormed back into the room and glared at Tasha. She smiled: My old boyfriend. I told you about him, remember?

I did remember. She'd always described him as a pretentious jerk, but now apparently he was someone with superior musical taste.

Barbara laughed: You haven't seen him in years, have you?

Tasha shook her head: Thankfully not.

I said: But *Graham* knew his music, didn't he? Unlike the dumbass hippie you're currently dating.

I knew I was sounding like a jealous jerk, but I couldn't fight the feeling of betrayal. Barbara looked alarmed and said: Hold on a second.

She flipped through a stack on albums on the floor beside her chair. She put a record on her turntable and said: Try this.

The music was impossibly weird, horns and keyboards of various kinds filling the room with abrasive angles of sound, no rhythmic or melodic pattern at all. I told myself it reminded me of Schoenberg, though I'd only heard Schoenberg once and had no definite recollection of what his music sounded like.

I made a face and said: What's this?

Barbara smiled: This is jazz. Does it sound like something your parents would listen to? Lounge music?

It didn't.

Barbara said: It's John Coltrane's *Ascension*. And if you really want to hear the future of music, you can close your eyes now and let the pictures come.

I recognized her allusion to a recent Rolling Stones song, but I didn't want to see the pictures Coltrane's music would have made in my head.

Tasha shook her head slowly and said: It's a shame he died last year—such a huge loss. He was definitely one of the two or three great geniuses of twentieth-century music. Who's playing with him on this album?

Barbara looked at the album cover and said: Freddie Hubbard, Pharoah Sanders, McCoy Tyner, Elvin Jones, Archie Shepp, a lot of great people.

I'd never heard of any of them, though Tasha nodded eagerly as if she knew the names well. I felt like the dumb student hiding out in the back row of a music appreciation class.

Still, the appreciation part of it wasn't entirely lost on me. The music was starting to remind me of Pink Floyd's "Interstellar Overdrive," a sound collage I prided myself on liking even though—or perhaps because—all my friends hated it. Or maybe it was more like Jimi Hendrix doing "Wild Thing" at Monterey, the sounds that came out of his burning guitar as he smashed it into the stage. I knew Hendrix and Pink Floyd had done their share of acid, and that some of their music was designed to be listened to on acid, so I wondered if Coltrane was tripping when he made the music I was liking more and more, now that the Paper Sun was fully taking effect, and everything in the room was rippling and throbbing. But the thing that ruined it for me was the album cover, a picture of Coltrane wearing a three-piece suit with a saxophone on his lap.

I held up the cover and said: This music is incredibly strange, like he made it on acid or something. But why is Coltrane wearing a fucking suit?

Tasha and Barbara looked at each other, then started laughing hysterically. Barbara finally said: You can't wear a suit and do acid? Who says?

Suddenly I was dying, dying of thirst. Nothing sounded better than a glass of water, and I was moving down the dark hallway again, past the piles of old books toward the kitchen, and the water coming out of the faucet looked like a series of colored scarves pulled out of a magician's hat, and soon it was traveling everywhere in my body, making my internal organs glow and throb, as if in response to a shift in basic metabolic arrangements, messing up the words that normally kept the past in the past and the future in the future, leading me into a small dark room with a couch and more piles of books and a huge aquarium. I wasn't sure where I was at first, but then I remembered Barbara saying something about her meditation room, the place where she went when she wanted the words in her mind to move like colorful fish from distant parts of the world. I watched them gliding and flashing through the miniature world she'd made for them, castles and caves and coral reefs and swaying plants in pale blue light, but the words in my mind were doing more than naming what I was looking at. They were making it something else, as if the world were nothing more than raw material for language, as if the aquarium were a magic machine, where images could be summoned by pushing buttons, a massive network of pictures on a glowing screen, where a face that might have been mine at first was looking back at me from the glass, changing into a face I knew I'd seen somewhere before but couldn't place, someone with glasses dressed in a Superman t-shirt, then dressed as a cave man clubbing a saber-toothed tiger, then wearing a Che beret and a Karl Marx beard, then looking stoned with Einstein hair and a blackboard filled with equations, computations made of spoons and crescent moons and pitchforks, then playing tenor sax in a basement bar, then strapped in the electric chair on the back of a Cheerios box, then rising like a smiling cartoon sun above Manhattan, where planes were circling the Empire State Building shooting at a giant ape, becoming a face of tiny mirrors reflecting my face looking into the glass, but some of the mirrors were angled and facing each other mirroring empty space, gaps in my face that loudly collapsed in a heap of glass on the floor.

I hurried back into the kitchen to get a broom and paper towels. I heard Barbara's voice from the other room: Everything okay?

I said: I just dropped a glass of water. I'll clean it up right away.

She laughed and said: No problem.

I said: Really?

She said: Really.

But I knew she wasn't telling the truth, and the word *truth* got stuck and stopped, then began to stretch like a rubber band, and I was scared that it might snap, so I said: Really?

She said: Really. No problem at all.

I knew this couldn't be true. There were never no problems at all. It was just a phrase failing to conceal its own instability, trying to make itself seem to be more than a verbal construction. The word construction got stuck and stopped, as if to remind me that there was only one syllable of difference between construction and destruction. I thought of classes I'd taken back at Berkeley, where hip young professors and long-haired classmates talked about language as a virus or prison. I told myself that silence was the only way out. I spoke the phrase out loud, making it sound as dramatic as possible: *Silence is the only way out.* Suddenly, I was convinced that I knew why silence played such a crucial role in meditative practices all over the world, so I wasn't surprised when I moved back into the living room, forgetting about the broken glass I'd left on the floor, and looked at the *Ascension* liner notes and found that Coltrane's later music had been inspired by a meditative experience during his withdrawal from heroin addiction. For a second or two, I assumed that my thoughts about silence would help me appreciate Coltrane's music. But there was nothing silent about *Ascension*, nothing I would have wanted to hear while trying to meditate.

Instead, it seemed to be subtracting segments of time from their place in the linear sequence. First I was reading the liner notes, and then I was outside walking, holding hands with Tasha. Whatever happened in between was gone. I heard our footsteps on the pavement, saw that we were moving along a waterfront of abandoned industrial buildings, with silhouettes of pointed housetops and factory smokestacks in the background, a thick layer of clouds reflecting the lights of the city. Coltrane's music had become psychedelic sound waves pouring from every open door and window in the neighborhood. It was like we were suddenly back in the night before, and I wondered if I'd felt the same thing the night before, that we'd already been there, walking along the waterfront of music, wondering how many times we'd been there before.

Then it seemed like a month before, a late-night conversation back in the flat with Family, laughing at an M.C. Escher black light poster I'd just finished taping to the wall, a giant praying mantis in a castle on the moon. They'd asked me to listen carefully to "Summer 67," a song they were still working on at the time, trying to get it ready for their next album. I wasn't expecting to feel critical. I figured the song would be just as impressively weird as all their other songs, even though they'd warned me that they weren't sure what to do with it. Instrumentally, it was pure magic, moving through a series of striking transitions held together by an eerie violin riff. But the lyrics were lame, little more than a heap of stale images and phrases, a clear indication that the Summer of Love was over, that we didn't need another song about it. When the music ended, I tried to look pleased, then awkwardly praised the violin part and tried to change the subject,

240

something I've always been able to do quite skillfully. But they knew I was holding something back, kept asking me questions, and before too long I was telling the truth, scared that they'd be offended, that our friendship would soon be over.

But they handled it well. I could tell they meant it when they all thanked me for being honest. They invited me to come to the studio with them a few days later, then took my suggestion to cut the vocals entirely, to let the instrumental tracks stand on their own. I remember the moment clearly, listening to the new version, knowing it was right. Without the clichés about love and flower power, "Summer 67" was compelling and mysterious, like it might have been composed in a lunar palace, music designed to enchant a praying mantis. They were so pleased that they offered me partial composition credit, which I refused. It was enough for me that they had done so well with a comment I'd been afraid to make. It brought us all together in a powerful way, and set the stage for our final interaction, which began on a very cold night near the end of my time in London, a few months later.

I hadn't been feeling well and had gone to bed early, disappointed that I didn't have the energy to go out with the band and hear them play. They had a gig at the Marquee Club, the top London venue for progressive rock bands once the UFO Club folded. It was hard to believe I was too sick to get out of bed. But I felt much better when they came back at three in the morning, waking me up to get stoned with them. Charlie and Roger, who wrote most of the group's material, wanted my opinion on a new song called "The Nearsighted Assassin." I can't recall exactly how the lyrics went, but the song mentioned Gavrilo Princip and Archduke Ferdinand and warned against using weapons without clear vision. Charlie Whitney, a guitarist no one remembers even though he was as at least as good as Hendrix or Clapton or anyone else playing at the time, was particularly concerned about the "weapons without clear vision" idea, which he and vocalist Roger Chapman had come up with after talking with a friend of Tasha's at a recent performance. I knew immediately that they had to be talking about Ivo Jovanovic, and I was amazed that Tasha had gotten him to attend another concert.

I wanted to ask her how she'd talked him into it, but she and I were on the outs at that point, ever since I'd gone to bed with Barbara and then tried to lie my way out of it when Tasha asked me about it later. It wasn't so much that I'd cheated on her, since Tasha and I had established right from the start that we both wanted to be free to sleep around. What pissed her off was that I felt I had to lie about it. I've always had trouble trusting people who claim that they're above telling lies, and I didn't hesitate to tell Tasha that I didn't think lying was the real problem. She finally admitted that she and Barbara had been lovers for a long time and had an unspoken agreement that Barbara was only supposed to sleep with men if Tasha was involved. I didn't understand this at all, but Tasha refused to explain it. Instead, she told me bluntly that I had a month to find ways to start paying my rent, that "working" in her gallery wasn't an option anymore, so I made quick plans to move back to the States. The band was sad when I told them I was leaving, though they agreed with me that Tasha probably wasn't kidding when she said I'd have to start paying rent, that they'd never known her to change her mind once she made a decision.

So I was only a week away from flying to San Francisco. I was planning to crash with a friend who was living in a room above a Haight Street record store where he had a part-time job. We'd talked on the phone several times and he was eager to do more acid together and turn me on to some cool new albums.

Of course, San Francisco was known for its hip music, rock groups that are so famous for their connection to the Woodstock generation that there's no need to name them. But I knew there weren't any bands like Family there, or anywhere else in the world for that matter, and their trust in my critical intelligence was giving my long-haired ego a major boost. It was sad to be leaving that special feeling behind.

I had an especially strong connection with Charlie and Roger, since they both seemed to like talking about music as much as they liked making it. I'd never seen them apart from each other, which somehow led me to think of them as comedy team, especially since Charlie looked like a long-haired Charlie Chaplin, and Roger, who had more hair on his chin than on his head, always looked like he was on the verge of laughing. If they didn't have plans to go out, they spent their days in flannel pajamas. I'd always liked people who spent their days in pajamas. But that night they were wearing their Salvation Army performance outfits, jeans and denim shirts under baggy sweaters.

I told them I'd met Ivo Jovanovic a few months ago and knew his story about not wearing glasses on the day when he was supposed to shoot the archduke.

Charlie said: The bloke was so strange I didn't want to talk to him at first, and the feeling was apparently mutual. But then he started raging against our encore song, "How-Hi-The-Li," like it was communist propaganda. I mean, sure, it mentions Chou En-Lai and the Eastern Bloc, so I guess you could say it makes references to communist situations, but it doesn't tell people to become communists, whatever that means. It ends with, "We only want to turn the whole world on," but that's about getting stoned, not becoming a communist. I know some people think getting stoned and becoming a communist are more or less the same thing, but after the final words the song dissolves into a saxophone solo, so if you really want some kind of message—

I looked across the room at the saxophone player, Jim King, who'd been doing increasingly wild solos when the band performed the song in concerts and clubs. I was thinking he might have something to say about messages in music, since his contributions to the band were mostly nonverbal. But he just sat there slumped against the wall and shrugged and gave me the same vague look he used in all situations, as if there was nothing to say beyond what he'd already said with his horn.

Roger said: I'm not even sure what that song is about, but this guy—what did you say his name was again?

I said: Ivo—I...V...O. Tasha told me it's a pretty common name in Yugoslavia.

Roger said: Okay, so Ivo seemed to think our song had some kind of dangerous underground message, and when I told him I didn't know what he was talking about, he said he wasn't surprised because the most damaging propaganda is the kind you don't know you're transmitting.

Charlie said: It was like he thought everyone was sending out sinister messages to each other without knowing it.

Roger said: But that story about the assassination—was that real? Was he really planning to shoot someone even though he didn't have his glasses on?

I said: I thought the guy was just crazy at first, but Tasha told me that as far as she could tell the story was real. And the guy spent four years in jail, even though he couldn't get the gun out of his pocket.

Charlie said: The story's almost too weird to be fake. But why does he go around telling it? Why does he want everyone to know that he couldn't pull the trigger? It's not like the story makes him look like a hero. My grandfather was killed in the trenches in World War I, and in a way Ivo and Gavrilo Princip and the others were responsible for a war that didn't really have to start. So why would he want to take credit for starting it?

Roger said: From what I've heard, the war would have started anyway. It was just a matter of time.

I said: Right. There was something about the way Europe was set up at the time that made war unavoidable. All the major nations were spending huge amounts of money on weapons, Jolly Old England included. Not all that different from the way things are today, with the Arms Race and everything, except there was no time for a Cold War back in 1914 because Europe was on such a short fuse. The assassination just set things off, and—

Charlie nodded and said: But still, the guy's story makes him look like a fool. And what about the guys he was working with, who knew he was nearsighted and recruited him for the assassination anyway. What were they thinking?

I said: From what I remember from a class I took last year at Berkeley, they were working with a secret organization—the Black Hand or the Unseen Hand or something like that. Anyway, the day before the planned assassination, the Black Hand told them not to go through with it, but somehow they ended up doing it anyway. Things got crazy—bombs going off at the wrong time, cyanide pills that didn't work, a real tragedy of errors, and the only reason Princip was able to fire the fatal shots was because the archduke's driver took a wrong turn. It was almost like a slapstick assassination, crazy behavior by starving students stoked up on revolutionary literature. Don't get me wrong. I'm not trashing students with left-wing reading interests. Obviously, I'm one of them. But it's hard for me to picture getting caught up in a situation as crazy as the one Ivo Jovanovic was talking about, doing the things he and the others were planning, and—

Charlie said: So you think they were just confused?

I said: Sounds like it. I know I would've been. I'm the same age now as Princip and Jovanovic were then, and if someone hired me to shoot Richard Nixon, I'm pretty sure I'd be totally freaked out, even if I thought it was the right thing to do. I'm amazed Princip could even pull the trigger and I'm not surprised that Ivo lost his nerve, especially since he couldn't see anything except—

Jim King was suddenly grabbing my sleeve: Hey, can we have some popcorn? I've got a bad case of the munchies!

He was giving me the goofiest grin in the world. It was the first time I'd ever seen anything like pleasure on his face. I was never sure why Jim was so distant, especially compared to the rest of the group, but it might have had something to do with his heroin habit, which was starting to get out of hand, as everyone knew. Within a few months, if I'm remembering correctly, he had to drop out of the band and check into rehab, and as far as I know, he never played music again. He was like so many other sixties musicians who burned themselves out, leaving themselves with no future, in music or anything else.

But now he had a magical expression on his face. I assumed he'd been smoking that night and not shooting up, since he had such a craving for food. His smile was so intense it looked like it might become permanent, like the face of a smiling cartoon sun, rising over a town of laughing people, a place where joy wasn't always just a bad imitation of itself, where people felt pleasure that didn't always quickly turn out to seem stupid. I started laughing, couldn't figure out why, tried to stop but couldn't. The feeling quickly established its own momentum, kept building on itself. Soon all of us were laughing, Jim and Charlie and Roger

246

and I, and even the band's rhythm section—Ric and Rob, who'd gone downstairs to have three-way sex with Jenny, an art student who'd been hanging out with the band for the past few weeks— even they began laughing wildly. We could hear them through the floorboards, though of course they couldn't have known what we were laughing at. Maybe they were laughing just because they could hear us laughing. It was so intense it felt like the building was shaking. I went to the window expecting London to be dark, maybe a few lit windows here and there, but instead there was a vast configuration of lights, thousands of rooms where people were still awake at three in the morning. It should have been a quiet, contemplative moment. But I told myself that in every room there were people laughing their brains out, all of them somehow sharing the same absurd pleasure.

I don't remember what happened after that, how long that crazy moment continued, or what brought it to an end. But I do remember that a few days before I left London, Family played two parts of "The Nearsighted Assassin" for me in the studio, a melodic segment with lyrics, and a partially improvised instrumental passage that was one of the greatest things I'd ever heard, taking "Summer 67" a step further. Jim King was especially inspired, with flute and saxophone work worthy of the jazz masters Tasha claimed he was trying to imitate. But the "weapons without clear vision" line made the vocal part of the song sound awkward and preachy, so I urged them to cut it, let the message emerge through a combination of images, the strange details Ivo Jovanovic had provided—the cyanide pills that didn't work, the man jumping off the bridge into an empty river, the blurred image of the archduke in a panic, shouting and waving his arms in the street, the young man without glasses losing his nerve, missing his chance to shoot his way into the history books of the future.

Jim and Ric and Rob nodded as soon as I made the suggestion, apparently remembering my response to "Summer 67," eager to keep exploring the song's instrumental possibilities. But Charlie and Roger said that they still liked the vision imagery and wanted to figure out a way to keep it in the song, though they agreed with me that the lyrics in their current form were too obvious. I'm not sure what they finally did with the song. I know it didn't show up on subsequent albums, though it's possible that parts of it were redesigned as other songs. Or maybe it turned up on some live album that was never released in the States. I'd like to think so. The nonvocal passage I heard that day was so inventive, so alive with surprising transitions, so brilliant in the space it provided for inspired solo playing and dialogue between instruments, that it's hard to accept that it simply got lost, that it doesn't exist anymore. But lots of things disappear in the past, and there's no way to bring them back.

The last few days of my stay in London are just a blur at this point. A few months later I was back in school at Berkeley, and then the rest of my life happened—other cities, other people, other classes, degrees and advanced degrees, job after job after job after job, some of them worth doing, some of them not. But no matter what happened, no matter how much I drifted away from my interest in the British art rock scene of the late sixties, I tried to preserve what I remembered about "The Nearsighted Assassin," especially the instrumental passage. The trouble is, I've listened to so much other music since then that it's hard to sort out my recollections. When I try to focus, it's like someone is changing channels in my head, quickly moving from station to station, back and forth on a radio dial. But something happened recently that made me feel like I was still back there, in my top-floor room in 1968 with Jim and Charlie and Roger, laughing wildly. The thing that triggered the memory wasn't much, not even a minor incident really, but it clarified something for me, if only briefly.

I was in the Pacific Beach section of San Diego, where I've been working for the past twenty years as a community college history professor. I'd been fighting the urge to go to the bathroom, hoping it could wait until I got home, but I finally gave up and decided to use the men's room at The Left Coast Café, and maybe sit for a few minutes with a Bloody Mary. I chose a corner table and asked the waiter to bring me my drink, and I would have gone straight to the bathroom, had it not been for an old guy wearing shades paging fiercely through a small black notebook a few tables away. He finally stopped turning the pages and smiled, apparently having found what he was looking for. He sat for a minute reading carefully, nodding slowly. Then he looked at me with the goofiest grin in the world, and suddenly I remembered that night in London, not as a few vague images, but as a full scene I could briefly inhabit: a sky blue oval rug beside my bed, an M.C. Escher black light poster on the wall, a double neck guitar and a tenor sax on an old brown sofa, a coffee table covered with books and records, a dormer window framing the lights of the city, and laughter so intense it was still in my body, waiting for me to remember how good it felt.

Back in 1968, I might have invited the man to sit at my table and show me what he was reading. It might have been part of a story called "The Nearsighted Assassin," based in part on an aging man's traumatic recollections, the awkward part he played in one of history's crucial moments, a stumbling confession that nonetheless inspired a forgotten rock band's greatest moment, even if that music is gone forever, even if nothing can really bring back what doesn't exist anymore, a feeling that so many people shared back then, that something strange and important might have been happening, something that was changing what it meant to be important, taking the word off its pedestal, making it learn to laugh at itself, a story that wouldn't have ended with an account of what really happened, how everyone moved on and finally left the great music behind, or decided that the music wasn't as great as it seemed at the time, decided that they were better off not doing acid, that they needed to keep their minds as clear as possible just to get by, to avoid making stupid mistakes that couldn't be fixed up later on. In 1968, I would have had a long conversation, letting the old man tell me why such a crazy smile had appeared on his face, and why he'd chosen to share it with me—someone he didn't know, someone who might have just ignored him.

But I'm not who I was back then. I put my desperate need for the bathroom first, and when I came back out the man was gone.

MORE DANGEROUS

Gabe repeats the magic words: "The laws of history are obscured by the accidents of history." He's not sure where he first came across this line, and he's not even sure he understands it. But he likes the way it sounds, and he assumes that others will too, especially if he can deliver it with confidence, with the tone and facial expression of someone who knows what he's talking about. He imagines himself at work or on a date or at a party or bar, having what seems like a normal conversation, then tossing off the line like it's the kind of thing he says all the time, like it just popped into his head and hasn't been carefully prepared. He's eager to see the expressions on people's faces, the obvious respect the line will command.

He isn't quite ready. He hasn't been able to memorize it yet, so he takes it on a yellow Post-it everywhere he goes. Now he's got it between his legs on the seat of his car as he drives to work. He reads it, looks at the road, reads it again, looks at the road, reads it again, pauses a minute, then says it out loud, "The accidents of history are obscured by the laws of history." It doesn't sound right. He looks between his legs and makes the correction, "The *laws* of history are obscured by the *accidents* of history." He knows he can't afford to make a mistake like that when he finally delivers the line. What would people think? He imagines looks of contempt, blunt ridicule, amused questions. Or maybe no one would notice. Maybe the line would work even if he messed it up. After all, he lives in San Diego, where tanning seems to be more important than thinking.

He comes to an intersection of two-lane roads. He knows that there's never much traffic here, so he doesn't come to a full stop. Out of the corner of his eye he sees a car approaching on his right. He decides to keep going, turning left onto the intersecting road, figuring that the other driver has plenty of time to slow down and let him go first. He's confident that there won't be a collision. After all, the laws of history aren't obscured by accidents on the road.

But the other driver hits his horn, roars out into the oncoming lane, passing and cutting back and stopping suddenly, forcing Gabe to slam on the brakes, narrowly avoiding a collision. The driver jumps out of his red Corvette, gives Gabe the finger, shouting obscenities. Gabe wants to shout back, but he can see that the guy is powerfully built and has a dark tan, as if his muscles were made of San Diego sunlight. Gabe lacks physical confidence. He's pale and flabby and spends too much time reading books he doesn't understand. So he stays buckled into his black Honda Civic and takes the verbal abuse, terrified that he might get yanked out and beaten up. He's so freaked out that he doesn't think of using his iPhone to call the police, or securing the power windows and doors and driving away. Instead, he stares at the digital clock on the dashboard, worried that he might pee in his pants or start crying. Finally, the guy stops yelling, smirks and gets back into his car, revs the engine several times and roars away, leaving rubber.

At first, Gabe is relieved, glad that he didn't get his teeth knocked out. But then he wants to kill. He feels pathetic, like the wimpy guy who got sand kicked in his face in the Charles Atlas ads that appeared in sports magazines he read in his early teens, back when he used to memorize baseball statistics. The guy in the ads transformed himself, became muscular and self-assured and sexy. But Gabe knows he'll never become the new Charles Atlas. He's too lazy, too undisciplined, and eats too much junk food. He feels helpless, so disgusted with himself that he calls in sick and goes home and makes himself a bowl of buttered popcorn.

He's always done his best thinking on popcorn, and he's only halfway through the bowl when he gets an idea. He can still remember the driver's vanity license plate, HOTCAR, and he uses it in an Internet search, finding out that the driver's name is Duke Archer, a personal trainer who lives only five blocks away. Soon Gabe is taking time each day to follow HOTCAR through the city, learning that early on weekday mornings Duke travels to a gym on a dead-end road near Lindbergh Airport, a neighborhood of abandoned factory buildings. He unlocks the place, turns on the lights, inspects the equipment, then does paperwork at the front desk. He opens the doors an hour later, when a few early birds arrive to work out. But in that first hour, when Duke is there alone, Gabe never sees anyone on the road to the gym. The situation is perfect for what he has in mind. His anger is filling him with a determination he's never felt before. He buys a gun and goes to a firing range five nights a week, imagining Duke Archer's face in place of the target, the faces of guys who pushed him around in the past. Five weeks later, he tells himself he's ready.

He waits at an intersection about a mile from the gym, watching the sun come up behind the dark industrial buildings. When Duke's Corvette approaches, Gabe pulls out in front of him. Duke does exactly what Gabe expects, passing and cutting him off and braking suddenly, jumping out and firing off the same insults he used before. Gabe watches him for a minute, amused by the performance. Then he steps calmly out of his car and returns exactly the same offensive language. Duke throws off his sweat shirt, showing off his big muscles, advancing firmly. He looks like Charles Atlas.

Gabe pulls out his gun. Duke freezes, then flashes a tough guy smile and keeps moving forward. Gabe puts a bullet in Duke's right foot, knocking him down onto the blacktop. Gabe pauses to enjoy his work, fully taking in the shock in Duke's contorted face, then orders him to get up and take off his clothes. Duke is writhing in pain, unable to respond at first, but when Gabe puts the gun to his head, Duke staggers up and takes everything off. Gabe has memorized a string of clever insults he found on the Internet. He presents them in the clinical tone of a scientist giving a paper at a conference, informing Duke that his birth certificate is a letter of apology from the condom factory, that he's so ugly it looks like his face was on fire and someone tried to put it out with a fork. Then he tells Duke to get down and beg. When he hesitates, Gabe puts a bullet in his left foot, and Duke is quickly on his knees, pleading through tears and clenched teeth.

Gabe thoroughly enjoys Duke's pain and desperation. If he weren't so busy holding his gun with both hands like they do in the movies, he'd be filming the scene with his phone. He looks quickly back down the road to make sure no cars are approaching. The coast is clear. But the San Diego skyline in the background, the sunlight flashing off the cluster of tall glass buildings, briefly leads him to question what he's doing: Shouldn't someone who enjoys the privilege of living in America's finest city behave in a more dignified way? Shouldn't the sunny skies have made him mellow enough to come up with kinder, gentler ways of resolving his problems? Gabe knows the obvious answers, but he's never liked the predictably cheerful weather, the oppressively polite people smiling and telling him to have a nice day. He turns back to Duke and says: Repeat after me—The laws of history are obscured by the accidents of history. Duke gives him a strange look, so Gabe slams the gun across his face, drawing blood from his nose and mouth. Gabe smiles and snaps: Look me in the eye, motherfucker! Repeat after me—the accidents of history are obscured by the laws of history.

Duke looks Gabe in the eye and timidly asks: Which way do you want it, the first way or the second?

Gabe snarls: Both ways at the same fucking time, dumbass!

Gabe wants to prolong his enjoyment of Duke's panic and pain. But he thinks that the last thing he said sounded lame, that he failed to pronounce the words *fucking* and *dumbass* with the necessary sting. He thinks he can see contempt beneath the terror in Duke's eyes, and he almost loses control. He grabs Duke's curly black hair and yanks his head back, jams the gun into his mouth and prepares to pull the trigger.

For a second or two, the only sound is the music booming from the open door of Duke's idling car. A song ends, another one starts. It's one of Gabe's all-time favorites. He pulls the gun out of Duke's mouth and says: Is that your music, or just something on the radio?

Duke says: It's from a CD I made of my favorite songs. It's Steely Dan's "Don't Take Me Alive," though at this point I'm kind of hoping you'll ignore the lyrics and take me alive.

Duke sounds smarter than Gabe expected him to. His enjoyment of a clever band like Steely Dan tells Gabe that Duke might deserve to live, even with his offensively stupid license plate. Gabe can't keep himself from smiling. Duke sees the change in Gabe's attitude and quickly says: Look, I'm really sorry I jumped out of the car and started cursing you out. It's a bad habit I'm trying to break. I've even signed up for an anger management class. It starts next week. If you want, I can text you the information, and—

Gabe says: Text *me* the information? Why would *I* want the information?

Duke tries to smile: I mean, you know, just in case you wanted to take the class too?

Gabe snaps: Take the class? Why would I want to do something like that? *You're* the one with the problem, douchebag! You flipped out on me once before, a few weeks ago. But you probably do it so often that you don't even remember me—or any of your other victims, for that matter.

Duke says: Listen, if you put away your gun, I promise I won't press charges about the bullets in my feet. I'll even let you sleep with my girlfriend Susan. She's tanned and blond and utterly gorgeous, the perfect San Diego girl. She's damn good in bed and—

Gabe says: I can't stand beach bimbos. I hate how aggressively dense they always are. There's no way—

Duke says: No! Listen! Susan hates the beach! She's really smart. She's got advanced degrees in history from Stanford. She's even got published articles. You can look her up on the Internet.

Gabe laughs: If she's really so smart, what's she doing with a dumb fuck like you?

Duke says: I met her at the gym. I was her personal trainer for a while, and I got her a free membership. We're good between the sheets.

Gabe hates it when people claim that they've got a good sex life. He imagines them with deep tans, tight abs and perfect teeth, covered with designer sweat, making all the right moves and all the good sounds. He can't picture himself being anywhere near as telegenic in bed. But he has to admit that Susan sounds amazing: a San Diego blond with brains! Someone who might be impressed by the line he's trying to learn! He says: She'd really sleep with me to save your life?

Duke says: I'll call her right now and explain the situation, and you can listen to the whole conversation on speakerphone.

Gabe takes a step back but keeps the gun pointed at Duke's head. He says: Okay, dial. But don't try anything funny. Make sure to tell her you'll be dead meat if she calls the police. I'd hate to shoot a fellow Steely Dan fan, but I don't like it when people make me feel like shit.

Duke quickly nods, pulls out his phone and speed dials Susan's number, switching to speakerphone.

Susan isn't really his girlfriend. She's just been using him for sex. Duke Archer isn't the type of guy she usually dates. She plans to drop him as soon as she can find a more sensitive man, someone who's not so desperate to seem tough and decisive. Right now she's five miles away, in Pacific Beach, rushing out of a small glass office building. She's excited because she's finally worked up the nerve to quit her job, pleased that she took her boss by surprise, interrupting his early morning coffee, making a fierce and well-rehearsed speech and then storming out of his office, slamming the door behind her.

She feels her smart phone vibrating in her pocket. She pulls it out to check the number, but she's not watching where she's going and bumps into someone. Her phone gets knocked onto the sidewalk, where a man accidentally steps on it with the sound of a snail getting squashed. He quickly apologizes, bending to gather up the shattered pieces, handing them back, a short young man wearing an old three-piece suit and a black fedora. She starts to tell him there's no need to apologize, but something about him prevents her from getting the words out. It's not just that he looks like he's been clipped out of an old black and white magazine and pasted onto a postcard version of a clear San Diego morning. It's also that he's looking at her like he doesn't know how to look at a human face, as if she had no face and he was just pretending to see her.

She finally says: It's no problem. I hate smart phones anyway.

He says: Smart phones?

She shrugs: I don't know why I've even got one. I almost never use it. All the special features make me crazy.

He says: A smart phone? How is it different from a stupid phone?

She laughs: I'm starting to think all phones are stupid. But everyone here in San Diego is totally in love with them.

He says: The thing I just broke is called a smart phone?

She laughs again, more tensely this time: You don't know what a smart phone is? An iPhone?

He shrugs: It looks like a mechanical device. How can it be smart—or stupid, for that matter? Isn't it just a thing you can use to get something done?

She looks at him like he's got to be joking, but there's no humor in his eye, just quiet confusion. She tells him to have a nice day and turns to leave, but he says: Excuse me, I know you're probably busy, but can you take me to the beach? I've heard it's a nice place to go.

She's been brought up to be a nice girl, so she turns back to him and says: The beach is just a few blocks away. She points toward the ocean, which is visible at the end of Grand Avenue.

He says: But it would be nice if you came with me, in case there are things that need to be explained.

She says: Things that need to be explained? There's nothing at the beach to explain. It's just a bunch of idiots lying on the sand.

He says: But surely they're enjoying the sound of the waves crashing on the shore.

She says: They're not even listening to it. They've all got pods in their ears. The only reason they're there is to work on their tans.

He looks puzzled: Work on their tans? Is a tan something you can work on?

She laughs: The idiots in this town seem to think so.

He says: But you have a tan, and you don't seem to be an idiot.

Susan smiles: I go to a tanning salon. That way I don't have to bother with the sun.

He still looks puzzled: But you're always bothering with the sun here, aren't you? I've only been here a short time, but I keep hearing people praising the weather, how wonderful it is that it's sunny all the time. It sounds like they're boasting about it, like it's something they've accomplished. But I don't think I would want to live in a place where the weather is so predictable. I think it would get boring.

She says: It's worse than boring. It's deadening. It makes people dumber and dumber the longer they stay here. I'm a good example. Ten years ago, I would have laughed at people who went to tanning salons.

Susan can hardly believe that she's having a negative conversation about the San Diego weather. It's the first one she's ever had or even heard. She feels like she's violating a sacred understanding, saying subversive things that she might get punished for, especially if this weird little man turns out to be more dangerous than he seems, and his awkward behavior is just a cover-up, a way of concealing sinister connections. Normally, she wouldn't talk to a stranger, but he seems so misplaced, so out of context, that she can't just walk away. She's fascinated by his slightly mechanical way of talking, as if the words were being projected through his mouth from a remote location, or perhaps from a place that doesn't exist anymore. She says: Why don't we get out of the sun? There's a nice café right around the corner. What did you say your name was?

He says: I didn't say my name. Do you want me to say it?

She nods and smiles: Sure, why not? By the way, I'm Susan.

He nods and comes close to smiling, but happiness doesn't seem to be part of his facial routine. It's like he's afraid to show his teeth, afraid to reveal the darkness in his mouth. He finally says: Hello, Susan. My name is Gavrilo.

Susan starts to smile with all her teeth, but stops herself and says: Gavrilo? Like Gavrilo Princip? The guy who shot the archduke in Sarajevo a hundred years ago? The guy who set off the chain reaction that ended in World War I, the war to end all wars?

He looks disturbed: That's my full name—Gavrilo Princip.

She smiles: In a more intelligent city, having a name like Gavrilo Princip might be a problem. But here in San Diego, no one knows anything about the past. It's like the people here assume that only what's happening right now makes any difference, like history is something that happened long ago and far away. Especially here in Pacific Beach, you'd have trouble finding ten people who would know that you've got the same name as a famous assassin.

He looks even more disturbed, then says: If my full name makes you feel strange, you can call me Gavro.

She says: Is that what your friends call you?

He says: I don't have any friends. They all died a long time ago.

She says: Oh, sorry.

262

He says: There's no need to apologize. They did what they had to do, and after that there was no need to continue.

Susan isn't sure what to say. Though she knows it would be weird to say *cool* or *awesome*, the words so many San Diegans use when they don't know what to say, she also feels that it's her turn to talk, that saying nothing would be impolite. But when she hears herself say *wow* she feels like an idiot. It's another sign that she's been in San Diego far too long.

Gavro tilts his head and says: Wow?

She says: I mean, that's really impressive—that your friends had what it takes to do what had to be done.

He shrugs: I suppose it was better than the cowardly alternatives.

She starts to say *wow* again, then starts to say *cool*, then catches herself and takes a deep breath and says: Okay, so I mentioned a nice café right around corner. Let's get ourselves out of the sun and drink something cool.

Gavro nods, and they walk in silence to a small café surrounded by palm trees. On the flagstone patio, sleeveless men and women sit at plastic tables, typing and reading text messages and nursing caffeine drinks with Italian names. Inside it's dark, with three round wooden tables beneath slowly turning fans. There's a small wooden bar on one side, a unisex bathroom on the other, and a back door opening onto a street, where a celebration of some kind is in progress, or perhaps a reenactment, since everyone is wearing outfits that went out of date a long time ago, in some other part of the world. Susan is surprised that the door is open. She's never seen it open before, and she's always assumed that it faced an alley with garbage cans, not a tree-lined boulevard lined with old buildings.

They sit by the back door. The waiter comes and she orders two Bloody Marys. She winks at Gavro and says: It's my treat. It's not every day that you get to have drinks with a famous assassin.

Gavro says: That's very nice of you, Susan. But can you buy me a sandwich instead? I'm terribly hungry, and I don't have any money.

She nods and tells the waiter to bring only one Bloody Mary, and a glass of water for Gavro. The waiter gives Gavro a puzzled look, like he's looking at a celebrity whose name he can't remember. Gavro returns the same look, and for less than a second Susan thinks they've traded faces, or that they're twins, even though the waiter is tall and tanned with long blond hair and a tropical shirt, the typical San Diego surfer look. She thinks of Gavro riding the waves in his old black suit and fedora. She wants to laugh, but she knows that it would look like she's laughing at nothing, and people have always told her that she looks weird laughing at nothing. She's learned to keep it under control, though the impulse is hard to avoid in San Diego, where she often finds things ridiculous without knowing why. For now she decides to act like things are normal. She looks at her watch and covers her mouth and starts coughing. The waiter finally manages the smile his job requires, says that he'll be right back and goes to get their drinks. Susan asks Gavro what he wants, pointing to the list of sandwiches on the blackboard behind the bar.

Gavro stares, creasing his brow, as if the menu were a list of coded instructions. He finally shrugs and says: I'm not sure what I want.

Susan looks at him carefully, wondering why she's spending time with such a strange man. In the past, she never had trouble walking away from people who made her uneasy, but with Gavro she feels like she's under a spell, an impression that's more embarrassing than disturbing, since the concept of being under a spell would have seemed silly to her five minutes ago. With most of the men she sleeps with, like Duke Archer from her gym, she's firm and assertive, but with Gavro she feels like she's been taken from the place where she's lived for the past ten years and dropped into a place she doesn't know, a substitute San Diego that exists for the sole purpose of replacing the real San Diego, though Susan knows she would never use the word *real* to describe San Diego.

The waiter puts their drinks on the table, and Susan tells him to bring a grilled cheese sandwich. Then she looks at Gavro expecting him to speak, to at least say thank you. But he's looking intently out the back door, like he's expecting something or someone. He reaches into his pocket and pulls out an old gold watch, studies it for a second or two, then slams it facedown on the table, breaking the crystal. He looks surprised at what he's done. He picks up the watch with his thumb and index finger, treating it like a squashed insect that might still be alive and try to bite him, carefully placing it face up on his napkin. The numbers peel themselves off the face of the watch and stagger out onto the table, looking around as if trying to get their bearings. Then they collapse and dissolve into the dark stained wood beside Susan's Bloody Mary. She blinks and grabs her purse and starts to get up, but again something stops her, the strong sense that something important is waiting to happen outside, carefully assembling itself in the carnival atmosphere, something that won't properly take place unless she's observing it. The sunlight from the back door plays on the broken bits of crystal on the table, taking her back to her freshman year at Stanford, an angry social science professor from somewhere in Eastern Europe—no one seemed to know exactly where, though there were rumors that long ago he'd written a manifesto calling for ethnic cleansing in the Balkans, and Susan often wondered why such a sinister person was teaching at a great American university. But what comes back most forcefully now is a phrase he kept repeating like a mantra throughout the semester: The laws of history are obscured by the accidents of history—a line from Tolstoy, or maybe Trotsky, he kept getting them confused, as if the famous names of the past were nothing more than a deck of cards to shuffle.

The waiter brings the sandwich and asks if he can get them anything else, but before Susan can shake her head and smile and say no thanks, Gavro is biting fiercely into the toasted bread, quickly chewing and swallowing, then taking another big bite. In less than a minute the sandwich is gone. He leans back in his chair, resting his back against the exposed brick wall, and something close to a smile settles into his face, like he's just had really good sex. He closes his eyes and says: Thank you, Susan. That was truly wonderful.

Suddenly there's a loud noise from the back door. He looks up and squints into the light. Susan can see a grand and beautifully kept old car with its top down trying to back up, a man and a woman in the back seat wearing elaborate old costumes looking confused, someone dressed in what might be a Halloween general's uniform shouting at the driver, who keeps shaking his head and grinding the gears. Gavro gets up from his chair, pulls a revolver out of his inside jacket pocket, steps quickly out the back door without even a glance in Susan's direction.

She sits with her Bloody Mary, not sure what to do next. There's a pause that feels like a hundred flashbulbs punching the sunlight out of the room, turning the moment into a black and white photograph framed in a dusty museum, a place that will soon be closed because no one goes there anymore. Then she hears two gunshots, screams and shouts bursting in through the door. History feels more dangerous than it ever did before.

SANDWICHES

He's not sure what to do next. The plan has apparently failed. He thinks of the gun in his inner coat pocket, thinks of the man he was planning to kill. The crowded street is filled with noise. It's hot and there's too much light. The only thing he's clear about right now is that he's hungry. He's spent his life being hungry. But it's never been this bad.

Schiller's delicatessen is right across the street. He went there for the first time a few days ago with Tanya, right after having sex for the first time in his life. He'd had a cheese sandwich he liked so much that he'd gone back the next day and had two more. He would have had another one if he hadn't run out of money. He doesn't have money now, but he figures he can eat and leave without paying, disappear into the crowd if anyone tries to stop him.

He hears someone calling his name and sees Tanya waving to him near the deli's entrance. They parted on uncertain terms a few days ago, without making plans to meet again, but she looks so excited to see him now that he starts to feel the same way. He waves and returns her eager smile, hurries across the street. He likes the way her black hair curls down onto her bare shoulders. She's wearing a blood red dress that fits her perfectly.

She takes his hand and says: Did you hear what just happened?

He shakes his head: I heard an explosion. People were screaming. Then the archduke's car drove by. Crowds of people were in my way, so I couldn't see him clearly. I tried to move closer but—

She says: Someone threw a bomb at him. It bounced off his car and exploded in front of the car behind him. It came within seconds of killing him. They got the guy who threw the bomb. He tried to drink poison. Then he threw himself into the river.

He says: He drowned himself?

Tanya says: He tried to. But the Miljacka this time of year is only three inches deep. Imagine how stupid he must have felt when he realized that the river was almost dry!

He shrugs and says: The archduke was stupid to come here. Hundreds of people probably wanted to kill him. And he chose Saint Vitus Day for his grand appearance! I know you're not Serbian, but if you were you'd understand what an insult it was for the Habsburgs to send him down here on a day that's sacred to us, the day we celebrate our martyrs. Then he was stupid enough to drive right down the Appel Quay in an open car with swarms of people on either side. Anyone in the crowd could have shot him at any time! I'd shoot him right now if I could. I wish he hadn't gone by so fast a few minutes ago. But there were people in my way, and his car was gone before I could reach—I mean, before I could fully understand—before I could—

She laughs and says: Before you say before again, let's go inside. You look like you need a good sandwich!

The deli's dim light is a nice change from the glare of the late morning sun. Behind the counter, big chunks of meat and cheese hang from the ceiling in mesh bags, just waiting to be sliced and used in sandwiches. A counterman with a face of tiny mirrors takes their order, quickly makes their food, and Tanya pays. The place is crowded, but she spots a corner table. Ceiling fans fill the broad oak floorboards with turning shadows.

They sit, and before she's even had time to put her sandwich on the table, he's already taken a big bite out of his. He smiles and leans back in his chair, closing his eyes, chewing slowly. People talk loudly all around him, and he can pick out parts of what they're saying, but he doesn't care. Right now the only thing that matters is that he's got good food in his mouth and more good food in his hands. He swallows and takes another big bite without opening his eyes, leans further back in his chair so that it's propped against the wall. He wonders briefly if Tanya's getting annoyed. After all, she bought him food, and now he hasn't even looked in her direction, let alone tried to start a conversation. But he's so lost in the pleasure of his sandwich that he just keeps chewing. He wants the taste in his mouth to last forever.

He finally opens his eyes and says: When my friend Nedjo heard I'd gone to bed with you, he said you'd already slept with half the men in Sarajevo and your goal was to sleep with the other half.

She smiles: Any problem with that? It's more or less what I told you at the café a few days ago.

He says: I didn't believe you.

She says: Why would I lie about something like that?

He says: To get attention.

She smiles: To convince you that I'm a slut?

He shakes his head: To convince me that you're not just another boring bourgeois person, that you're willing to do wild and dangerous things.

She laughs: Why would I need to prove that to someone like you?

271

He says: You seem to want me for something.

She says: I don't want you; I want your dick.

He thinks he's supposed to laugh, but suddenly she's not smiling, so he puts a serious look on his face and says: It doesn't bother you that I'm angry all the time?

She says: Nothing turns on a sexy woman more than an angry man.

He says: Some angry men are angrier than others.

He bites eagerly into his sandwich and closes his eyes again, chewing slowly. He thinks back to their meeting at the Semiz Café, how surprised he'd been when she singled him out for conversation, making strong eye contact, smiling and nodding eagerly at everything he said, leaning over the small round table and touching him lightly on the arm, telling him all about herself, her contempt for the wealthy life her parents had given her, her respect for young men willing to go beyond mere discussion and take serious action. She told him how intrigued she was by Young Bosnia, the student groups she'd seen so many times in the cheap cafés, how she imagined being part of what they were planning, even though she wasn't a Serb and had nothing to gain by supporting radical agendas. Her smile was nice, but the longer she talked, the more dubious her attitude seemed to him. He wondered if she really shared their convictions, or if she was just fascinated by the Young Bosnian mystique, the secrecy they insisted on, even as they made themselves easy to identify with the three-piece suits and fedoras they wore so often. He enjoyed getting bold attention from such an attractive woman, someone who made herself sound so experienced in bed, though she said she was only eighteen, a year younger than he was. But members of Young Bosnia were supposed to abstain from sex, and besides, he wondered what she would do if she had to face real danger, the kind he and his friends had sworn themselves to. Would she be so excited about the Young Bosnian underground if she had to face bullets and prison time? The risks she talked about seemed so safe to him, and he felt contempt for the pride she took in the so-called rebellious things she was doing, like wearing dresses that fit so well she was bound to get lots of attention, like sleeping with men she barely knew, men she knew her parents would never approve of, like laughing at people who called her a nymphomaniac.

He's not sure what to think of the word nymphomaniac. He knows it probably means that she's got problems, the kind that might require years of psychoanalysis. But at this point, he's more concerned about his own behavior, that she seduced him so easily, that it took so little to get him past one of the central Young Bosnian beliefs, that drinking and sex were bourgeois distractions, ways of taking young men away from the crucial thing, the political struggle, the need for true Serbian independence. He recalls how nervous he became when she practically forced him to take her back to his room, where she questioned him so carefully about the radical books and pamphlets piled beside his bed that he wondered if she was a secret agent of the Habsburg Empire, if she knew about his dangerous plans and was probing for more information. But now that he's with her again, and the plan to kill the archduke has apparently come to nothing, he's not sure what to care about, or if it even makes sense to care about anything. A few minutes ago, when he told her he'd shoot the archduke if he could, she seemed to take it as a joke. Maybe that's all it's ever been, something to tell himself so that his life doesn't seem so pointless. Maybe he lacks the nerve to pull the trigger. He wolfs down the rest of his sandwich and wants another one.

She says: You know, I just realized that I don't even know your name.

He keeps his eyes closed and keeps chewing. He finally says: Gavro.

She says: Really? Short for Gavrilo? Like "Gavri'el" or "Gabri'el" from the Old Testament? The messenger angel?

He says: You sound like a Hebrew scholar.

She nods: My uncle is a Hebrew scholar, and he's always at our house talking in Hebrew with my father. Half the time I can't understand a word they say. They wanted me to learn Hebrew, and I had some instruction, but I got tired of it pretty quickly.

He finally opens his eyes: I might be a messenger of some kind, but it's got nothing to do with God or God's angels.

She nods: I didn't think so. But Gavrilo is still a nice name for you.

He stops chewing and says: Fine. But if we ever end up in bed again, don't use that name. In bed I want you to call me Archduke Franz Ferdinand. Or maybe just Archduke. Or just Duke.

She puts a playful look on her face: It might be difficult. I've seen pictures. His mustache is different from yours and his face is fatter.

He says: He eats better, and much more often.

She says: You really hate that guy don't you? But I'll bet you've never met him. How can you hate a guy you've never met?

He says: I know everything I need to know about him.

She says: Like what? My father knows people who know the archduke personally, and they say that he's got big problems controlling his anger, which sometimes leads him to make a fool of himself and others in public, but aside from that he's a pretty nice guy. My father told me that he married his wife even though the Emperor didn't approve, and he was only allowed to marry her after he signed a piece of paper saying that any children they had wouldn't really be Habsburgs and couldn't inherit anything. Just imagine: She's a titled woman! The Countess Sophie Chotek. Her family goes back more than a thousand aristocratic years, and still the Habsburgs think she's not good enough for them. At state dinners, she's not allowed to sit at the main table with her husband. She has to sit with the so-called commoners in the back of the room. She's not allowed to ride in the royal car with him in Vienna, which is one reason why they were pleased to come to Sarajevo, where for some reason they're allowed to appear in public together. And the archduke? Of course, he's a Habsburg too, but he gave up everything and married for love.

He says: That's nice. Sounds like something you'd read in a popular novel, not that I've got time to read popular novels.

She says: But really, can someone who's willing to sacrifice everything for love be such a bad guy?

He imitates her voice: "Can someone who's willing to sac- rifice everything for love be such a bad guy?" Of course he can! Just because he's nice to his wife and kids doesn't make him a good guy. His uncle is going to be dead soon. Archduke Franz Ferdinand will soon be the Habsburg Emperor. And it's clear that he doesn't want an independent Serbia. He wants us under his thumb, like we're all just a bunch of idiots from the provinces who wouldn't know what to do with ourselves if we didn't have people from advanced cultures ordering us around. Maybe you don't care because you're not Serbian and your family has con- nections with powerful people in Vienna. But for Serbs like me, the man is sinister. Think about it: If I shot him, I'd be famous. My name would be in all the papers and history books. But if I behave myself and obey the laws, I'll just be another faceless peasant the archduke doesn't care about. And from what I've heard, it's dangerous to be one of those people he doesn't care about. Someone told me that if the archduke is standing on a train platform and a fly lands on his head, the station master gets fired. And besides, the archduke likes to kill animals just for the fun of it. He publicly boasts that he's murdered hundreds of deer with his gun.

She says: He calls it murder?

He says: Probably not. But that's what it is.

She shrugs: Lots of men like hunting. Are they all murderers?

He says: If he killed animals with his bare hands in a fair fight, I wouldn't have any problem with it. But he shoots them with a gun they can't defend themselves against. And it's not like he's killing them because he needs the food. It's just his way of showing off with a rifle. Don't get me wrong. It's not that I can't stand the thought of killing animals. I grew up in a farming village where killing animals was part of our lives. But we killed them because we needed food and clothing. We never killed them just for the fun of it. Killing a pig isn't fun, especially for the pig. And the archduke has openly said that all Slavs are pigs.

She smiles and pretends to clap her hands, as if in response to a speech. He gives her a hard look, so she says: You're quite a talker, aren't you? It's funny. When I first met you in the café, you sat back and let me control the conversation, and you did the same thing later in your room. I didn't mind, since I like to talk, and people say I'm a good talker. But right now it feels like I should let you do most of the talking. It's an awkward feeling, since I'm not usually anyone's audience, but you're fun to listen to.

He says: Really? How can something that gives you an awkward feeling be any fun? Is it some kind of skill you've mastered, maybe something you've learned from your father? He must get lots of practice with awkward feelings when he's around the Habsburgs up in Vienna. After all, he's Jewish, isn't he? Isn't the archduke known for his hatred of Jews?

She says: No one up there knows he's a Jew. Or maybe they do but they act like they don't. Officially, we all became Catholics a long time ago, though my mother's parents were Turkish. So I'm not sure what I am, and I don't really care. What's wrong with just being a person?

He says: Nothing. But that's not how the Habsburgs see it. Just ask Countess Sophie.

She starts to say something, but stops when she sees that his plate is empty. She offers him her sandwich. He takes it without hesitation, takes a big bite and looks quickly around the room. It's even louder than it was before, and everyone seems to be talking about the same thing: the attempted assassination, different versions of exactly what happened, though they all agree that the sky was filled with blackbirds and the river was only three inches deep. A woman sitting at a table near the open doorway is eagerly describing what happened at City Hall, the archduke's rage when he met the mayor of Sarajevo soon after the bomb went off. The mayor acted like nothing had happened, reading a prepared speech joyously welcoming the archduke to the city. The archduke had a prepared speech too, but it was covered in blood, and he could only read part of it. The woman telling the story is getting on Gavro's nerves. She's pronouncing each word with care, pausing between phrases, gesturing fiercely with her hands, as if she were giving a performance. He wants to take out his gun and blow her head off. Yet he also knows that she might have information, that she might know where the archduke is now, if he's he's still at City Hall or if he's been smart enough to leave town. Gavro wants to get up and approach her with questions. But the woman sees someone she knows passing by on the street, quickly says goodbye to the man she's been talking to, and hurries out.

Her departure makes him nervous, like something important might be on the verge of happening, and he might miss out on it. He pulls out an old gold watch and sets it on the table, staring at the numbers, adding and subtracting in his head, making mistakes and correcting them, then correcting the corrections.

Tanya says: Where did you get that amazing watch? It looks like it might be expensive—I mean, really expensive, or maybe an heirloom of some kind.

He says: I'm sure it's an heirloom, but not from my family.

She says: So where did you get it?

He says: I stole it.

She says: You stole it? Really? From a rich person?

He says: From the archduke himself.

She smiles like he must be joking: Really? How?

He says: I ran into him on Thursday at the bazaar. First I stared him down, and I could tell he was getting nervous because he pulled his watch out of his pocket without even looking at it. So I looked up and shouted: Up there! Look! Up in the sky! He and his wife and their bodyguards all looked up, and I snatched the watch from his hand and put a pencil in its place. When he looked back at me and then at the pencil in his hand, I looked back at the sky and said again: Up there! It's coming closer! They all looked up again, and I lost myself in the crowd.

She looks at him closely, as if she were trying to see if he's lying. He shrugs and says: It's true. How else could I have gotten a watch like this? It's hundreds of years old. It's not the kind of thing you can find in stores.

She takes the watch and examines it carefully and says: What are these letters inscribed on it? FF? I guess it must mean Franz Ferdinand, right?

He says: Wrong! It means Fuck Face.

She starts to smile: You've got a very weird sense of humor, don't you?

He takes the watch out of her hand and puts it back in his pocket and says: Some people think it's weird. Some people don't even notice it.

He looks at Tanya's hands on the table, tries to imagine her holding a gun, then looks at her face, the plump lips he kissed a few days ago, the smooth complexion that's slightly darker than his. But she's staring past him at something that isn't there when he turns to look. For a second, the room seems larger than it was before, then smaller. Tiny reflections come and go in the counterman's face, as if his head were the eye of a giant insect. Ceiling fans turn the warm June air in lethargic circles. The dusty light in the street goes flat as a blank page against the tall arched windows on either side of the doorway. He takes another bite of her sandwich, chews it slowly, leaning back in his chair, closing his eyes, thinking back to a night three weeks ago, he and Nedjo and Trifko slipping and stumbling and shivering through mud and cold rain on the Bosnian border, finally finding shelter in an empty hut, collapsing on the dirt floor and laughing wildly at their crazy adventure, carrying illegal weapons through a dismal countryside because they'd seen in the papers a few months ago that Archduke Franz Ferdinand, heir apparent to the Habsburg throne, would soon be visiting Sarajevo, and they'd convinced themselves that the man should be killed, that they were the right men for the job. He remembers learning to shoot the guns that the man from the Black Hand gave them, target practice in a park on the outskirts of Belgrade, how he got to be a crack shot, how the Black Hand people gave them food and sometimes even a place to stay.

He opens his eyes, looks around the room in surprise, as if he's seeing it for the first time. He says: I can't remember what we were just talking about.

She takes his hand and says: Hurry up and finish your sandwich. My parents are going to be at a party all afternoon. We can go back to my room and have fun. I'm on the third floor, and there's a great view from the window beside my bed. You can see all of Sarajevo's minarets and church towers and the mountains in the distance.

He smiles: Just like one of those colored picture postcards.

She says: Even better than that. And I've got a big bed, so we won't have to use that stupid room of yours again.

He says: I like my stupid room.

She says: Really? Why? There's nothing to it. A desk, a bed, and a pile of books on a bare wood floor. Not even a rug. And the bed is so small!

He says: I like my stupid room because it's just a stupid room. I spend lots of time there.

She says: Doing what?

He says: Playing cards.

She says: By yourself? Solitaire?

He says: Not solitaire. I don't like solitaire.

She looks at her watch and says: What do you play?

He says: Cards.

She says: But what's the game called?

He says: Cards.

She says: Cards? There's a game that's just called Cards?

He says: That's the game I play.

She says: How do you play it?

He says: You put the cards on the table and you do whatever you want.

She laughs: No rules? How do you win or lose?

He says: You don't. I don't like winning or losing.

She says: Then what's the point?

He says: The point is to play.

She shrugs and says: But what's the fun of just putting cards on the table?

He says: You can do whatever you want.

She makes a face: It's all just random?

He says: It goes like this. I start with all the cards face up and I make combinations. I try to surprise myself. I avoid the obvious, like putting a nine of clubs on a ten of clubs or putting a nine of clubs on a nine of hearts. Instead, I might match up a two with a five, since a two is like an upside down five turned backwards, or maybe a three with an eight, since a three is like an eight that hasn't quite happened yet, or maybe a four with a nine, since a four is like an angular nine, or an ace with a seven, since an ace is really a one, and a one is like an unslanted seven that hasn't finished itself on top. But the real fun comes with the royalty cards. What could be more humbling for a king or queen of spades than getting matched up with a two of clubs? What could be more absurd for a one-eyed jack than getting matched up with—

She says: I don't get it. I can see why it might be fun to fool around with the deck for a minute or two, but doesn't it feel pointless after a while? There's no challenge.

He says: I don't like challenges.

She says: Why?

He says: Six of my nine brothers and sisters died before they were five. Sometimes we had food and sometimes we didn't. My father sent me away because he couldn't afford to keep me. If I'm going to play games, I want to feel good. I don't feel good when I lose. One time I was sitting in my room doing nothing when Danilo came in and asked me—

She says: Danilo? The same guy who told you I'm a slut?

He says: That was Nedjo. Nedjo Cabrinovic. The guy who threw the bomb.

She looks alarmed: You know the guy who threw the bomb?

He's stunned that he's just revealed a crucial secret, something that could easily be used against him later. He quickly says: Not really. But Nedjo's the type who might talk about throwing bombs, and he would make it sound like he meant it, but then he wouldn't really do it, though he might say that he'd really done it, and he'd sound so convincing that you'd believe him. But Danilo's different. He wouldn't talk about throwing bombs. He'd write articles about it, and they'd be so convincing that you'd end up thinking that you didn't need real bombs, that all you really needed was clever language.

She tries to smile, though she still looks disturbed, glancing tensely around the room. She finally says: So Danilo's the one who threw the bomb, drank poison that had no effect on him, then threw himself into an empty river?

He shakes his head and tries to laugh: No, that was someone else. Forget about him. The cops have him now, and they're probably pulling his fingernails out one by one, trying to get information. He'll probably end up giving them all the names they want. So forget about him. Danilo's the guy whose mother owns the house where I've got my room. He lets me stay there for nothing. Two weeks ago, he came into my room and asked me where I'd been for the past five days. I said, "I've been right here." He said that my room had been empty for five days and

282

nights and no one could figure out where I'd gone. That's when I started playing Cards. It helps me keep track of myself and it keeps me happy. No rules, no challenges.

She looks at her watch again and says: A few minutes ago you were talking about shooting the archduke. That would be a big challenge, wouldn't it? You don't sound like someone who doesn't like challenges.

He thinks of the Browning revolver in his coat pocket. He says: A challenge like that is in a category by itself. You do it once and then you drink cyanide and your life is over. But when I'm just playing a game, I don't like challenges.

She puts her hand under the table between his legs and says: Let's hurry up and go to my parents' house. I'm glad it makes you happy to play Cards by yourself. But I know other ways to make you happy.

He says: I want another sandwich after this one.

She says: So order another sandwich and have that guy with the face of mirrors wrap it up for you. We can take it back to my parents' house and you can eat it there after we set the sheets on fire.

He says: I might want another one after that one.

She says: Really?

He says: And another one after that one.

She says: Finish your damn sandwich. Let's get out of here!

He says: Why don't you go back to your parents' house? I'll meet you there in about an hour.

She looks like she wants to slap him, then smiles and gets up and starts to walk out and says: Okay. But you better show up!

He says: Aren't you going to give me any money?

She turns, looks angry, moves her face about an inch from his and whispers fiercely: Money? You want *me* to give *you* money to have sex? Do I look like someone who has to pay?

He says: I spent all my money a few days ago on sandwiches. I don't have anything left. It sounds like your parents have money. I need money for more sandwiches.

She pulls coins out of her purse and smacks them down on the table one by one.

He says: Aren't you going to draw me a map?

When she looks puzzled, he says: How else will I know how to get to your parents' house?

She goes up to the counterman and asks him for something to write on. He rips off a piece of sandwich paper. She looks at his mirror face and starts to say thank you, but suddenly she's trapped in a hundred reflections, which take her face apart and reassemble it incorrectly. She quickly turns away and tries to catch Gavro's eyes across the room, but he's looking down with pleasure at the sandwich in his hands. She starts to hate him. She thinks he's just using her to get sandwiches, that eating and politics are the only things he cares about. He was horribly awkward in bed with her a few days ago, coming too soon and then not knowing what to do when she sat on his face, and he couldn't get her out of his room fast enough. Young Bosnia sounded so important and mysterious when she first became aware of it a few months ago. She'd heard that they talked in code, made secret signals to each other, as if they were Masons, and weren't afraid to let women participate. When she'd heard they abstained from sex, she thought it might be fun to seduce one of them, and she'd even made a bet with a friend that she could do it on the first date. But now that she's actually won her bet, Young Bosnia seems extreme and violent, and she doesn't think violence ever solves anything. And it sounds like Gavro might know people trying to kill the archduke! It suddenly seems crazy that she's with him at all, and she tells herself that she's got to stop choosing to be with weird men when she could easily do better. She cringes as she remembers the silly things she said to him when they first sat down with their sandwiches, nonsense about liking angry men and wanting his dick. She hates herself when junk like that comes out of her mouth, and she always tells herself she won't talk non-sense in the future, and then she does it with the next guy and feels like a fool all over again. She thinks of telling Gavro to get lost, shooting him down in front of everyone in the room. But she's never liked making scenes, so she tells herself to keep smil-ing at him until their afternoon is over, teach him a few things about giving beautiful women pleasure in bed, and then to forget about him, find someone else. She knows that she won't have any trouble, that any man who sees her will want to have sex with her.

She comes back to their table and says: When you get your new sandwiches, don't look at the counterman's face.

He says: Why not?

She says: You won't like what you see.

He says: I usually don't.

He bites fiercely into his sandwich. She puts the sandwich paper down on the table and draws a map with a few quick strokes. He squints at the page, nods and smiles. He pulls her close and kisses her with his mouth full of bread and cheese, us-ing his tongue to push the food into her mouth. She pulls back, slightly annoyed, then chews and swallows the food, laughs and turns and walks outside.

In the open transom above a side door, an eye the size of a pig's head looks inside, scanning left and right, up and down, then closing and turning away. Gavro starts to get horny. He feels like he's getting away with something, breaking the laws of erotic attraction, going to bed with someone who's much more attrac-tive than he is. She's also got to be five inches taller. He's always

285

thought he was too short, a feeling confirmed when he tried to enlist in the Serbian army the year before and was bluntly told that he wasn't big enough. But now he's apparently big enough for the sexiest woman in Sarajevo.

He gets up and goes outside, intending to move quickly through the streets, beat her to her parents' house and surprise her, playfully point his gun at her from the front porch. But the dusty sunlight hits him in the face. His eyes have trouble adjusting to the glare, and in the blindness of the moment he sees himself on Saint Vitus Day in 1389 at the Battle of Kosovo, sneaking into the Ottoman sultan's tent and stabbing him in his sleep, ecstatic in the knowledge that he'll quickly be caught and killed by the sultan's men, that the blood on his hands will make him a Serbian hero, a Serbian martyr. But now on Saint Vitus Day in 1914, there's too much sunlight in his eyes, and he wants to fall back into the darkness of the deli, get another sandwich, watch the turning shadows on the floorboards.

There's a man with a black hat standing beside him smoking a cigar. He drops it on the sidewalk and stomps it out with his foot. He looks at Gavro like someone looking through a darkened window. He says: You're a ghost in a town where no one believes in ghosts. You're reading a book on a park bench beside a wall that's not a wall, a wall that's really a book in another dimension, a book that's really a wall in another dimension, though you know that other dimensions don't exist. You're a stray dog haunted by moonlight in a town on the other side of the world. You're in the yes of no and the no of yes. You're the ace of lightning.

Gavro says: I'm the ace of lightning.

The man smiles and turns away and disappears around the corner. Gavro starts to follow him, then stops. There's too much light in his eyes. There's an open car on Franz Joseph Street coming to a stop right in front of him, the black and yellow banners of the Empire dangling over the hood. Gavro takes a close look at the people in the car. He's there—Gavro remembers him clearly from three days before—Archduke Franz Ferdinand, plump in a pale blue military outfit, dark green feathers spouting from his black helmet. His wife, Countess Sophie, is there beside him, smiling beneath the big flowery hat that all the rich ladies wear at public occasions. They're waving at their future subjects, the crowds of people cheering on the street, while another man in the car, the Austrian governor of Bosnia, General Potiorek, is shouting something at the driver.

Gavro can't react at first. It sounds like the general is telling the driver that they've made a wrong turn, that their plans were changed at City Hall and they're not where they're supposed to be and they'll have to back up. The driver is shaking his head, clearly confused. Gavro is confused too. It doesn't make sense that the archduke would be back in his open car, driving down the streets of Sarajevo, risking his life and the life of the woman he loves, when only an hour ago someone threw a bomb at him. Hasn't it occurred to him that someone else might want to kill him? Gavro knows of at least six other people planning to murder the archduke—the three students Danilo hired at the last minute, along with his old friends Trifko and Nedjo, but Nedjo of course has already failed. Gavro thinks back to their meetings in Belgrade, the guy from the Black Hand who gave them weapons and cyanide and made them swear an oath to kill themselves once the job was done. And now the archduke is close enough to spit on. Everything Gavro has been preparing for since March is just a bullet away.

He reaches for his gun, but stops when the archduke turns and looks directly into his eyes, and they share what feels to

Gavro like a shiver of recognition, as if they represented for each other a future prepared by everything that's ever happened, not prepared as if divine forces were at work, but shaped by a complex accumulation of discrete events, slowly building over the centuries to result in the present situation, which can only lead to worldwide violence and disaster, stupidities and horrors beyond belief. Gavro isn't sure what to do with this feeling. It's like he's just been punched in the stomach by a clown with a painted smile and a big red nose, and he can hear people laughing somewhere in back of him, trying to stop and then laughing even harder, while circus music plays so far away that he's not sure it's really there, though he can't stop listening to it. He's got his hand on his gun in his inner coat pocket, but his grip goes limp when the music gets faster and louder, then abruptly stops. The moment splits to become two pieces of bread, moving at the speed of light from opposite ends of the universe, meeting only when a large chunk of cheese comes between them, covered with spices and sauce and reducing Gavro to raw hunger, driving him back inside where he orders another sandwich, tries not to see his face a hundred times in the counterman's face, slamming Tanya's coins down one by one on the marble countertop.

The archduke stares at the empty space that Gavro has left behind. He's sure he saw someone standing there with a gun a split second ago, possibly the same person who tried to stare him down a few days ago, then pointed at the sky and started shouting. The archduke shouts at the driver to get the car back on the Appel Quay. But the gears are jammed and the driver looks like he's not sure what to do.

The archduke turns to Sophie and says: Once they get this damn car going, let's cancel everything else and get out of here! I'm tired of smiling and waving.

She says: Ever since that bomb went off, I feel like every person I'm waving at might have a gun. And they're right to want to shoot us, aren't they?

He shakes his head and blinks in amazement: Dearest Sophie, what are you saying? Yes, there might be people here who want us dead, but that doesn't mean they're *right* to want us dead. You and I, we haven't done anything to hurt anyone.

She says: Haven't we? I was reading the Serbian papers on the train coming down here, and of course they're filled with propaganda, making your uncle and his friends look more sinister than they really are. But beyond all the half-truths and distortions, the propaganda isn't complete nonsense: They don't want the Habsburg Empire here. And why should they?

He says: Try saying that to my uncle. He'll be quick to tell you that if we let them rule themselves, they'll make trouble for us. We can't let that happen. We—

She smiles and says: We? Who's we? Your uncle and his people think they're too good for me. They won't even officially recognize me as your wife. And they always act like you don't know what you're doing and can't be trusted.

He looks down and quietly says: Disgusting, isn't it?

She says: I'm so sick of it!

He takes her hand and says: Why don't we just drop the pretense, forget about what we're supposed to be representing here? Why don't we just go back to our room and make love? That spa we're staying at—it's got such a nice view of the city, the minarets and church towers and the mountains in the distance. Let's go there and set the sheets on fire!

Thirty feet away, Gavro stares at the makings of his new sandwich on the cutting board. The counterman's hands move so quickly that Gavro can't follow what he's doing. The magic that makes the sandwich so unbearably good escapes him. It's like a piece of piano music composed in a rush of madness, a sound so bizarre that people can't explain why they like it so much, except to say that it makes them want to hear more of it, more madness, and he thinks of Saint Vitus, patron saint of madmen, of people bitten by snakes or hit by lightning, unofficial patron saint of Serbian martyrs. Gavro can't stop wondering why the Habsburgs chose Saint Vitus Day for the archduke's visit. Dani was probably right when he said that the insult must have been carefully planned. They must have known that the day was special, the anniversary of the Battle of Kosovo, the day of heroes willing to die in wars against foreign invaders. Were they hoping that someone might kill the archduke? Did they have good reasons to get rid of him, to put the empire's future into the hands of a less embarrassing man? Had they made secret plans with the Black Hand, like Dani said this morning? Had they been hoping all along to find Young Bosnian students to do their dirty work for them? Had the plan he and Nedjo came up with been exactly what they were looking for? Gavro has had these thoughts before, but they always lead nowhere, only to more and more questions leading nowhere, and nowhere is a feeling that he can't stand anymore. He can't bring himself to believe that he's just an unwitting tool of the Habsburg Empire, that he's nothing more than a hit man, not a hero.

The counterman wraps up the sandwich and turns. The face of a hundred mirrors makes the room seem larger and smaller. Gavro can't keep himself from ignoring Tanya's warning. His eyes are pulled into a mirrored space that multiplies his face, though each tiny mirror gives only a partial reflection, so it looks like most of him isn't there, an incomplete face repeated a hundred times, a face that's present mostly in its absence. He tries in vain to blink the image away. He feels like he might throw up. He pushes the sandwich away, reels outside again into the noise of the crowd, the smiles and waving hands, the grinding gears of the imperial car, the black and yellow banners moving slightly as a breeze comes up. He pulls out his gun. The archduke and Countess Sophie aren't facing the street anymore. They're facing each other with bedroom eyes, like nothing else makes any difference. Gavro thinks they look like they're on their first date.

He shoots twice.

ACKNOWLEDGMENTS

Earlier versions of some of the stories in this collection were originally published in *Altered Scale, Fiction International, The Literary Review, Morning Will Come, Quarterly West, Western Humanities Review,* and the anthology *Sunshine/Noir II* (City Works Press).